After completing a psychology degree, Alice Hunter became an interventions facilitator in a prison. There, she was part of a team offering rehabilitation programmes to men serving sentences for a wide range of offences, often working with prisoners who'd committed serious violent crimes. Previously, Alice had been a nurse, working in the NHS. She now puts her experiences to good use in fiction. *The Serial Killer's Wife* and *The Serial Killer's Daughter* draw heavily on her knowledge of psychology and the criminal mind.

By the same author:

The Serial Killer's Wife

THE
SERIAL
KILLER'S
DAUGHTER

ALICE HUNTER

avon.

Published by AVON
A division of HarperCollins*Publishers* Ltd
1 London Bridge Street
London SE1 9GF

www.harpercollins.co.uk

HarperCollins*Publishers*
Macken House, 39/40 Mayor Street Upper
Dublin 1, D01 C9W8, Ireland

A Paperback Original 2022

7

First published in Great Britain by HarperCollins*Publishers* 2022

Typeset in Sabon LT Std by Palimpsest Book Production Limited,
Falkirk, Stirlingshire

Printed and bound in the UK using 100% Renewable Electricity
at CPI Group (UK) Ltd

For Anne Williams
Seven years and counting.
Thank you for being the most wonderful agent.

Prologue

The delicate, wispy wing detached with one sharp tug.

Concentrating hard, the pink tip of the girl's tongue poked through the gap where her two front teeth had been a few days before. The thumb and forefinger of one hand pinned the helpless insect to the wooden picnic table as the fingers of the other went about dismembering the twitching butterfly.

A cabbage white. Common; plain; not special, her daddy said.

She didn't understand what *common* was, but she knew the other words.

She gently placed the top right wing, its two black dots like blank, dead eyes, to one side, before tearing the lower right wing from its body. The girl was focused, her gaze never leaving the butterfly as she lifted her other hand, releasing the vice keeping the creature trapped. She watched as its remaining wings fluttered, first furiously, then slowing. Giving up. They only lived for two weeks anyway – she learned that at school. It wasn't like she was killing it really.

And besides, now she was *making* it special.

A gentle breeze caught one of the severed wings and it flew across the table. The girl slammed her hand down hard on it before it could escape, and a white, dusty powder puffed through her fingers. She sighed. It was ruined now. She'd have to capture another and start over.

From the kitchen window, her mother watched – fear, mixed with a sense of inevitability, settling in her stomach. She knew this type of behaviour.

God, please, no.

Was history repeating itself?

Chapter 1

JENNY

Wednesday

I stare down at my hands – the gold band is missing from my ring finger. My heart flutters wildly as I try to recall what I've done with it, noting at the same time the thick, dark lines beneath my short nails – which, instead of their usual, manicured, rounded shape are rough and jagged. My fingers tremble as I hold them up, my brain fighting to connect what I see with a memory of how they came to be like this. A plausible reason for the dirt embedded there doesn't come to me.

A knock makes me jump.

'You all right in there, love? You've been ages.' It's Mark. Obviously. Who else would it be? Images flit through my mind's eye, like beetles scuttling to hide, but I can't grasp hold of any that make sense.

'Yes, I'm fine,' I call, my focus fixed on the grey, marble-effect tiles above the sink as I speak this lie. I daren't tell him I can't even remember getting out of bed, or that I woke on the cold, tiled kitchen floor, stiff and aching having spent God knows how long lying there before sneaking back upstairs and into the bathroom, where I locked myself in, fearful; afraid of . . . what? Something. The unknown.

It's been a while since I've had a blackout like this one. I've had night terrors, but no episodes of leaving the bedroom, or house, since . . . *Oh, God.* I take a deep breath and swallow hard, squeezing the panicky feeling back down. There's something lurking in the recesses of my mind – something bad. I might not be able to recall what that something is, yet, but I'm sure it'll rear its ugly head. It'll surface and present itself to me in a way that'll no doubt catch me off-guard.

'You're going to be late, Jen,' Mark says, his tone gentle. He can probably sense something isn't right. That, or he's found my discarded wedding ring and is worried it's happening again. The memory of the last time I slipped my ring from my finger and hurled it at Mark is still fresh in my mind. I cringe as I recall the stream of expletives and insults that flew from my mouth. It wasn't my finest moment.

'Be there in a minute. Can you hurry the kids along for me?' I do my best to keep my voice steady, despite the fear rising within me. Why is my ring missing, and why is there mud under my nails?

I scrub at them with a nail brush for what feels like ten minutes before leaving the sanctuary of the bathroom with my dirty pyjamas bundled in my arms. I lift the lid of the hamper and shove them underneath the other clothes. I don't want Mark to see them.

What the *hell* did I do last night?

4

Chapter 2

MARK

My eyes take a while to focus. I reach a hand across the bed, but it's empty. What time is it? I feel groggy – no doubt due to the bottle of red I polished off last night – and my head hurts. I'll pretend it's because of the 'my body isn't used to getting that much sleep' story I like to tell myself, all the while knowing it's simply because I'm hung over. Midweek drinking is never a good idea. Although, every time I choose to partake, I seem to forget that. *It was a celebration*, the voice in my head says. Indeed, I do like to celebrate every achievement, however small – and last night's was because I've reconnected with an old uni chum who is going to propel my IT business to new heights. Or so he repeatedly promised me. The details of *how* he's going to help me accomplish this are hazy.

I slowly extricate myself from the tangle of duvet and stumble towards the en suite. Water is running; Jen must be getting ready. I collapse back on the bed and grab my mobile from the bedside table. I squint at the display. It's

7 a.m. Damn. My alarm didn't go off. Not that I'm a creature of habit or anything, but I have set my alarm for 6 a.m. every morning for the past ten years. And every time it goes off, I get up. Even if, like this morning, I'm worse for wear. Why not today?

Because it's been turned off.

Surely I didn't do that?

Lying with my head turned away from the light filtering through the curtains, I attempt to retrace my steps. Jen was in bed when I came up last night, having gone up before me while I drained the last drops of wine watching a repeat episode of *Breaking Bad*. I kissed her goodnight, placed my phone on the table and went to sleep as soon as my head hit the pillow. I didn't even go on my phone, and I certainly have no recollection of switching the alarm off. I frown and swipe the alarm notification across again to make sure it goes off tomorrow, and get up again. Jen has been in the bathroom far longer than usual.

'You all right in there, love?' I ask through the door.

She says she is. I tell her she's going to be late, wondering if her alarm also malfunctioned. Then with a jolt I realise I, too, will be late. Jen asks me to get Ella and Alfie sorted and I suppress a sigh. I have to get them their breakfast and make sure they have everything for school. It's the last thing I need right now on top of being late – my day is already going down the pan. And just as I chastise myself for negative thinking, telling myself the day will be what I make of it, something shiny on the fluffy cream rug at the end of the bed catches my attention. Nausea sweeps through me as I duck down to pick it up. A groan sounds through my pursed lips as I hold it between my thumb and forefinger. Jen's wedding ring.

Shit.

Bar her need to remove it for work sometimes, it's only ever come off her finger once before during our ten-year marriage. And on that occasion, all hell broke loose. Did she throw this at me last night? I couldn't have been too drunk to remember. It was only one bottle of wine. But something made her take it off. And now she's hiding away in the en suite.

I look at the closed door, half afraid of what I'm going to be faced with when she opens it. Then the squealing noises from downstairs remind me that I must hurry the morning routine along. I leave the bedroom and head to the kitchen, relieved at the excuse to put off confronting the reason Jen is avoiding me.

Chapter 3

JENNY

Mark has everything running like a well-oiled machine by the time I reach the kitchen, dressed for work, my face plastered with my usual make-up and a smile. Ella and Alfie are in their school uniforms, each sitting at the table eating two rounds of Marmite on toast, glasses of orange juice poured ready for them to down before packing them into the car to drive to Coleton Combe primary. Mark was going to do the drop-off today for once and I the pick-up, so that I could make an early start at the practice, but I'm guessing, given the time and the fact he is in a state of undress, I'm doing both.

It's times like these I wish he'd made use of the ample space in our house to set up his office here – it would save a lot of bother as well as keep business costs down, but he was adamant he needed a place away from the home, somewhere he could separate his work and family life. So, for now, his workplace is in Exeter, about a forty-minute drive away. The plus with having my vet practice just on the outskirts of the village is that I'm there in minutes – no rush-hour traffic to cope with; no road diversions or traffic jams – so I usually take the kids. Because this morning hasn't begun as planned, the early start is out of the window.

Mark looks up at me as I enter, his large, dark eyes filled with concern. 'Morning,' he says, placing his mug back on the table. No 'love' at the end, like normal. I swallow down my anxiety and muster a cheery response, quickly sidling up to him, leaning down and planting a kiss on his lips. His shoulders visibly lower as tension leaks from them. He was clearly expecting a different reaction.

'Well, you two are being super good!' I go to Ella and Alfie in turn, kissing the tops of their heads, then ruffling their mops of dark hair.

'Aw, Mummy,' Alfie moans, patting his hair down again. Ella merely rolls her eyes without comment. Mark casts his gaze towards them, then back to me. The tension in his body may have gone, but it remains heavy in the atmosphere and I realise I have to be the one to make the first move here.

'Not sure what happened with the alarms,' I venture. 'Sorry to have hogged the bathroom – you go ahead and get ready. I'll take the kids to school.' I walk back to him and slip my arms around his bare shoulders, my eyes dropping to his sexy, brown torso. His hands reach up, covering mine and, for a moment, my anxiety melts away with his warmth. Then, he abruptly drains his mug of coffee and stands. He's a foot taller than me, slim but with impressive, well-defined muscles in his chest and upper arms. He keeps himself fit with regular gym sessions and cycling. His strength has always been something I've adored. It was one of the things that drew me to him when we first met eleven years ago, yet it's also something that scares me sometimes. As much as I'd been determined to choose a life partner who was as opposite from my father as possible, they did have that in common.

I push those thoughts away as Mark takes my hand and turns it palm-up, dropping my wedding ring into it and giving me a questioning look.

'Are we okay, Jen?'

My throat constricts. 'Yes,' I say, keeping eye contact. 'I don't remember taking it off,' I admit. I slip the ring back on and Mark takes me in his arms. Warm. Safe. Secure. Or, that's how it used to be not that long ago. 'I wish we could stay like this all day,' I murmur into his smooth chest, then pull back, smiling up at my husband. The man who has stood by me all these years, the father of my children. He's a good dad – *really* good. He puts Ella and Alfie first and spends time with them, never raising his voice or losing his patience, always giving them his best. He's present, doesn't disappear for days on end like my own father used to. Doesn't leave them alone with a disturbed mother.

Or, maybe he does.

Am I disturbed? I have night terrors and, more worry-ingly, unexplainable moments in time where I'm unaware of what I'm doing. There've been occasions, like last night, when I've woken up, not in bed, and can't recall where I've been. So, maybe I am disturbed? But I have to believe I'm as good a mother as he is a father. We're a team. Despite what he did last year. However hard I try to dislodge it, though, an echo of mistrust remains wedged inside my mind like a cork stuck fast in a bottle.

'So do I, love. But the bills won't—'

'Pay themselves,' we say in unison.

'Look,' Mark says, 'if there's something playing on your mind . . .'

'We'll talk later,' I say, smiling to reassure him. I need the next eight hours to come up with a suitable explanation – a reason why I'm feeling this way. One that doesn't involve me telling him the truth.

Chapter 4

JENNY

I'm hot and flustered by the time I fling myself and the kids out the house to jump into the car, shouting goodbye up the stairs to Mark before I slam the door behind me and press my key fob to release the central locking.

'Why isn't Daddy taking us?' Ella asks as she pulls her booster seat from the rear of the car and positions it in the passenger side of my Volvo estate.

'Er . . . come on, missy,' I say, my brow furrowing. 'You know you have to sit in the back, it's—'

'The laaaaw,' Ella finishes, her expression mocking as she yanks it back out. 'Was worth a try.' The fact that as a family we're all able to finish each other's sentences screams at me that we repeat the same things often. It's like *Groundhog Day*.

'And it's because our alarms didn't go off this morning, we're running late and Daddy has to be in work by nine-thirty.' I'm thankful Alfie has at least quietly climbed into his own booster seat and has secured his seatbelt without me having to ask or help. 'Good boy, Alfie,' I say, shooting Ella a 'see – your six-year-old brother is better behaved than you' glare.

'*Whatever*,' Ella says, then pokes her tongue out at me.

'Ew! You're not going to put that thing back in your mouth, are you?'

'Ha-ha, Mum.'

I swear Ella has already begun the process of becoming a teenager, despite only being eight. As I walk towards the driver door, my gaze drifts back to the front of the house, and a black bin liner bundled beside the step catches my attention. I must have missed it when we rushed out. There's no time to mess about, so I shouldn't check now. I'll see what it is later. My hand hovers on the handle. No. I can't leave it – I have to know what it is and why it's been left there.

'Curiosity killed the cat,' I mumble to myself. 'Two secs, kids,' I say, and jog back to the step. There's nothing on the bag – no identifying labels or anything. It's not secured with its green drawstring; the top is just twisted around. Maybe Mark put it there ready to throw into the wheelie bin. But then I remember that we don't have black bin bags – I only buy the white ones specific for my Brabantia swing bin. My stomach lurches, a buried memory fleetingly resurfacing as I pick it up. It's quite heavy. Something makes me hesitate and suddenly I don't want to know what's inside.

'Hurry up, Mum!' Ella shouts from the car.

'Yes, sorry. Just got to bin this.' I take the bag and have a quick glance around. The long gravel drive is empty, and there is no noise from the neighbours – we can't even see their houses from here. I nip around the side of the house, where the wheelie bins and recycling boxes are kept. Out of sight of the children, I place the bag at my feet and crouch down. My hands shake as I carefully untwist the top, adrenaline shooting through my veins. It's like my body knows what's inside before I do.

The smell hits me first, and I gag.

'Jesus!' I automatically withdraw my face from it.

Inside is a mushy mess. The remnants of an animal, possibly a cat by the size and shape. Why on earth would someone put this on my doorstep? I've had *live* animals left outside my house before – presumably by those who knew I was a vet. Mark had joked that I was the local answer to unwanted pets – the equivalent to an abandoned baby being left at a hospital for a caring nurse to find. But leaving the *remains* of a pet is something else. There's no possible reason for it. Other than to shock; disgust. Tears burn my eyes. How could someone do this to a defenceless domestic animal? I really hope it didn't suffer. I'm about to twist the top of the bag again when I notice something else.

My heart plummets.

Gently rolling the top down, I uncover more of the mutilated animal, its tail, ginger and striped, curled to the side of the guts. More or less intact, albeit bloody.

Poor thing. Definitely a cat, then.

But that isn't what makes me gasp.

It's the dead butterfly lying on top.

Stumbling back from the bag, I lurch to the side of the house and throw up.

That can't be a coincidence.

Someone must know.

15

Chapter 5

JENNY

'Morning, Jen – thank God. I was beginning to worry.'
Hayley scoots her chair out from the reception desk and
stands, reaching over the counter to pass me a piece of
paper. 'These are the early morning animals in for surgery.
Nisha has done the preliminaries; Vanessa is organising
the operating room and I've booked them in.' Her voice
is clipped.

'Thanks so much – sorry I'm late.' I'm flustered, more
than I've ever been before. 'Samir not here yet?'

'No, and nor is Abi. I don't know what's going on
this morning; everything is out of whack. You know, the
place can't run smoothly if we're not all here on time.
Wouldn't be as bad if you hadn't expanded the services
we offer.' Her cheeks are pink, but the rest of her face
is pale. She looks tired. Hayley is the longest-serving
staff member, apart from myself and Samir. He and I set
up the Well Combe Pet Care practice after many long
discussions, which began over a pint and a large wine

at a dinner celebrating another vet's practice opening. I'd worked as a vet since qualifying but always for someone else. And, hitting thirty-five and realising I didn't want that forever, I had drunkenly divulged my 'big plan' to Samir – who, it turned out, was equally fed up with being stagnant in the current practice. It was a divine intervention, we'd decided.

We were lucky to have the money to buy the premises and accompanying land, thanks to Samir's parents and to Mark's grandparents, who'd left him a significant sum when they passed. Mark saw it as an investment opportunity, with the hope that eventually a small building to accommodate his IT business could be added within the grounds.

To begin with, the vet practice didn't even have any veterinary nurses – we only had a small client list and Hayley ran pretty much everything while we did the direct pet care. Our plan had always been to build the business, though – and three years ago, things finally came together when we hired Vanessa, who is the senior nurse now. Nisha came on board more recently, at the same time as Abi who Hayley is training up on the reception but who also has her eye on becoming a veterinary nurse; she's bright and enthusiastic and young enough to 'mould'. It's a happy practice. We all get along – each bringing a unique set of skills to the table.

Hayley's been under the weather lately with a flare-up of her arthritis, and I don't like to think I've caused her any stress. 'You go grab a cuppa. I'll call Samir and Abi – I'm sure they're on their way. I don't know if there's been an accident or something, because the roads are busy and there seems to be a lot of activity for a Wednesday.'

'Maybe there's an issue on the main road then – often people use the village as a cut-through to town if there is.' Hayley tuts and bustles off in the direction of the staffroom while I take some deep breaths and attempt to regain control of the day. I have a weird feeling, but it's one I can't place – like déjà vu, but not quite. As I'm about to call Samir, he bursts in.

'Bloody hell – what a shit morning.' His arms are loaded with a cardboard box and some files, topped with a Marvel Avengers lunch bag – 'temporarily borrowed' from his seven-year-old son because Duffy, the family cockapoo, destroyed his own when he left it lying around at home. Ella and Alfie are so desperate for a dog but if I'm honest, I'm afraid of the added responsibility. I've promised them a rabbit instead – although not given a specific date for its arrival. I'm hoping to put it off for another year or so.

I smile at Samir, shaking my head. His cursing is terrible, but he says it in such a way that it never sounds offensive. I think it's his accent, which gives his bad language a certain charming quality, although it's diluted since I first met him back when we studied at Plymouth university. There isn't a huge Indian community locally and as he's been living in Devon for almost twenty years, sometimes I catch a Devonian dialect slipping into his conversation. I have asked him to refrain from spouting profanities when clients are around, but he lets loose when it's just us.

'Not just me, then?' I say, replacing the receiver. 'Our alarm didn't go off. I rushed the kids to school, practically flinging them into class late, then got stuck in traffic, something that *never* happens here – the whole day is on the wrong track now.'

'Don't you let Mark hear you saying that. Isn't he always declaring, "The day is what you make of it"?'

'Hah! Yeah – he's all about positivity, that one.' I raise my eyebrows. Samir laughs as he hurries through the reception, turning and bumping the swing doors open with his back, before disappearing into his consulting room. We've been friends long enough to be able to comfortably take the mick out of our respective spouses, as well as each other. I couldn't ask for a better business partner and friend.

Returning my attention to the phone, I dial Abi. Her mobile rings twice then diverts to voicemail. I leave a brief 'hope everything's okay' message, a niggling feeling creeping over my skin. Maybe she's just caught up in traffic too. I walk towards my own room, the sound of barking greeting me as I open the door. Surprise mingles with relief when I see that it's Abi, struggling to manage a large golden retriever – all I can see is fur and arms as she attempts to get him to sit on the weighing scale.

'Oh, you're here!' I say, finally shrugging off my coat to hurry to her aid. 'When did you sneak in?'

'Nisha . . . let me . . . in . . . the back.' Her words escape her in fits and bursts as she grapples with Goldie. I try not to laugh.

It takes several attempts to steady Goldie long enough to get his weight, but eventually we manage it, and Abi records it on the system. She straightens her uniform then redoes her ponytail, which had come undone during the wrestling, brushing the long, black-treacle-coloured strands with her fingertips, dragging it back and securing it with the band.

'This isn't really in your job description,' I say. 'But thanks.'

'I wanted to help, seeing as I was a bit late. Felt bad when I saw clients waiting – thought I'd offer my assistance to speed things along. But, given my failed attempt at this, maybe I should stick to the desk job.' She throws her head back, laughing awkwardly, then rushes out the door.

Too late, I realise I should've corrected her, praised her instead of letting her think she'd done a bad job, but my mind is not quite here. I need to make sure it is, though, because in twenty minutes I'm going to be operating on our first animal with Samir and Vanessa.

Get your head in the game.

During a quiet moment in the lunch break, the image of the mutilated cat barges into my mind. I'd successfully kept it at bay during operations, but now it's forced its way in. Who would do such a thing? If it hadn't been for the butterfly, I might've dismissed it as roadkill or something – maybe the cat had been hit by a car right outside our house and the driver had used what they had to scoop up the remains and deposited it on my step because they assumed I was the owner. A nice, neat explanation. But the butterfly ruins that theory.

The butterfly ruins *everything*.

The staffroom door swings open and I catch my breath, startled out of my thoughts.

'Oh, Abi,' I say, somewhat breathlessly. She walks in carrying a small, pink-striped box.

'Cream cakes from Kelly's – couldn't resist. Sorry, it's why I was late – had to wait for her to open up, then she took a while to serve me. Thought it'd be worth it?' Abi gives me an apprehensive look as she stretches out her arm, offering me the open box. Does she think I'll chastise her? I hope I'm not that kind of boss. I smile, keen to make up for my earlier omission, too. My gaze catches on the skin of Abi's arm as her long-sleeved polo shirt rides up, revealing a succession of raised white lines that run horizontally along the inner forearm. Echoes of trauma, I think with concern, and I avert my eyes.

'Thanks, Abi. They do look good.' I reach in and remove the cream-filled chocolate choux bun and take a bite. 'Oh. My. God,' I say between mouthfuls. 'Haven't had one of these since I was a kid. My mother used to—' I break off.

'Used to . . . ?' Abi prompts.

'Oh.' I wave a hand dismissively. 'Nothing.' I stuff my mouth with another chunk, so that I can't speak any further. I don't want to make the day any worse by bringing that woman into my conversation. It's the first time I've actually thought about her for ages. Every now and then, out of the blue, something random triggers a memory to pop into my head – but most of the time I manage to keep everything I ever knew about my mother locked up in the dark, cobwebby recesses of my mind. It's been over twenty years since I had to see her hard-featured face.

'Has she passed?' Abi says, her expression soft. She obviously thinks that's why I don't want to continue talking about her. It would be so much easier if I were to just say 'yes', but I find myself telling the truth.

'No. Or, at least, I don't think she has. I wouldn't know. We're not in contact.' I give a strained smile.

If she's shocked by my admission, she masks it well. 'Sorry,' she says. 'That's sad.'

I shrug. 'I guess it is, in many ways. But I'm better off without her.' I feel a stirring of discomfort talking to Abi about this – she's young, a relatively new employee, not a friend. But then, that may well be why I've chosen to open up to her. That's enough for now, though, and I divert the attention away from myself. 'You have a good relationship with your mum?'

'Ah, you know – hit and miss, really.' Now it's Abi waving her hand dismissively. 'She has her moments, but I feel sometimes she regrets having had me.'

I blink, not sure what to say – as much as we might have an uncaring mother in common, I don't know her situation. But I can guarantee it's not the same as mine past that one similarity. A memory of mother pulling away from the front door as my friends walked by on their way to school pops into my head. She was afraid her little girl was going to bolt, make a run for it and escape the confines of the four walls, leaving her there alone. 'You aren't like them; you are better off learning at home with me. You love spending time with Mummy, don't you?'

I squeeze my eyes closed for a second, before casting around for a change of subject. 'Thank you for stepping in to help this morning – I'm glad you're thinking of undertaking veterinary nurse training. Being a receptionist is great, but I can tell you've got far more ambition.'

'Yes, I have!' Her face lights up. 'I'd love to be like you. You've got a fabulous career and a family. You've really got it all – I'm in awe.'

'Oh, Abi – that's very kind of you to say.' I give a nervous laugh. If only she knew what was really going on. 'Sometimes you have to fight to escape your past, and have faith in yourself.'

'I'm a little lacking on the self-confidence front.' Abi drops her gaze. 'Hard to see your own worth when others tell you you're never going to amount to anything,' she says, her voice quavering.

A lump forms in my throat, her words sparking empathy. 'Well, you will prove them wrong, Abi. I have every confidence in you – make sure you back yourself. You're doing really well here already. I'm so pleased we employed you.'

'Yeah, me too.' She flashes me a wide smile. Her features – high, sharp-looking cheekbones and small, round eyes – transform from severe to striking. She reminds me of Snow White, with her black hair and creamy complexion. I mean it when I say I'm pleased I hired her. There's something about Abi that makes me want to take her under my wing. But I have to admit, I'm not sure whose benefit I'm doing it for – hers or mine. It's like I'm compelled to do something really good, to make up for my family history; for all the badness. I suppose that's partly why I chose to become a vet: I wanted to heal, where they hurt.

Chapter 6

MARK

My heart thuds against my ribs. I stand over the linen hamper, its lid gripped in my hand as I stare at the clothes inside. The edge of Jenny's pyjamas caught my eye when I deposited my jogging bottoms, and now I'm almost doubled-up as though I've just been punched in the gut. I can see that the material is damp, and I can tell that the brown stains are mud even without dragging them out to give them a closer inspection. These were the pyjamas she was wearing last night, and yet they're beneath other dirty laundry. Like she's purposely hidden them. Her wedding ring, flung to the floor for whatever reason, might've been dismissible on its own. But together with her increasingly strange behaviour, this discovery makes it impossible to carry on brushing my fears aside.

I've always known that Jen held back certain aspects of her life from me – one of the first things she said when we met was that she'd had a 'complicated and unsatisfying' childhood, culminating in her leaving home as soon as she could – going off to university and never returning to her roots. She'd told me the bare minimum, then asked that we never speak of it again. When we married, none of her family were guests – it's the way she wanted it.

And, to this day, I've never once pressed for details. Even in the throes of one of her night terrors, where she awoke screaming and terrified – shouting 'they're coming for me' and repeating the words, 'I'm not like him' – I didn't question her. Even after the times I found her passed out on the kitchen floor, or in the garden, cold and shivering as she'd been lying there for hours, did I ask her why she had these nightmares and blackouts; what it was in her past that haunted her.

And she's never offered up an explanation.

It's one of *The Unknowns*, as I refer to them, about my wife – of which there are a few. I find myself wondering sometimes if it's just me she keeps in the dark, or whether she confides in Roisin. But, from the times we've spent with her best friend and her husband, Harry, Jen's always changed the subject if the conversation ever touched upon our childhoods, so perhaps Roisin doesn't know her as well as she thinks either. Despite having gaps in my knowledge, though, I've supported Jenny. Loved her. Trusted her.

She doesn't trust me, though. It's been festering just beneath the surface since last year, threatening to push through and spread its poison – destroying our marriage bit by bit. As I stare down at the bundle of dirty clothes, I realise that's why she'd been locked in the bathroom this morning – why she was hiding from me.

It's happened again.

How could I have missed it?

You were drunk.

I replace the hamper lid and plonk myself down on the bed. The sleepwalking – the *blackouts* – have been occasional; it's mostly night terrors she suffers from. But they were more frequent last year. Dredging up the memories makes my stomach churn. After all, it was my fault. But I did everything I could to stop her from harming herself, including barricading the door one time. That failed as Alfie had needed us during the night and was distraught when he couldn't get into our room. Jen was furious so instead, since then, I have made sure to intercept her – preventing her from leaving the house by following her, coaxing her back to bed.

But she must've slipped through the net on this occasion. That's only happened once before that I know of.

I wonder where she went this time.

Chapter 7

JENNY

The day, starting off as badly as it did, has actually ended up being a good one, and I'm feeling calm and relaxed as I steer into the driveway and park up next to Mark's Audi. Maybe I over-reacted to the situation this morning – to both my blackout and the mutilated cat. The simplest explanations are often the right ones and I'm more confident now that I jumped to the wrong conclusion. Let's face it, it wouldn't be the first time. Someone from my past somehow finding out where I live seems unlikely after all this time, especially given the fact I'm a couple hundred miles away from my hometown and don't even go under the same name anymore.

I mean, how could they have found out? I've managed to keep it a secret from my own husband for eleven years, and there's absolutely no link between my ex-family and me. The butterfly is just a weird coincidence. Has to be. Probably got bundled into the bin liner accidentally, having landed on the bloody mess and getting itself stuck to it. I almost feel stupid for having reacted so badly this morning.

The smell of jerk chicken greets me as I step over the threshold, and I inhale deeply as I enter the kitchen.

'Oh, my God, that smells divine,' I say to Mark. He's brandishing a plastic ladle and has donned a blue-check apron. He flamboyantly stirs the dish. Alfie and Ella are laughing at him as they sit at the table, knives and forks in hand. 'Thanks for picking the kids up from after-school club. Hey, kids,' I turn my attention to them. 'Good days at school?'

Ella wrinkles her nose and I wait for her to respond with her usual 'I don't remember what we did' answer. 'It was good,' she says instead. 'We're doing a nature project. It's cool.'

'Oh, *is* it?' I raise my eyebrows, surprised to hear excitement in her voice. Lately, she's not been showing much interest in schoolwork and even though I've kept it to myself, I was getting worried. I'd begun to think maybe she was being bullied. But she certainly seems happy in this moment as she's rambling on about habitats and something about the physical characteristics of insects. I drop my bag on the worktop and go across to Mark, giving him a kiss. 'And how's the love of my life's day been?' I almost wince at my choice of phrase. It's been a while since I referred to him in that way, and judging by his expression, he thinks the same.

'It's been productive. A bit stressy, though. You?' There's only a hint of a smile on his face and I sense there's more to the abrupt 'you?' question. It's loaded. I feel as though he's angry with me, and I don't know why. I explained the ring this morning – was quick to reassure him – but there's something unspoken between us now. I take a step back, scrutinising his face for clues. Suspicion clouds my mind as apprehension surges, my muscles tensing. It's like he knows something I don't.

'It was busy, the way I like it, really.' I attempt to keep my voice steady, in spite of my rising anxiety. 'I think the new team are all working well together and I had a good chat with one of the newest members today. She kind of reminds me of my younger self.' I go to dip my fingertip into the pot of jerk chicken and it's swiftly batted away.

'Nooo! Do not spoil the chef's special dish, Mrs Johnson – you must wait.' The children laugh, but his tone is sharp and I can tell he's being serious.

'Sorry,' I say, trying to catch his eyes, but he avoids mine. 'Is there something you're not telling me?' I keep my words hushed, so as not to alert Ella and Alfie to the newly tense atmosphere.

'Didn't you hear the news?' He covers the simmering pot of food and walks away from the oven, heading into the lounge. Assuming he doesn't want to share whatever was on the news in front of the children, I follow.

'No. Haven't had the radio on today. What's happened?' We're standing just inside the doorway; the TV is on with the sound muted. Mark's eyes flit from it to the floor, looking anywhere but at me. There's a lump in my throat, and I cough to clear it. Whatever has happened must be pretty bad to cause this reaction in Mark. Maybe I was right: there *was* an accident this morning, causing the increased traffic through the village. Was it a fatality? Someone I know? My pulse jumps about – oh, God – something's happened to Roisin. We've not had a catch-up in weeks. But no, I think. Mark wouldn't be telling me like this if my best friend had been injured or died. I take a deep, calming breath. 'What, Mark? For God's sake, what is it?'

'All day it's been filled with reports of a local woman who's gone missing. Didn't return home after a quiz night at the pub last night.'

'Our pub?' I ask, shocked and appalled. It can't have happened here, in Coleton Combe – I'd have definitely heard that.

'The one and only Union,' Mark says, finally looking at me. 'They started the search early this morning, apparently, when her partner raised the alarm.'

'You'd have thought we'd have heard the commotion then.'

'We were late up. And I slept so heavily,' he says, shrugging. 'You don't usually, though – didn't you hear anything at all?'

My mind whirrs. I can't confide about the blackout in this moment – not when I don't yet know what I did. I decide to play dumb. 'No, nothing. Actually slept well for once. Hence us both oversleeping. You know how it is, when you sleep heavily, it's like your body was craving it and wanted more.' I use one of his own beliefs. 'Who is it, anyway? Who's missing?' Acid churns in my stomach as I wait for his reply. It's a village where everyone knows everyone else, so it stands to reason I'm going to know the name he utters.

He stares at me intently, not blinking. It's like he's analysing me, trying to see something behind my eyes, and I find myself hoping to God that whatever he's looking for isn't there. Sighing, his face crumpling, he very quietly says: 'Olivia Edwards.'

My innards twist and the ground seems to shake beneath my feet. I stumble to the sofa and sit down heavily, before I fall. My heart bangs against my ribs, its vibrations spreading through my body, and all I can hear is the whooshing of my own blood, a pulsating cacophony in my ears.

I *do* know Olivia Edwards. We both do.

She's the woman Mark had an affair with.

Chapter 8

MARK

Since hearing the news on the way to work this morning, I've thought of nothing else. By the time I reached my office – a room I'm temporarily renting on a floor of a communications building – my head was banging again, despite the paracetamol I'd taken for the hangover. The details were sketchy at that point, but hearing the murmurings of shocked and concerned villagers and seeing the local news discussing Olivia's last-known movements, a fresh horror swept through me like a tidal wave.

Now, Jenny's ashen face, her features frozen in a thousand-yard stare, drives this horror up even further. It's not just shock I see, it's fear – her dilated pupils almost obscure her forest-green irises. My pulse smashes hard in my throat. The last time I saw her face like this was last year, when I brought her out of a trance-like state by taking her by the shoulders and shaking her. She had no recollection of what she'd been doing for the hours previous to me finding her like that. I'd been drinking that evening, and she'd got out of bed without me hearing.

I still don't know how long she'd been gone before I awoke and found her side of the bed empty; cold. I'd had no choice. I *had* to go looking for her. Even now, I can still feel the sheer panic in my gut as I drove around searching the streets. Can still feel the tug of guilt when I realised where she was. The vision of her standing there, in Olivia's garden, a rock in her hand still vivid. I shudder at the memory.

Jen sits mute in front of me, her lips twitching. The entire village, and now the whole country, are talking about Olivia's disappearance, but I'm only interested in what she has to say.

'They're saying she was taken from the street.' My eyes implore hers as I try to snap her from her thoughts.

'Taken?' The word is a whisper.

'Yes. Abducted.'

'Shit.'

I feel a twinge of irritation. Isn't she going to utter more than single-word responses? 'I mean, that's really scary, isn't it? In our little village. Who'd do something like that?'

She shakes her head, then sucks in a deep breath. 'Right,' she says, blinking rapidly, then straightening. 'We can't talk about it now. Let's have dinner. I don't want the kids to know there's something wrong.'

I stare at her. *Let's have dinner?* How can she be so calm after what she's just learned? Before I have chance to ask, she gets up from the sofa and heads back into the kitchen. I stand frozen, dumbstruck. I'm not altogether sure what reaction I expected, but it's not this. A little voice in my mind says she's acting like this because she already knew. She's definitely been behaving oddly and what with the muddy pyjamas, her wedding ring flung to the floor . . . 'No. Don't do that,' I whisper, rubbing my hands roughly over my head to silence the voice. It was a coincidence she had a blackout last night, that's all.

'Are you dishing up, then?' she calls from the kitchen.

'Yep – two secs.' I exhale forcefully, pushing my shoulders back in an attempt to compose myself, then join them at the table.

All smiles.

All forced.

Am I going to ignore the red flags that are waving madly in my mind?

I choke on a mouthful of food and feel Jen's eyes on me as I gulp some water down. I could really do with a glass of red, but I need a clear head in case Jen has another episode tonight. I glance at her, catching her eye and we hold each other's gaze for what feels like minutes. The unspoken accusation hovers invisibly over us. I can't blame Jen entirely for the mistrust that's engulfed our marriage this past year.

Not when I'm the one who caused it.

Chapter 9

JENNY

Tiredness consumes me, yet I lie awake, my eyes wide and staring. The glow of the streetlamp leaks through the curtains into the darkened room, throwing shapes onto the ceiling and walls like a child's night-light projecting ocean waves to soothe them into a blissful sleep. Sometimes I wish I was a child again so these things might work. Then I remember my childhood and am grateful I'll never have to live through it again.

Mark is quiet and still beside me. How do men do that? Just fall asleep before you can even count to ten? Annoys me no end. I have the urge to prod him awake so he might join me in this insomniac nightmare. Occasions where I fall asleep within an hour of slipping into bed are rare. Since that awful time last year, the sleep disturbances from my childhood have returned. I flip from nights of sleeplessness to those filled with night terrors and sleep-walking. If that's what the moments of nothingness I experience are – I've never sought medical advice, too terrified the truth will be exposed for all to see. So I do my best to deny they happen at all, burying each episode alongside acknowledgement of my parents' existence.

Mark's always referred to them as blackouts, if we ever speak about them, that is. They've been part of my life, on and off, for almost as long as I can remember – but if I think about it hard enough, I can pinpoint their onset. I'm sure if I were to ever see a psychologist, or counsellor, they would also home in on the exact moment they began.

It was when my dad was first taken away from me.

'Jane! Jane!'

Jane's body jiggled on the mattress as her mother's hands shook her shoulders, bringing her out of a deep sleep. She blinked her eyes open, a feeling of fear beginning in her tummy and bubbling up, making her feel sick. Her mother's face was inches from hers and looked ghostly white. Tears streaked down it like she was leaking. Jane swallowed down a scream.

'What, Mummy? What's wrong?' Her voice was squeaky, through tiredness or fright, she wasn't sure. What was going on? It wasn't morning – time to get up – because it was still dark in her room. She hadn't needed the night-light for months now, finally feeling grown-up enough to forgo the added security; she already had her tatty, beloved bear – Daddy said she didn't need the light as well. Now her mum flicked the bedside lamp on, further illuminating her face, and Jane noticed her mummy's eyes were red, wide; her mouth twisted.

'You have to get up,' she said, her voice a raspy whisper. The duvet was ripped from her; cold air touched her bare arms. Her mother fumbled with a jumper, shaking hands trying to feed Jane's head then arms through.

'Mummy, you're scaring me. Am I dreaming?'

'It's not a dream, Jane.'

'Claire, where the fuck are you?' Her daddy's voice boomed through the quiet night. And just as he shouted, causing a new ripple of terror to spread through her body, Jane saw flashes of blue light coming through the curtains.

'Coming! We're coming!'

'I'm scared,' Jane said again as her mother dragged her, still barefoot, from her bedroom and then down the stairs.

'It's too fucking late,' Daddy yelled.

Jane couldn't see him, only heard his voice as it exploded in the hallway. Her mother pushed trainers roughly onto Jane's feet, squeezing them, making her wince.

'I need socks with these; they give me blisters.' Tears sprung to her own eyes now, as bewilderment over-whelmed her.

'No time. Gotta go.'

Jane didn't resist being pulled by her arm away from the hallway, through the lounge towards the kitchen, then to the back door. 'Daddy?' Her eyes implored his as he came into view. They were wide, his face unsmiling, his chest heaving with fast breathing. He was scared, too. Seeing him like that immediately doubled her own fear.

'Hey, Princess.' He lunged forward, scooping her into his arms. 'I'm sorry. We're going on a night-time adventure.' His arms felt strong around her. Usually she'd feel comforted, but tonight it was all wrong. 'You got everything, Claire?'

'No, Paul! What the fuck! You expect me to have packed for this occasion?'

Jane wrapped her arms more tightly around her daddy's neck, twisting her legs around his middle, her own breathing now rapid, almost matching his. 'Is someone trying to hurt us?'

Her question went unanswered as he turned and opened the back door. Cool air surged inside and curled itself around her, momentarily snatching her breath away.

And then, lights. So many lights blinded her. Yelling filled her ears. So many different voices. Sheer panic flooded her little body, and she slammed her eyes shut, screwing them up as tightly as she could. High-pitched screaming echoed in her head.

Then . . . she was falling.

'Jen. Jen, love.' My shoulders shake; my body rocks on the mattress.

'What! Do we have to go?' I bolt up into a sitting position, the duvet sliding from me. The room is dark. Memories hurtle into my mind and blind panic sends me shooting out of bed and towards the door.

'Jen!' Mark is suddenly beside me, gentle hands on my arms, his soothing shushing warm against my ear. 'You were dreaming, love. It's okay – you're safe.'

I take a slow, juddering breath. It *had* been a dream. I was Jenny now, not the frightened little Jane anymore. Nothing is wrong now. Mark guides me back to bed, and I let him tuck me in as if I were a child. If only it had happened like this that night, when I was eight years old. If only my father hadn't been snatched from me, leaving me with *her*. A shiver runs down my spine, a memory of Claire digging her nails into my neck as she shoved me into the living room, yelling that I have to stay home with her for my own good. 'You can't go out like the others, Jane. No one likes you. I'm the only one who loves you enough to stay with you.' Every evening ended with me curled up in my bed, crying myself to sleep while wishing for a different life.

'Can you hold me until I fall to sleep?' I lift the duvet cover and shuffle my body towards Mark, turning on my side so my back is against his chest. He immediately wraps his arm around my middle and we nestle together. I feel his breath against my hair, and his warmth as he pushes against me.

'I do love you, you know,' he says.

I want to say it back, but my lips press together, the words refusing to leave my mouth.

Chapter 10

JENNY

Thursday

'You all right this morning?' Mark joins us at the kitchen table, sliding into the chair opposite me. He's addressing us all, but I know he's really asking me, because of last night. Unlike the blackouts, I can usually recall the fact I've had a nightmare. I eventually fell asleep after hours of thinking about *them*. I know I shouldn't give them headspace, but every now and then, they take hold of my thoughts. It's allowing them to have control, I know that – and I fight with everything I've got to stop myself from giving them any opportunity to ruin my carefully constructed life. Sometimes I win; sometimes they do.

'Raring to begin the day,' I say, with as much enthusiasm as I can muster. 'What say you, kids?'

'I'm in charge of Fudge today,' Alfie declares, his eyes wide with excitement at the prospect of looking after the class gerbil. 'Kaz had him yesterday and let him loose in the classroom!' He slaps a hand to his mouth, but a chuckle escapes. 'Mrs Fleming made him stay in at break to find him and it took Kaz aaaages.'

'Well, I hope you do a good job today and keep him safe, eh?' I say.

'Do you get to bring him home in the holiday?' Ella says. 'I did that – do you remember, Mummy? But it was terrible because—'

I suddenly realise where this is going and shoot Ella a warning glance, waving my hand in front of my throat in a slashing motion. I quickly interject. 'I don't think they do home visits for the class animals anymore, Ella – do they, Alfie?'

'No.' He lowers his head. '*Apparently*, it's not safe to let them leave the school building – only with one of the teachers.' I smile at the way he says 'apparently'. Bless him, he's growing up so quickly.

'I think that's best,' Mark says, taking a slurp of coffee. 'Every animal needs love and care, however small they are. Isn't that right, Mummy?'

Even though I know Mark is aiming this at me because I'm a vet, and obviously it's my job to care for all animals no matter what, the comment feels pointed. Like he knows what I found on the doorstep yesterday, and somehow blames me. Of course, I also know my own anxiety and guilt is causing me to think this way. He could equally be referring to the pet Ella has just mentioned – the incident that occurred during Ella's summer break when she brought Hammy Hamster to stay. Ella has always blamed me for the hoover sucking him up – not questioning her own decision to let him have run of the lounge without telling me.

46

'Absolutely. They are all important, even the flies.' This, I don't believe in the slightest. I loathe flies.

'They only live for a month,' Ella pipes up. 'Did you know that?'

'Not in here they don't,' Mark mutters under his breath as he winks at me. I almost laugh.

'Then they should have a good month, shouldn't they. Live life to the full,' I say.

Ella giggles. 'In that case, can we buy some treats for them, like you give the dogs at the vets'?'

'Let's not go that far. But the point is, every animal and insect is a living creature. They deserve to be treated well. And, Alfie – if you're responsible for Fudge today, that means thinking about his needs first. It's lovely to be able to take them out of the cage, but if it's not in a controlled way, with Mrs Fleming's knowledge, then you have to think of another way to have fun with him. Like, you could get some old cardboard rolls and ask her to pop one in his cage so you can watch him running in and out of it, or something like that, okay?'

'Yes, Mum. I'll do it all properly, I promise.'

'Good. There's an empty roll in the bathroom, and the kitchen roll is about to run out, so you can take those with you if you like.'

We finish up breakfast and once Alfie has collected the cardboard rolls, we say our goodbyes to Mark. We've not discussed the nightmare I had last night; it's brushed aside together with any mention of Olivia's disappearance – both topics too difficult to bring up easily. The ten o'clock news didn't add anything we didn't already know about the abduction. Maybe the police are keeping developments close to their chests, or maybe there are absolutely no leads and they've zero theories or suspects. Either scenario chills my blood. I really hope they find her today.

'I might be a bit late tonight, by the way,' Mark says as I'm bundling the kids out the door.

'Oh, why?'

'Do you remember my old uni mate, Brett, who said he was going to help me build the business? The one I was speaking with the other night?'

My stomach lurches. 'Vaguely,' I lie. I'd left Mark chatting away on the phone, annoyed he was being so loud and preventing me hearing the TV, so I hadn't heard much of the conversation. 'Strap yourselves in, please,' I tell the kids as they run to the car.

'Well, he's driving down from Somerset today to talk his plan through with me in person. And you know what it's like – we'll end up feeling the need to finish off the meeting in the pub.'

'But, you're driving . . .'

'Oh, I'm going to come back here, drop the car and walk to The Union with him.'

My heart sinks at the mention of The Union. I can't believe they're going to the pub Olivia went to before she was taken.

'And what about Brett?' Brett crawling out of the wood-work now isn't good timing. Why is he flavour of the month all of a sudden? I don't like it. I'm aware I also went into business with someone I went to uni with – I know it can happen. But Samir and I had been in touch that entire time. Prior to the other night Mark hadn't spoken to Brett since he first introduced us back when we got together. That was, like, eleven years ago – and Brett had unsettled me then, so I was glad they lost contact.

I wonder why he's back in touch now? I bet Brett has some hare-brained get-rich-quick pyramid scheme thing going and Mark is gullible enough to fall for it.

'I didn't think you'd mind – I said he could crash here for the night?'

What? My breath catches in my chest. I want to shout 'no way', but know that would come across as an over-reaction. 'On a weeknight?' I grimace. Having Brett staying in my home with everything going on at the moment is the last thing I need. What if I have a night terror while he's here – or even worse, a blackout? But there's no time to put up any kind of argument – prob-ably why Mark chose not to tell me before. Annoyance edges my voice as I call back, 'Sure, if you want.' And then, mutter, 'It's already a done deal whatever I say anyway.'

Closing the door, I plaster on a smile for the kids. It drops from my face immediately as I spot a black bin liner to the side of the doorstep, and my breath hitches in my chest.

Another one? My mind spins with all the questions and implications. I don't understand. Whoever is doing this can't know I will be the one to find it. I don't always leave the house first, although lately that has been the case. Is someone watching the house? The hairs at the base of my neck prickle at the thought, my eyes frantically searching the driveway. Our house is one of three large detached properties along this lane, all have quite long driveways and opposite the houses the lane is lined with trees, beyond which are fields. It would be easy for someone to conceal themselves just behind the trees, to spy on the properties. I stare down the length of the driveway. I can only just see the trees from here, and I wonder how much of my house can be seen from there.

Without bothering to look inside the liner, I grab it, jog around the side of the house and deposit it in the bin. I'll deal with it later – I'll pop back before I head to my meeting this afternoon. As I climb in the car, I glance at Ella and Alfie through the rear-view mirror. Seeing their innocent, light-brown faces staring back fills me with love. They need looking after, to have security and unconditional love. They certainly don't need their mother to lose her mind.

I glance back at the house as we drive out and wonder how much it would cost to get a security camera.

Chapter 11

JENNY

Slade Lane, the road we usually take to the school, is blocked by a large lorry, and I want to scream in frustration. Why they try and drive these narrow lanes is beyond me. One cottage, on the corner approaching the post office, was smashed into last year – the lorry took a chunk of the building clean off. After that, villagers petitioned to prevent large goods vehicles from coming through, but to no avail.

It put the fear into a few homeowners along that road, though; I remember the furore well. Caroline Brewer, who's lived in Coleton Combe her entire life, put a camera on the front of her house angled towards the road – all apparently above board – and rumour has it she spends pretty much all day sitting watching the vehicles go by and as soon as she spots a lorry, she darts out and 'oversees' their safe passage past her home. I laughed when I was told this, but actually, I don't blame her. I just hope this lorry isn't wedged, or worse has ploughed into another house.

When I finally lose my patience, I hook a right to circumnavigate whatever chaos might be occurring. Then, as I drive around the bend, I realise my mistake with a sharp stab of alarm. Police crime scene tape stretches the width of the road ahead of me. It's the location Olivia Edwards was believed to have been taken from en route to her house.

'Dammit,' I mutter, while attempting a three-point turn that ends up being a six-point turn. I grumble under my breath about the estate car being too long for a simple manoeuvre, but really I know it's because seeing the police cordon has made this all so very real and my nerves can't take it. This is madness; there's never been anything like this happen before in Coleton Combe. And all the added police presence, journalists and news crews have created more traffic, more congestion for our little village. It's a selfish thought, but I'm tempted to arrange a holiday to get us all away from the rigmarole until it dies down. *If* it does. What if they don't find Olivia? Icy tendrils tickle my spine. The worst-case scenario crosses my mind and I shake my head to rid myself of it.

'What's the matter, Mummy? What are we doing?' Alfie says.

I force my attention to the here and now. 'I thought it would be quicker to come this way because of the stupid lorry, but I was wrong.' Beads of sweat prickle my forehead. 'It's a warm one today.'

'You need to be more patient, Mum,' Ella says. I give a short, sharp laugh. She's right, of course. Although I'm fairly used to little or no sleep, I admit I'm more irritated than I should be.

I wonder why!

My finger-drumming on the steering wheel intensifies with each passing minute, until finally I see movement ahead. The lorry makes it through, thankfully without leaving a path of destruction in its wake. As I reach where it'd been, I see the problem. An ITV news van is parked on the double yellow lines, narrowing the road even further. I grip the wheel a little tighter. It's parked near to where Olivia lives. Every now and then, you hope for something exciting to happen in a sleepy village. But this isn't the kind of exciting I like or need. A flashback to my nightmare last night brings bile into my mouth.

'Daddy's had to leave,' her mum said. Tears stripped away lines of her dark-beige make-up, leaving streaks of paler skin. She looked like a Frazzle crisp.

'Why did the police take him?' Jane said. She had been flung to the grassy area in the back garden as men surrounded her daddy, their flashlights ablaze, voices loud and scary – yelling for him to 'get down on the ground, now!' That had been the last thing she remembered before waking up in a strange bed. Her mummy said she'd been asleep for ten hours, but she found that hard to believe. How could she have gone to sleep after what had happened? Fear still made her heart pound as she waited for her mum to say something. Explain why her daddy had been taken.

'He's helping them with something, that's all.'

Jane knew a lie when she heard one. 'I'm eight, Mum. Not a baby. And I'm *not* stupid.'

Claire sighed and shook her head. 'Look. It's me and you now. We only have each other, and we're all that's important, okay?'

'No. No, it's not okay. I want my daddy. Where is he?' Panic rose up inside her, like she was filling with hot air and would burst.

'Jane, sweetheart.' Claire put her head in her hands, then took a deep breath and looked Jane straight in the eye. 'The truth is, your daddy did something wrong.'

'What did he do?' Tears made her voice thick.

'It's complicated. But he was trying to look after us. Make sure we had enough money. So, he took a little bit, to help us. But I'm afraid he did it more than once and now, because he can't pay it back, he has to give them his time instead.'

'I don't understand.'

'You've heard about prison?'

Jane nodded. Her body felt numb, like she was there, but not there. 'It's where people are punished.'

'Well, yes – their punishment is being kept from those they love for a time.'

'How long will Daddy have to be punished?' Jane asked. She watched her mother's face crumple. She was silent for ages and Jane pushed her hands into her mother's chest. 'How long?' she shouted.

'Sorry, Jane. I know you love your daddy. But, like I said, it's just you and me now. He's not coming back.'

Jane felt her heart bang fast and hard. In her chest, in her ears, her stomach, everywhere. Her breathing shallowed and, for the second time, everything went black.

Even though I hadn't understood then, my life was changed forever in ways no child should ever have to experience. As we pass the news van, I untuck my hair from behind my ears and pull it forward to cover my face as much as possible, just in case there are cameras. I can't be seen on national television. There's a very real danger *she* will see me and track me down. And if she did that, there's every chance she'd ruin my life all over again.

'Love you two,' I say, smiling at my beautiful children when we've safely passed by. *Our* beautiful children. We're good parents, Mark and I. Despite my emotional baggage, my tainted heritage, I've tried to make good in every area of my life. I know I'm not doing so well with my marriage since *the affair*, but he said that was nothing; just a one-night stand. I still struggle to fully believe that. But he didn't leave. That's something, surely. There's still time to make up for the mistakes and for me to forgive him.

Olivia's disappearance is a wake-up call. It's made me realise some home truths. I have to learn to trust Mark fully again. Quickly.

Chapter 12

JENNY

We reach school with a few minutes to spare. I'm not as quick as I hope dropping Ella and Alfie off, though, getting waylaid by a group of gossipy mothers instead. The gaggle of gossips, as I like to call them. I try to avoid playground politics as a rule, but today I infiltrate the group because I want to know the latest news about Olivia.

All the parents are known to me one way or another – through school or community events, and a lot use my practice for their pet care. The five women currently huddled with me in a circle near the gate are mums of the pupils in Ella's class. From them, I learn that Isabella is being kept home for the moment by Olivia's partner, Yannis. He's not Isabella's dad – none of us knows who is. Or, at least, no one's telling if they do.

'Did you know they'd been having . . . *issues*? I mean, they always look at the partner first, don't they?' Frankie says. She's an operator at the police contact centre at

Middlemoor in Exeter, so she's the one person in this group who has any kind of inside knowledge.

'Liv did confide in me that they were arguing all the time. Said she was forever trying to keep the peace, not wanting to yell in front of poor little Isabella.' I thought Willow, who I generally find aloof and puts herself way above anyone else, would pull the 'I know Olivia the best' card, and she hasn't disappointed.

'Sounds like most couples,' I can't help but say with a snort. All heads turn sharply to me, their eyes wide. 'We all have our arguments, surely?' I lift a shoulder in a half-shrug, but when none of them respond, I carry on, feeling my cheeks turning red. 'Just because they've argued a bit, doesn't mean he's, you know, involved in her disappearance for God's sake. We really shouldn't jump to con—'

'We're not jumping to conclusions, Jenny. And where've you been? You've clearly not heard the update.'

My spine tingles at Frankie's tone. 'No, I haven't. What is it?'

'Detectives are confident it isn't a simple missing person's case – they believe she was abducted on the way home from The Union late Tuesday night.' I almost stop her to point out this had already been on the news and wasn't new information, but she's in full flow now. 'There's some form of evidence or other, but they aren't releasing the details. They're interviewing pub staff, neighbours, knocking on doors – it's so scary.'

What could the evidence be? My heart stutters, skipping a beat. *I must cut down my caffeine intake,* I think, choosing to believe that's the problem. 'Have any of you been interviewed?' I ask.

'I have, and so's Rach.' Rachel nods her confirmation silently, and Frankie continues. 'I've seen coppers everywhere in Coleton Combe. I guess they'll leave no stone unturned.'

'But there haven't been any leads that you know of?' I ask.

'Nothing on the village grapevine indicates there is, no.'

'It's so weird. How can someone just vanish like this?' Rach says.

'No one else thinking what I am?' Zari, who up until now hasn't said a word, asks, her large brown eyes filled with worry. There's silence for a moment, and my stomach clenches. 'I think we have to consider the possibility that police are looking for a body.'

As if to confirm it, a helicopter passes low overhead, its dark underbelly ominous. All our heads tilt upwards to watch its progress. The distinct yellow top identifies it as a police helicopter. As it reaches the outskirts of the village it hovers, seemingly over the fields and wooded area. We all watch in silence as it very slowly circles.

'Christ.' Willow breaks the spell and it feels like the whole group lets out the breath it's been holding. 'Not being funny, but if they really think she's been killed, couldn't we all be in danger?'

'Don't be ridiculous; this isn't *CSI*,' Frankie snaps. But her voice is shaky, and I can almost feel the atmosphere change. I shudder.

'No need to be condescending.' Willow purses her lips and shifts her gaze from Frankie to the rest of us. 'In any case, we didn't think one abduction – or murder, or whatever we're looking at here – could happen in Coleton Combe. If I'd suggested this happening last week, you'd have all said the same thing then. Now look. It's not that much of a jump to think this could just be the start.'

'The start of what?' Zari says, her eyes wide.

'Nothing,' I say, physically moving in between them. 'Come on, there's no evidence yet. Let's not freak ourselves out, eh?'

'Well, I still say we shouldn't be going out alone. Not until we know what happened to Olivia,' Willow says.

'It's a fair point. Maybe we should create some kind of rota? Make sure we're always with at least one person if we go out after dark?' Rachel's face is like a white mask.

'Sounds a bit over the top,' Frankie says, frowning. 'And anyway, just because Olivia was taken at night, doesn't mean another woman will be taken in the same way.'

'Isn't that what serial killers do? They repeat the same MO.'

'Really, Willow,' I say harshly through gritted teeth. 'Serial killer? Enough. I realise nothing like this has ever happened here, but please, ladies, let's keep some perspective. Olivia went missing on her way home from the pub. The police seem to think she was abducted, not murdered—'

'But only high-profile people and kids get abducted – and usually in return for a ransom. How many women are just kidnapped? They're nearly always found dead.'

I shoot Willow an incredulous glance. My head starts pounding and I know I need to leave this conversation now. 'I have to get to work,' I say, my voice tight. 'See you guys tomorrow.'

'Don't forget, Jenny – don't go out alone.'

Without responding, I pivot on my heel and keep walking until I get to the car. I jump in and switch the radio on, turning the volume of the music up as loud as it can go.

Chapter 13

JENNY

The noise of the helicopter is deafening when I park in my reserved space at Well Combe Pet Care, next to Samir's grey Toyota Prius. There's a high-pitched whining that goes right through me, and the din of the helicopter's engine and rotor blades combined makes my pulse race. I've never been good with low-flying aircraft – some fear or other dating from childhood. Come to think of it, most of my fears originate from childhood – but that may well be the same for everyone. *It's not all about you, Jenny; you're not the only one with a troubled past.*

The sound seems to come closer then moves away again. I crane my neck to see if I can spot it as I walk to the entrance, but there's no sign of it. It must be low, the trees obscuring a clear view. I imagine on the other side of the fields, where the gates are, there'll be dozens of police vehicles too. Maybe even forensics. Frankie's curt comment to Willow about *CSI* comes back to me. Frankie jumped down her throat, but it really could all blow up, just like a TV crime show.

Especially if they find a body.

A shiver runs down my back. 'Someone walk over your grave?' my mother's voice intrudes, and I wince. I suppose it's inevitable my thoughts will drift to her, to my father, right now. Hard not to let them during darker moments. If questions about my history ever come up, which is rare, I tell people I left home to go to university and stayed in Devon in order to complete vet training, then remained because I loved the West Country and had a placement at a practice I wanted to take up. Anyone who knows me well enough has given up asking why I don't visit family. Mark used to press me about it but even he stopped asking due to my reaction.

The truth of it is, though, I planned a 'gap year' prior to attending university purely so I could escape my mother earlier – so I might claw back some confidence and learn to socialise again before meeting other students. Keeping it from Claire so she couldn't stop me going had been one of the hardest challenges. How do you keep secrets from someone who's always breathing down your neck? When I found my bedroom in disarray one day, I knew she'd sensed I was keeping something from her and she'd searched it. But I was one step ahead; I guessed she'd do that. She didn't know *all* the secret hiding places I'd had as a child and luckily she'd failed to find the one I'd hidden my tickets and itinerary in. It seemed she under-estimated my ability to utilise the floorboards around the house. A week later, I was gone – and finally free.

I worked hard at progressing, pushing myself all the time to be better. Although to begin with I was cripplingly shy, I forced myself to be outgoing, to join in, living by the saying 'fake it till you make it'. Mostly it worked. It wasn't all so easy, though. Her lies were the worst. They had the biggest, most far-reaching and longest-lasting consequences. 'I only lied to protect you,' she'd said. No. She lied to protect herself and to keep me close. In the end, all she accomplished was to drive me away. If I know her, though, despite twenty years having passed, she's still searching for me.

Like the police are searching for Olivia.

Perhaps *she* chose to run away, too.

I walk into reception and Hayley hands me the list of today's consultations. 'What a racket eh?' she says, her eyes squinting. 'Do you think it'll be like this all day?' She rubs at her temples, and I note her swollen knuckles.

I shrug, not sure what she wants me to say. Why would I know any more than she does? I ask if she's doing okay – if the new arthritis meds she's been given have begun to work. I know the consultant advised a different kind, but by the look of her physical symptoms, they aren't yet taking effect. She must be in pain, though she won't let on. She smiles thinly.

'Yes, yes. I'll be fine, Jenny.'

'If you need anything, please do let me know. Okay?' My words are almost drowned out by the helicopter.

'Glad there's no surgery booked in today,' she says, raising her voice needlessly to make a point.

'We'll keep the main windows closed – that should block out most of the noise.' Neither of us mentions the reason the helicopter is right by the practice. Some of the woodland it appears to be hovering over also belongs to us. It extends from the land that we acquired as part of the purchase of the vet practice. There's an old covenant attached to the deeds, but we've never really looked into having it removed. All I know is it's protected, so we can't build on that part. Samir knows more about it than me; he's a keen conservationist.

'At least you only have to be here for the morning,' Hayley says, cutting into my thoughts.

'True. About time the veterinary society meetings had a purpose beyond updating me on the latest technological advances.'

'How come Samir never gets to skive off to them?' Hayley gives me a sideways glance as I laugh her comment off and head for my room. Whilst there's no scheduled surgery, it doesn't mean an emergency won't crop up, but thankfully it's mostly a morning filled with check-ups and diagnostic imaging, then this afternoon it's vaccines, which the nurses will take care of. I'm relieved it's currently shaping up to be an easy day, because I think we're all feeling the pull of worry, anxiety and – in my case at least – fear.

The chatter from the school mums earlier plays on my mind despite my best efforts to concentrate on the pets and their owners. But they don't help – almost every client so far has mentioned how terrible it is, how shocked they are, how appalled they are that something so awful could happen in our lovely village. And especially to quiet, unassuming Olivia. 'The absolute loveliest person I know,' one man said. I manage to block the helicopter noise and zone out a few times, but those moments don't provide me with any respite. Instead, my mind focuses on the mutilated cat, and whatever else was left on my doorstep today. The only way of finding out who is leaving them is to either stay up all night keeping watch, or get a camera. I make a mental note to ask Caroline Brewer about hers.

It's not until 11 a.m. coffee break that I catch up with the whole team together in the staffroom. A newspaper is on the low coffee table. The front page carries a photo of Olivia leaning back in a chair outside a café, her long brunette hair loose around her shoulders, a pretty purple chiffon scarf lying along her collarbone. She's smiling – no, beaming – her white teeth popping against her olive complexion. It's a beautiful photo. The headline reads: **Woman snatched from village street as she walks home.**

I decide that now is a good time to put some feelers out to find out what each of my employees knows or thinks. Nisha and Vanessa are sitting together, sharing a punnet of strawberries, and I sidle up to them.

'Did you hear anything about the lead-up to Olivia's abduction? Like, had anything happened beforehand?' I don't preamble; there seems little point when it's practically the only topic of conversation anyway.

'You mean, like, did she have a stalker?' Vanessa screws up her nose. 'God, that's a scary thought.'

'Yeah. It is,' I agree. 'But surely it would make more sense. It's just so . . . unlikely, to be taken from the street like that in a village, isn't it? And our village at that. It's not your average crime for a community such as this. Makes me think there was something specific about Olivia – that she was targeted.'

'True. Opportunistic offenders are more usually found in child abductions, not those of adults,' Vanessa says thoughtfully, echoing the gist of what the playground mums were saying. 'You're right,' she says with more conviction. 'Adult victims are more likely to be taken by those they know, or by someone with an obsession . . . Or a grudge.'

I smart at the last bit, resisting the urge to scowl at her. Did she give me a funny look when she said that?

Those I work with didn't know that Mark fancied Olivia and then embarked on an affair, as far as I'm aware. Not at the time, anyway. But I do wonder if Olivia's neighbours or any of the village gossips have said something since her disappearance. People like to dig up the past at times like this. I have first-hand knowledge of that. Even though when it was happening to us I didn't understand it, I grew up with a lot of hatred being aimed my way. I thought the only person privy to my continuing mistrust and paranoia regarding Mark and Olivia was Roisin, and she wouldn't have ever uttered a word about it, I'm sure. Which reminds me, I must give her a call to arrange a meet-up for coffee. Or better, wine.

'It could mean we're likely to know the bastard responsible,' I say.

'Christ, I hadn't considered that.' Vanessa puts a hand to her mouth.

'It was the *first* thing I thought,' Nisha says with enthusiasm. 'And in my head, I went through the likely suspects. After I had to scratch her partner off the list, that is.'

'How come you took him off?'

'Had an alibi. He was taking care of the kid while Olivia had a night out.'

My naturally suspicious mind immediately questions this. 'Okay,' I say. That seems a solid alibi. *If* he didn't then sneak out while the child slept. But I suppose the police will consider that. 'So, who's on your list, Miss Marple?'

'Miss who?'

My mouth gapes and I shake my head. 'What? You don't know who Miss Marple is? I know I'm older than you lot, but I thought living in this neck of the woods, you'd know she's a character in Agatha Christie's novels! Torquay is the birthplace of one of the most revered crime writers in history – you do know *that*, at least, don't you?'

'Okay, thanks for the literary-slash-history lesson. Now do you want to know my thoughts or not?' Nisha raises an eyebrow.

'If you promise to Google Agatha after, yes – do proceed.'

'Yes, boss. So, we know Olivia was at the pub on Tuesday evening. Quiz night. And who runs the quiz? Creepy Colin. Suspect number one. Then, we have Dopey Dave—'

'Hang on,' I say, putting a hand up. 'Have you named every villager in this way?'

'Yes, absolutely. Anyway, Dopey Dave used to go out with Olivia, back in the day – before Yannis came onto the scene – and she dumped him. By text, no less.'

'I thought that's how it was done these days,' I say.

'It's brutal! Anyway, he spent many a drunken night in the pub after it, bad-mouthing Olivia and telling everyone who'd listen that she would regret giving him the elbow.'

'That puts him as suspect number one, then, surely? He has motive. Creepy Colin not so much. That we know of anyway.'

'Mmm . . . but I don't call him Dopey Dave for nothing. Not sure he'd have the ability to carry out an abduction.'

'Don't necessarily need brain power for that, though. It's a bit like smash and grab really. It isn't as though it was a crime needing intelligence.' I realise I'm getting into this far more than is wise.

'I guess not. Maybe the next candidate meets with your approval, then.'

'Go on,' I say.

'Gorgeous George.'

There's a prolonged silence as this name sinks in. We all know who Nisha is referring to. George Penworth is new to the village. Or new to most people's minds – he moved here two years ago, lives alone and is around thirty years of age. No one knows much about him, and over the years a few theories have transpired. The main one being he was located here following a stint in the local prison. He's reticent, keeps himself to himself on the whole, but does frequent The Union on an almost-daily basis according to the village grapevine.

'That's a good shout,' Vanessa says. 'He gives me the willies – staring like he does, like he has bloody x-ray vision and can see your naked body. He might be good-looking, but that's all he's got going for him.'

'Mustn't start rumours, guys,' I say. As much as I think she's got a point, I don't want the poor bloke's character assassinated – living with the repercussions of that aren't fun. I know. Though, in my case, it wasn't accusations or harmful gossip – it was the truth.

'Olivia's parents live next door to me,' Nisha says, and we all turn to look at her. I can't believe this hasn't already been brought up – I'd forgotten Nisha has temporarily moved in with her parents. I fight my impulse to ask her to do some digging – it would seem like an odd request. But she offers some information anyway. She tells us that since she's been there, she's only spotted Olivia visiting the house next door on a few occasions, and mostly at weekends, with her little girl.

'Have you seen police there? Do the press know they are Olivia's parents?' The urgency in my voice surprises me.

'Not sure about the press, but Mum said she saw a police car outside early yesterday.'

'Can't believe the news didn't filter through earlier yesterday. I had no idea until Mark told me last night.' As I slump back in the chair, I catch sight of Abi's stony, faraway expression; she's been silent during our conversation. She's not living in the village – she's three miles away, in town – but she's new to the area so I'm guessing all this talk of stalkers and abduction is a bit freaky, plus she doesn't know anyone on Nisha's suspect list so can't really contribute. I suddenly feel bad for both frightening and boring her. 'Let's talk about something else, shall we?' I jump up, collect the mugs and take them to the kitchen counter. 'Has anyone got any great film recommendations? Mark is out with his mate tonight and I want to take the chance to watch something he'd hate,' I say, forcing a laugh.

The thwacking of the helicopter becomes louder until it sounds as though it's directly overhead. We stop speaking, all eyes moving upwards to the ceiling. I swear I can feel the room vibrating. I wonder why they're focusing their attention over the woodland . . . and now here.

I glance down at my hands, which are gripping the worktop, and the mud that was embedded under my nails yesterday flashes in my mind. Where had it come from?

Whatever I'd been doing, the fact it was the night Olivia was taken stabs at my conscience like a syringe needle jabbing directly into my brain.

Chapter 14

JENNY

The putrid smell of decay assaults my nose as I lift the lid. I hadn't noticed a strong odour this morning when I'd quickly thrown in the new bin liner. Now it's got my full attention, I see maggots dripping from the bin lid like wriggling rice grains. I cough, covering my mouth and nose with the crook of one arm. I've dealt with many a gruesome thing during my training and practising as a vet, but this is different. Maybe it's because my mind conjured all the bad things from my past, all the things I found out, and attached them to this mutilated cat. I lower my arm from my face and shut the lid again, my mind frantically searching for an explanation. I only put the cat remains in the bin yesterday, so how could there be maggots already? Flies must have got inside beforehand and been feasting on food remnants I failed to put in the composter. That, or the remains of the cat weren't fresh.

I've left work early to attend my monthly meeting, so

I'm not expected back for this afternoon. Samir will take care of any consultations and the nurses will handle the vaccinations, while I make the journey to the usual location. It's not too far away, but it's always seemed pointless to return to work afterwards – I'd barely have time to fit in one client before close of business. So, I now have an hour to myself to bundle the remains up securely. Later, when everyone's left the practice, I'll label the poor cat as animal by-product, ready to be collected and taken to be incinerated along with the rest.

I spread out a large plastic sheet I took from the practice, then take out the newest bag as it's on the top, and put it aside while I deal with the least fresh specimen. I tip the wheelie bin on its side and reach in with a broom to scoop out the garbage onto the plastic so I can get to the buried liner. I'd piled a couple of white bags on top to hide it, in case Mark saw it – not that he ever puts the trash out. Only now, with the contents of the bin in a heap, do I spot another black bag. For a moment, my brain falters. I look to my side to check I really did remove the new one. Yes, I did. I frown at this one, which is a bit smaller than the one containing the cat. It's nearer the top of the pile, so it must have been closer to the bottom before I dragged it all out. This is where the maggot infestation appears to be originating.

With my gloved hands, I sweep the majority of soft, wriggling larvae from the bag, my breath held to prevent gagging, and then carefully take the edges and tip it up, giving it a shake to expel its contents. What appears to be a brown rabbit – in a stage of active decay – lands at my feet. I stagger backwards. Leaning against the wall, panting, I fight to comprehend what I'm seeing.

There was another bin liner left at the house before the ones I found. *When?*

And who put it in the bin? The only person who could've done it is Mark, surely? I mentally scroll through the last few days' interactions with him. He's been a little off with me, not really engaging in much conversation. If he'd found the mutilated rabbit, I would've thought he'd come to me straight away given that I'm the vet. Clearly, he hid it from me for some reason. Are we back to keeping secrets from each other? I push out the thought from my mind that shouts: well, *you* are, so why shouldn't he? Perhaps he just forgot to mention it.

My mind continues to reel as I check the pile of waste for evidence of other black liners. I'm relieved to not find any further animal corpses. But as I turn my attention back to the bag I found today, tension mounts in me once more. Yesterday's cat was not a one-off. I can no longer write it off as just someone who'd accidentally run it over and thought it might've belonged to this household.

No. Someone was targeting us. *Me.*

Have I upset anyone? I rack my brains. The only person I can think of is Olivia Edwards. The troubled expression on Mark's face when he told me about her abduction is etched into my mind. It was uncomfortable for both of us, but I'm the one left with a sense of unease – Mark appeared unperturbed when he left for work earlier, whistling as he crossed the driveway to his car. Or, at least, that's the way he was *trying* to come across.

I first came face to face with Olivia when she brought their family dog to the practice for a general check-up. She was quiet, unassuming, didn't easily make conversation. I remember it well because she barely looked at me during the consultation and her olive skin flushed a deep red each time I asked a question. It was the strangest thing.

She left my consulting room and went to book in a follow-up appointment at reception, as I'd asked her to. I happened to walk past the desk and catch her saying, 'Can you make sure to book Rex in with the other vet next time, please? I did ask for Samir for this appointment, but it wasn't him I've just seen.' I'd been so taken aback, I rushed on past, embarrassed she might turn and see me and realise I'd heard. I couldn't think of a single reason she'd feel that way. Not then.

Of course, I managed to find a reason eventually.

I close my eyes tightly, remembering my hoarsely whispered accusation; the look of guilt on Mark's face confirming I was right. The aftermath – his weak denial and then the desperate apologies. My whole body numb, the hurt not immediately surfacing as I went into shock. Shaking my head free of the images, I bundle the bags together. Putting them inside another, I place them to the side while I wrap the wheelie bin's spewed contents in the plastic sheet so I can chuck it all back in. Could I be assuming I'm the target when in fact it's Mark? I'm being quick to jump to the conclusion I'm the one these 'gifts' are being left for – the sign of a guilty conscience maybe? Seeing the butterfly caused my long-held fears to catapult themselves forward into reality, yet that really might've been a coincidence. I didn't find one among the rabbit remains. But then, the decomposition was already well underway with that corpse, so perhaps I missed it.

As I'm scooping the rubbish up, I catch sight of the bin bag I'm yet to look inside. I stare at it, somehow expecting it to move – like a scene from a horror movie. It's a few feet away from me, and yet, it's scaring me. Delaying opening it isn't helping – but I'm not keen to see the contents. If I don't look, I'll never know – a prospect that is appealing.

Bury your head in the sand, Jen. It's the only way.

Olivia's face flashes across my mind and I screw my eyes up to expel it. 'Taken from the street'. That's how it was described in the news. Just that line in itself brings back awful memories. It was one I repeatedly read in news reports and articles. I was seventeen when I found out the truth. Seventeen when, once again, my life shattered and splintered into tiny fragments and I lost my father for the second time.

I hear tiny taps as my tears drip onto a plastic bag. An intense heat builds in my stomach, slowly rising up until my face burns. I hate that I'm being forced into thinking about my parents – about who I came from. After all the running, hiding and burying I've done, how dare the source of all my problems rear its ugly head again now.

Refusing to acknowledge it won't stop whoever's doing this, though. Only facing them will.

I stride over to the bag and open it up.

The tufted brindle-coloured coat, bloodied, but with obvious rosettes identify my latest gruesome gift as a guinea pig. My brow furrows with a spark of recognition – do I know this pet? A link doesn't come to me. Gently removing it and turning it over, I see a deep incision has been made, the skin splayed to reveal its innards. I inhale sharply.

A perfectly preserved butterfly is pinned to it.

There's no mistake now. I am the target. And they,

whoever 'they' are, know about my past. They know what my father did – what he is.

My mother lied to me. My father isn't in prison for fraud.

I'm the daughter of a serial killer.

Chapter 15

The Painted Lady Killer

Inside the mind of serial killer Paul Slater

Paul Slater, now 65, is serving a whole-life sentence for the abduction and murder of five women, all of which took place between 1975 and 1987. During his twelve-year reign of terror, Slater had co-existed with the normal, everyday members of the community of Barnsley in the north of England, appearing to all who knew him as a good, solid family man – married, with a daughter he idolised. Quite how he'd managed to live alongside them, all the while preying on vulnerable females – and without raising suspicion – came as a devastating shock.

How does a monster such as this walk among us? And without detection?

These are just some of the questions posed by

many, and those the media have sought answers to, dedicating hundreds of column inches to theories and speculation. So much has been written over the past thirty years, with input from psychologists, psychiatrists, detectives, friends, even family members – but no one has yet asked the one person who holds all those answers: Paul Slater himself.

Until now.

Chapter 16

MARK

Jen is usually back earlier on the last Thursday of each month – a vet meeting she attends means she has most of the afternoon off – but the house is quiet as I enter with Brett, and he sits at the kitchen table while I make a brew. Perhaps she's avoiding being here so she doesn't have to get into a conversation with Brett. Or possibly it's me she's avoiding. It's been awkward between us since she found out about Olivia. She knows better than to bring up the past – neither of us wants to revisit that dark time – but sometimes I wish we could talk about it. I'm sure our worries and questions will eat away at us if we keep them buried. Like a poison, waiting to claim a victim.

Until recently, I'd always just accepted *The Unknowns* about Jenny. They hadn't mattered when we first met, on that snowy wintry afternoon in March when I was a day off thirty. A chance meeting – one I came to think of as fate – brought us together. Her car had been caught in a snowdrift along an embankment on the way into Coleton

Combe. The narrow lanes had taken her by surprise, she'd said. 'I've only ever driven main roads – I can't believe you're expected to have two-way traffic on *these*!' She'd gesticulated towards the lane her car was now trapped in, and I'd suppressed a laugh. She was pale, her eyes wide with shock as she told me how an idiot had practically run her off the road. 'Ignorant man. He clearly thought he owned the road – he was in the middle of it!'

I smiled as I offered to call a mate to help untangle her black Fiat and tow it to the garage. 'You should know, though – if you're going to drive these lanes again – that people tend to drive in the middle because it isn't wide enough for two vehicles to pass. You just have to reverse when you meet another car.' I felt like I was imparting bad news. 'You can reverse, can't you?' I'd said with a smirk.

She'd given me a sheepish look that told me no, she couldn't, and with a red face mumbled, 'I reversed around a corner for my test.'

And from that moment, me and Jen were connected. She told me she was moving to the village, so yes, she had to drive these roads. I agreed to teach her the ways of the lanes – including how to reverse without hitting each hedge on either side of the road in a crazy zig-zagging fashion – a manoeuvre I'd come to know well from grockles visiting this neck of the woods.

The Unknowns also hadn't mattered after our whirlwind romance, the dizziness of love overtaking all my sensibilities. My mum had been that enamoured with Jenny, so confident I'd found The One, I hadn't questioned Jen's reluctance to talk about her parents – mine were so welcoming, she said she thought of them as her own.

Mum got so wrapped up in helping Jenny with wedding plans, even she ignored her misgivings when Jen said she wasn't inviting her parents to the wedding. They so wanted to do things properly, my dad adamant I should ask Jen's dad for his blessing. But, the wedding went ahead without them and with each passing day, her parents were kind of forgotten. Until Jen fell pregnant. Having Ella was the icing on the cake. My mum and dad were so thrilled to hold our precious little girl for the first time and couldn't understand why Jen's parents weren't sharing the joy.

I can't ever imagine not being a part of Ella's and Alfie's lives. I'd go to any lengths to protect my children. How could Jenny's not have felt the same way? Yet, according to her, they didn't want anything to do with her. I wonder how much of that is the other way around.

As I think about parenting, my mind flits to Olivia. What must her poor parents be going through right now. Pure hell I suspect. I never want to know how that feels. From the moment I held Ella's tiny hand in mine I was both smitten and overwhelmed. She was so perfect, so needy. It was my duty from that day to ensure no harm ever came to her. Isn't that every parent's duty? What they strive for? How does it feel when they let their child down? That's how Jen always spoke about her parents – on the rare occasion she did. They let her down. Badly. I'm never going to be like that.

Ella and Alfie come first.

They are the main reason I didn't cause a huge fuss when Jen accused me of having an affair with Olivia. I tried hard to bury my head in the sand, to avoid terrible repercussions. I know the other reason I begged so hard for her forgiveness, lied about it being purely a one-night stand was due to the fact it had been more, but I couldn't have my cake and eat it. I didn't want the children to suffer. Our marital problems should not impact them; it's not fair. They need us both.

'You look deep in thought,' Brett says, and I turn to see him eyeing me quizzically. 'Whatever it is, mate, you aren't going to find the answer staring into tea leaves.'

'It's nothing,' I say, quickly composing myself and handing him his mug with a hasty smile. I can't think about it all now; I need to concentrate on the present. I tell him I'm merely contemplating our imminent chat. It's not like I can share what's really on my mind with him. With anyone, really. It's odd, now I'm thinking about it, that I don't have close mates here in Coleton. No one I confide in about meaningful things. I've never really been what's considered a 'man's man' – even through my school, college and uni days, I gravitated to girls and was more likely to be found hanging out with a group of them than playing football or getting rough with the boys. Even Brett was more of an acquaintance than a mate, really. It was probably due to my having three sisters – my natural default was to be around females. Not saying I was ever a womaniser, of course, but I was never without a girl-friend. Talking to women is something I'm comfortable doing and getting married didn't stop that. Jen didn't seem to mind it at first, but in the last year or so, it's become a problem.

More specifically, it was after what happened with Olivia.

I listen to Brett for a few minutes without really hearing him, and then he gets up and puts his mug on the side. He rubs his hands together just like he used to at uni – like he's preparing, gearing up for a 'good time'. I freeze, remembering those drunken, lairy nights, too many of which ended in a trail of destruction, or worse.

Hannah.

I suck in a deep breath. Her name is kept locked away in the dark recesses of my mind for self-preservation's sake, but in this split second, watching Brett, it comes to me and I shake my head. I wish I'd acted differently.

'Come on, Marky boy, lighten up. I thought we were celebrating.'

'Yeah,' I say, then hearing the lack of enthusiasm in my tone, follow it up with a confident, 'Let's do this.'

As I quickly change clothes, it crosses my mind that Brett is probably not here to sit and quietly discuss business, and as usual, I'm going along the road he takes me. Too late to change plans now, we're out the door and heading for the pub. It only occurs to me then that it might not be open. Could the police have closed it down? I hadn't thought about that possibility. It might be better if that's the case. We could get some cans from the shop and bring them home. I'm sure Jen won't mind – she can always go into the hobby room and read, or do one of her puzzles. She loves doing them to relax – and Lord knows we're both in need of that.

I text her as I walk to make sure she can pick the kids up from after-school club – maybe the vets' meeting is running late. I did tell her about my plans, though, so she'd have called if that were the case. She wouldn't want to leave Ella and Alfie standing in the playground waiting. Especially with everything that's going on.

'You ready to do this?' Brett asks as we walk around the corner and The Union sign comes into view. 'Because I haven't forgotten you being a wuss before.'

That was over twenty years ago and he's still bringing it up. My jaw clenches. I'm keen to put him right – tell him I was nothing of the sort – but I don't want to dredge it up again. It's a part of my past I'd rather not rake over. I'm surprised he would want to, either.

'Absolutely ready,' I say, picking up my pace and pointedly ignoring his dig. Cars are going in and out of the car park, so the pub is clearly open. I suppose it's not a crime scene – it's not where Olivia was taken. 'Looking forward to hearing how you're going to make me money,' I add, laughing. My light-hearted tone belies my guilt. I shouldn't be going about my life as normal, like nothing has happened. Olivia's family certainly won't be.

As we stroll down the slope leading to The Union's entrance, I catch sight of a police car parked on the adjacent road and my feet falter. I quickly regain my balance, pretending there's nothing wrong when Brett shoots me a curious glance. But, as I follow Brett over the threshold, I turn back in time to see a police officer knocking on a door. There's another standing outside chatting to the neighbouring one. My blood runs cold.

How long will it be before the police come to our door?

Chapter 17

Oh, my darling, I'll never forgive her for what she's done. I want you to know it wasn't your fault. None of this was.

It doesn't feel like that.

My father, God rest his shitty soul, always used the phrase 'a bad apple never falls far from the tree'. Although I hated him for saying it – because him quietly, menacingly, uttering those words over and over in my ear, meant he'd already given up on me – I'm beginning to believe it myself.

I really hope he was wrong. That you're wrong.

Maybe this family never stood a chance.

That's so defeatist.

I want you to know I wouldn't have given up on you. Despite what she might have told you, I wanted to be involved in your life – but she forbade it. She didn't want you tainted by my past. Although, she appeared to conveniently forget her own.

That about sums her up.

Murder runs in the blood, she said. She was probably right about that. It's not inevitable, though, Princess. The future isn't written yet. Don't forget that, will you?

I'll try not to, Dad.

But maybe it really does run in the blood.

Chapter 18

JENNY

The gravel crunches as I steer the car around to the back of Well Combe Pet Care, careful to avoid parking in view of the CCTV camera.

'Are we coming in to see the animals?' Alfie asks, excitedly.

'Not today, I'm afraid. It's all closed up now. Another time, sweetie.' My voice is tight, my stomach even more so. I explain I'm dropping something off and ask them to sit quietly in the car. As I climb out, I note there's still some activity going on in the fields to the left – but no helicopter hovering over the woodland at present. I'm not sure if that's a good or bad sign. Being hopeful, I consider they've maybe found Olivia. Or her body. I shiver and avert my eyes.

I pop the boot, surreptitiously remove the bin liner containing all the 'gifts' and walk to the rear door. I realise the CCTV will catch me doing this, so I don't know why I took the trouble to park out of sight really. In fact, why am I so worried about the camera anyway? I've nothing to hide. Still, I shoot it a furtive glance as I walk by – and realise too late that I probably look guilty of *something*. It's like when a police car is driving behind me, I automatically act differently despite knowing I'm keeping within the speed limit and my car is completely legal. And now, the weight of the remains heavy in my arms, I'm acting just as suspiciously. I need to relax. It's not as though I'm smuggling in human body parts and trying to pass them off as animal by-products.

Once inside, I check the coast is clear – no one's car was outside, but I want to be certain – and head to the waste room. I label the bag with a toxic sticker and leave it in the special container to be taken for incineration. A sudden feeling of déjà vu hits me so powerfully I pause, trying hard to grasp hold of a memory. But it's like liquid, quickly flowing away from me before I can catch it. I come in here to do this task on a regular basis, so I can't imagine it to be this particular act that has triggered the feeling. So, what did then? I glance at the clock: collection is in ten minutes – I've made it just in time. I need to get out of here now before the caretaker arrives to open the door for the transport company.

As I sit back in the car, a hiss of breath escapes me – a long, drawn-out sigh of relief. I say a silent prayer that I won't have to do this again.

'What's wrong, Mummy?' Alfie's doe eyes search mine in the rear-view mirror.

'Nothing, honey-bunch. Just a little tired.'

'That's because you keep getting up!' Ella glares at me, her brow low.

A trickle of sweat runs down my spine, making me shudder. What does she mean, I 'keep getting up'? I open my mouth about to ask her, but my phone rings and I snatch it from the dash. Unknown number. A scam call, no doubt. I throw it back down, annoyed it's not Mark. I replied to his earlier text to let him know I was fine to pick the kids up from club and asked what time he thought he'd be home, but I haven't received a response. Too busy reminiscing with Brett, I expect. I start the car, revving it more than needed. I really hope he and his mate are out all night – I want to be in bed when they get back. It's not my intention to see Brett and have to make small talk. It would be a task at the best of times, but right now, I'm certainly not feeling it – the thought of any conversation makes my stomach heavy.

Brett turning up again now has set alarm bells ringing. Up until his call the other night, I'd pushed him out of my mind. It's strange, the more I think of it – how Mark doesn't have any mates to speak of. He's lived in Coleton Combe for almost twenty years, yet isn't close with anyone. He said he came here because one of his sisters settled here with her family. But, not long after we met, she bought a house in the north of Devon – because of schools, she'd said.

To be fair, I suppose we've been self-sufficient mostly. When we were first married, we were so besotted, we didn't need, or want, anyone encroaching on our perfect marital bliss. But after I had Ella, I realised I needed friends – girlfriends who would relate to my changing role. I met Roisin at a mother and baby group – although she wasn't the one with the baby. She'd gone to support her sister, but we hit it off straight away and our bond was formed over a discussion about her cat. *Her* baby. The only type she was ever having, she'd said with an exaggerated eye-roll towards Tobias, her then-screaming nephew. 'Babies are too much like hard work,' she'd whispered in my ear.

'Can we have some sweets for film night?' Ella asks the second we get back on the road.

'Sure. I'll swing by the corner shop on the way home.'

I told them they could pick a film – as long as it was PG – and have tea on the lounge floor, like a picnic. I'll watch my choice on the TV in the bedroom when they've gone to bed. Vanessa's suggestion of *Game Night*, with Jason Bateman – my teenage crush – seems like a good idea. Nothing too taxing, nothing serious; my mind won't focus on detail or enjoy anything sombre.

The twenty-mile-per-hour speed limit through the village gives me an opportunity to slow down enough to discreetly check out Olivia's house as I pass by. All the curtains are closed – I can't see any movement. I shiver, pressing my foot down on the accelerator again, then slam my brakes on as someone walks out in front of the car.

'Jesus!'

'He's a silly man, isn't he, Mummy?' Alfie says from the back seat.

'Good job we were going slowly, isn't it?' I say, glaring at the man, who's still standing by the bonnet. I throw my arms up in a 'what are you doing?' way but he just stares right back. Then I recognise him. It's George – or Gorgeous George, as Nisha referred to him. My skin tingles. Why is he looking at me like that? I rev the engine, and he finally walks to the pavement, his eyes still on me as I go past and park up outside the shop. I was going to leave the kids in the car while I popped in to get them sweets, but now, with my nerves tingling, I drag them in with me.

*   *   *

It's almost midnight when I hear the men come back; baritone voices penetrate the peaceful house as they step into the hallway. They don't sound blind drunk, but they're certainly merry. Their deep, booming conversation echoes, making it hard to decipher their words, but I think I catch a name.

I creep out of bed and hover at the top of the stairs so I can hear better. Of course. They're talking about Olivia.

Mark shushes Brett and immediately my interest piques.

'You reckon she knows more than she's letting on?'

I assume by 'she', he means me.

'I don't know. Look, I'm sorry I mentioned it. I don't want to talk about it. Let's just get some sleep.' I take a step back, in case they come up the stairs and catch me listening. But then, the voices become quieter as they move towards the kitchen. Obviously he does want to talk about it. I take a chance and edge down further so I can still hear them.

'Mate, really – I'm here for you. Don't bottle it up – that's not a good idea. A problem shared . . .'

'There's just a few things – like, *stuff* you know – from her past, that she won't ever talk about. And I know I'm overthinking, trying to make something out of nothing, but . . .'

'But what?'

'The night Olivia was taken she . . . Jen . . . she had a blackout.'

My hand flies up to my mouth. What? He's confided in Brett about Olivia *and* my blackouts? Hearing him tell some bloke he hasn't spoken to in over a decade feels like a betrayal.

'Yeah. Which isn't to say she did anything – I mean,

91

she most definitely couldn't have somehow abducted Olivia. That's madness to even suggest.' He laughs, awkwardly. Gooseflesh prickles my arms.

'I sense a *but*.'

There's a prolonged silence; my booming heart is all I can hear right now. I don't want to miss whatever's coming next – I need to get closer. With my breath held, I tiptoe all the way down the stairs and across the hall. If they come out of the kitchen suddenly, I'll just have to say I've come down for a glass of water. My scalp tingles as I hear Mark's voice, low and dark. Barely recognisable.

'I'd been celebrating – drunk a bottle of wine, after our chat. And I don't really remember much about the night either. But in the morning, she was locked in the bathroom and later I found muddy clothes in the hamper.'

My stomach drops. Shit. That's why he's been a little awkward around me. How come he hasn't confronted me?

'So, she'd been outside you reckon?'

'Yeah. I have an awful, niggling feeling she saw some-thing. Or even had something to do with what happened.'

'Whoa. That's big, mate.'

What the hell? How could he even suggest that? My muscles twitch. I want to burst in on them and hit him.

'I know. And I'm probably wrong. Like I said, I'm overthinking. If there hadn't been the issue with her accusing me and Olivia of having an affair, I wouldn't even be considering this.'

Oh, my God. I bite down on my lower lip. 'Accusing'? I can't believe Mark's exposing my secrets but is clearly sweeping his own under the carpet by making out he wasn't involved with Olivia.

'I always said you had a sixth sense though. Ever since that business with—'

'Don't even utter that name.'

What was *that*? I caught the edge to Mark's voice. What's Brett talking about?

'Still. If you feel something's not right, I would bet you're right.'

'I don't want to be right, Brett. But if it wasn't her, I'm really afraid . . .'

Silence. He's trailed off, or he's whispering and I can no longer hear them. I can't bear to listen to more anyway. My chest is tight, my breathing shallow. I feel as though I've been stabbed through the heart. It appears I'm not the only one with trust issues. My own husband thinks I'm capable of something bad. God only knows what he'd think, or do, if he knew I had a murderer's blood running through my veins.

Chapter 19

JENNY

Friday

I get up early, before the alarm, leaving Mark snoring as I creep barefoot downstairs. He'd eventually staggered into bed at 3 a.m., alcohol fumes wafting close to my nose as he turned towards me. I'd kept my eyes closed, hoping he'd think I was asleep, but I sensed he was staring at me, his putrid breath like hot whispers against my cheek. I knew him going out to the pub with Brett would be a bad idea. I'm still reeling from the snippets of conversation I overheard last night – unsure what to do about it. For now, I put it to the back of my mind. His suspicions might be the least of my worries.

My hopes of catching someone in the act of leaving a new gift are dashed as I open the front door – there's not a soul in sight. But, as feared, a black bin liner is sitting waiting for me on the step. My jaw is tight, my fists clenched as I rush down the driveway, anger engulfing me. This is really pissing me off now. I check up and down the lane, walk across to the tree-lined bank and scramble up it, my bare feet slipping on the dewy grass. Grabbing hold of a low branch, I manage to hoick myself up high enough to see into the fields. Bar a few sheep, there's nothing to see.

For a while, I stare back at our house, looking at it through the perspective of a stranger. It's one of the more contemporary, exclusive houses in the village – it screams affluence with its double apex façade and huge floor-to-roof windows. Flanked by these impressive sheets of glass is an integrated balcony offering far-reaching views towards Dartmoor. It wasn't our first house in the village – we had a modest mid-terraced property in the centre when we first married. Mark rented prior to meeting me, as did I. We were lucky to get this place. It was a new-build we'd always admired when we were newly-weds but never dared to dream we'd one day be living in it. I tell myself I deserve it, that despite the helping hand we had at the beginning from Mark's grandparents, we both work hard to afford the mortgage and so why shouldn't we live in luxury? Of course, I've never quite believed I deserve it. Any of it.

If my theory is correct, though, envy of our wealth is not a motive for what's happening right now. The creeping dread of realisation points to one thing. The person or people responsible for leaving the mutilated animals know who I am. Or who I *was*. And they want me to know they know. But to what end? If this stunt is purely to frighten me, hopefully the dead animals are as bad as it'll get.

But if it's revenge?

Could it be someone related to one of my father's victims? The thought fills me with horror. Because, if that's the case, dead animals might only be the beginning.

I'm struck by another possibility as I clamber back down the bank. One that stops me in my tracks and sends tiny shockwaves through every nerve in my body.

My mother has finally found me.

Leaving cryptic messages would be just the sort of thing she'd do – and *of course* she'd know about the butterfly. She never wanted to let me go, was hellbent on keeping me with her, seeing as no one else would give her the time of day. Proof she'd become one of the most hated people in the town was evident by the graffiti daubed over the front of the house, regular vandalism of her car, and the yells of abuse I heard outside my bedroom window most nights. Fear of me being attacked if I went outside to play was the reason she kept me inside, she'd said. I eventually came to realise the vile actions and comments were directed at her, not me, like she told me – and it was through her increasing dread of being alone in her hell that she needed me. I was a prisoner in my own home. Not a single one of her friends stuck around – I was all she had. I'm well aware me leaving her would've destroyed her. Made her bitter. She'd have tried everything to find me. It may have been over twenty years, but something tells me she wouldn't have entirely given up.

If she's trying to win me back, though, she's going the wrong way about it. Although maybe that isn't her intention. It's more likely she is set on hurting me, like I hurt her. Ruin my life, like hers was ruined. I want to eliminate her from my list of suspects, but equally I don't ever want to go back there, to the place I once called home. Even

97

the thought steals the saliva from my mouth. Besides, I don't want to give her the satisfaction of turning up at her door asking questions. Maybe I could get someone else to do it for me. The only person I could ask to do such a thing is Roisin. It's a big ask, but I'm sure she'd be up for doing a little digging for me. She covers hundreds of miles for her pharmaceutical company rep job, so I could ask if she'd make a detour between her appointments to check my mother's movements, find out where she's been the past few days, that sort of thing. Just to be on the safe side.

Being a victim of my parents' warped behaviour isn't something I'm going to allow to happen again; I need to be the one in control. With new-found determination, I march up my driveway and snatch the bin liner from the step. It lifts easily; there's no real weight to it. It's not an animal. Confident Mark and his mate and Ella and Alfie are still asleep, I take it and go around to the back garden. I really should've put shoes on before venturing outside, but it's too late now as they sink into the damp lawn, the coldness biting my skin. I unlatch the shed door and place the bag on the wooden workbench that runs along-side one wall of the shed. It clonks as it makes contact with the wood.

While it's a relief to not have to get rid of another corpse, my heart judders at the thought of what *is* inside. So as not to give my mind too much time to consider the options, I reach a shaking hand into the bag. My finger-tips touch something cool. Solid. I retract my hand, nervous of what it is. It would be preferable to simply throw it away without looking. I wish I could be that person. As I know I would spend the next week, month, year pondering what it was, though, I have to just do it. It's like tearing off a plaster – the quicker I do it, the less pain it'll cause. I thrust my hand back inside the bag and grasp it again. Then, I slowly remove it, my breath held, eyes screwed shut.

For a moment I hold it in my palm like I've been told to 'close your eyes and open your hands' and I'm transported back to being a child, and mother giving me my one birthday gift – usually a new item of stationery I could use for my home schooling. It was never anything personal – or God forbid something a young girl might enjoy. Dad had been the one who'd bought thoughtful gifts, took me on fun days out, bought me ice-cream and sweets, giving me his secret wink, which meant 'don't tell your mother'. Once he left, so did the fun.

I cautiously open my eyes.

In my hand is a silver bracelet; beautifully crafted with diamonds set between elegant wave-shaped links. Each has a word engraved on it. There's a fleeting moment of familiarity.

Where have I seen this before?

Turning it over in my hand, I read the words: *kind*, *beautiful*, *caring*, *wonderful*, *precious*, *unique*. Then I notice the delicate heart-shaped charm on the end of the chain. An initial is engraved on it.

O.

I drop the bracelet.

All I can do is shake my head like a nodding dog in the back of a car. I blow out a steady stream of breath while trying to gather my thoughts. This is Olivia's. I have Olivia's bracelet. *Shit, shit, shit.* Was she wearing this the night she was abducted?

If so, it would mean that the person who took her is the one who's left this on my doorstep. And, given each bin liner has been the same distinctive type, with a green drawstring to tie them up, the person who's left the animal remains too.

Why, though? It doesn't make sense. I stride up and down inside the shed, the vibrations shuddering the wood beneath my cold, dirty feet. There's only one reason that springs to mind.

I'm next.

Panic swells inside my chest. I'd asked the girls at the vets' if they'd heard if Olivia had mentioned any odd occurrences in the lead-up to her abduction. Whether she'd had a stalker. What if she had, and now the same person is targeting me?

No. I'm jumping to conclusions. The butterfly attached to the guinea pig, to the cat – and probably the rabbit too had it not already begun decomposition – was specific. Personal. Probably not related to Olivia at all.

Then why has her bracelet been left for me?

More to the point – what the hell am I going to do with it?

Chapter 20

The Painted Lady Killer

Inside the mind of serial killer Paul Slater

Paul Slater didn't get his nickname – The Painted Lady Killer – purely because he left the butterfly of that name pinned to each of his victims. The meaning ran deeper than that. It was discovered that two of the five female victims had a police record for soliciting, one had been an escort and one had a reputation for 'putting it about' with various locals. This led the media to dub Slater The Painted Lady Killer *because of its connotation to prostitution. Painted lady is an old English term thought to refer to whores – and taken together with Slater's painted lady butterfly calling card, it was deemed the reason he chose it and his victims.*

However, his fifth and final victim, Penny

Hargreaves, whose murder ultimately led police to Slater, was different. Rather than being involved in sexual activity with multiple men, Penny Hargreaves was thought to have been cheating on her husband with one man. The identity of the man she'd embarked on an affair with was later revealed to be Curt Porter, landlord of The Butcher's Arms at the time – a pub Slater had been known to frequent. Slater's MO hadn't changed, exactly, but his choice of victim seemed to have deviated slightly. Psychologists believed, had he not been caught, that Paul Slater might've continued to kill, but they think his latest victim marked a change in preferred target – possibly to women who were having an extramarital affair. Of course, this is now merely speculation, being that Paul Slater will never again be free to commit another crime against women.

But, curious to know if the psychologists' theory was indeed correct, this was an area I was keen to explore with Paul Slater, and his detailed response was both fascinating and deeply chilling.

Chapter 21

JENNY

Afraid to take the bracelet back into the house with everyone inside, I scour the shed for a suitable hiding place until I can return and remove it safely. Carefully, I wrap it back up in the bin liner and slide it down behind the old metal filing cabinet. It wedges about halfway – easy for me to retrieve, but not visible unless you move the cabinet. As it's been here, in this same position, for the best part of five years and is filled with tools, I'm confident it's a good place to conceal it for now.

After stepping lightly over the grass and back around the side of the house, I slip through the front door, wiping my damp, muddy feet on the mat. The harsh bristles hurt my soles, but I can't walk mud through the house. If Mark sees I've been outside again – muddy *again* – too many questions will be asked. Although, maybe claiming a blackout is the cause of my state might be a good plan. I can't answer any questions then, and Mark wouldn't force it because he knows I have no awareness when I'm experiencing one.

It's still preferable to avoid him seeing me at all, so I manage to sneak into the en suite just as Mark's alarm wakes him. I get in the shower, the jets of water loud in my ears, drowning out Mark's muffled words through the locked door. My heart pounds as the hot spray washes over me. I tilt my face up into the stream of water, my eyes screwed tight as thoughts scramble around in my head. The fact Olivia's bracelet has been left, not another dead animal, is a massive deviation if it's from the same person. So, why the animals first and not simply the bracelet? It seems a lot of trouble to go to, to get my attention. Unless . . . Is it possible they were testing me? Before leaving potential evidence of an abduction – even murder, although I'm very much hoping that's not the outcome – perhaps they were making sure I didn't go to the police with the first bin liners. Confident I didn't, they've now left this, knowing I'm unlikely to hand it over to police in fear of somehow implicating myself.

Which makes me think it really is someone who knows who I am. Because being the daughter of an infamous serial killer puts me firmly under the microscope. And I can't, with one hundred per cent certainty, say where I was the night Olivia was taken, which means I daren't take an item belonging to the missing person to the police saying I happened to find it on my doorstep.

I know, though, that my plan to hide it, alongside the other things I keep hidden from Mark, is only a short-term solution. Destroying it all is the only way to protect myself. I'm guessing whoever is doing this to me is doing it for a reason – the most obvious now being to frame me for Olivia's abduction – and the more I think about it, likely murder. Because, I reckon that's the next development.

Olivia's body will be found and the police will be led to me. That's their plan. I feel it in my gut. Olivia's murder will be pinned on me, like the butterfly pinned to the animal corpses. I've been marked.

I have to find out who is behind this before they destroy my life.

Chapter 22

MARK

'Great night, mate. Must do it again soon.' Brett shovels a piece of toast into his mouth, washing it down with a gulp of black coffee. My stomach churns watching him.

'Yeah, definitely.' I give a weak smile. 'Although, not so heavy on the alcohol next time.'

'It was that last shot that tipped you over the edge.' Brett laughs.

'Whose bloody idea were they?' I'm not sure why I'm asking, the answer is obvious.

'Er . . . yours! Think you were trying to show me you could drink me under the table. Epic fail, as the kids would say.'

I shake my head, immediately regretting it as my brain feels as though it's knocking against the inside of my skull. I don't believe him; I would never instigate shots. I know where they lead. I rub my temples. 'Well, thanks for allowing me to make a tit of myself.' I realise *he* isn't worse for wear this morning. How did he put so much away and manage to: a) recall all the events of the evening, and b) escape a hangover?

'Ah, how could I resist? It was always so much fun watching you work your magic with the women after you'd had a skinful. Felt like I'd gone back in time.'

'What do you mean?'

'You had them MILFs eating out the palm of your hand, mate!'

Nausea bubbles inside me as the memories flood back. What was I playing at?

'Don't look so horrified,' Brett says, slapping me on the back. 'It was just a bit of harmless flirting. They were loving it.'

'They', I now recall with dismay, were the group of mums of kids in Ella's class. This was not good. Not good at all. Such timing. How will it look – a married man flirting with a group of females in the same pub Olivia was at moments before her abduction? Before I can question Brett further, Ella and Alfie slope in, sitting in their chairs at the table, all bleary-eyed and unruly-haired. How wonderful to have that childhood innocence. Shame we have to grow up, become responsible and weighed down by life's harsh lessons. Brett carries on about last night, and I cough, indicating for him to shut up. Not the type of conversation I want in front of my children.

Brett laughs. 'Ah, right. I got you. Don't want your kids knowing Daddy has a fun side, eh?'

I ignore him and he finally gets the message. He seems to be revelling in my humiliation a little too much. Surely a mate would've stepped in. He should've told me to calm it down last night, not encourage my crass behaviour. I recall now how he was definitely more in control than I was, urging me on like some wild frat boy. I wonder if Brett even drank his shots. Thinking back, that was something he'd pulled back in the day – lining up shots and for every two I necked, he only took one, throwing the other over his shoulder or tipping them into a nearby pint. I hadn't even realised at the time; he'd owned up during a truth or dare game one night a year later. Did I fall for his immature trick again? God, he must think I'm a complete bellend.

Why is he even going out of his way to help *my* business? I'm doing okay without his contacts, really. And his idea of opening offices throughout the country is a bit too grand for my liking. I'm a family man, want the simple things in life. I'm allowing him to carry me on a wave, like he used to. A wariness creeps into my gut as I watch him alternate a bite of toast with a swig of coffee, his slurping noises in between annoying. Perhaps I was too hasty to accept his help – I very rarely act impulsively and on those occasions when I did . . . well, I don't want to think about them, but they didn't work out well for me.

And he knows about one of them.

I'm suddenly keen to get him out of the house before Jen comes down for breakfast. I know I said too much last night, and for some reason, I'm afraid Brett might try and cause trouble by purposely letting something slip. I don't know why I have this feeling – and I'm angry with myself for opening up to him and for trusting his assertions all he wants is to help me drive my business up a gear. I'm beginning to suspect Brett has ulterior motives for looking me up and needling his way back into my life. One of my weaknesses is that I've always trusted people too quickly, taking them on face value. Believing everything they say without questioning it.

You'd think I'd have learned my lesson after the first time I was burned.

Chapter 23

JENNY

I go downstairs at the last possible moment, not wishing to spend time with Brett. My stomach knots as I approach the kitchen. In truth, I'm not keen on spending time with Mark either after what I overheard last night. I don't make eye contact with him as I breeze into the kitchen, attempting to appear nonchalant. He and Brett are sitting drinking coffee while Ella and Alfie noisily slurp Weetos from their bowls.

'Mind you don't get chocolatey milk down your jumpers,' I say, adding an artificially cheerful, 'Morning, all,' before walking to the coffee machine and standing stiffly, my back to the table so that I don't have to face them yet. Hiding my past has become second nature to me; I find it easier to compartmentalise those things from who I am now. But these new, present-day events are threatening to pull my carefully constructed life down around my ears. And it's going to be so much harder to conceal. I feel that my worries, anxieties and fears must be visible on my skin, like newly inked tattoos branding me and alerting everyone to my predicament. If it all comes out – if my little family, my friends, colleagues and acquaintances learn about my father, I too will be vilified. And if Olivia isn't found safe and well, all fingers will point in my direction.

'You okay, Jen?' Mark asks, but I don't turn around; I very slowly pour coffee into my mug, drawing it out for as long as possible. If I look at him he'll see the hurt and disappointment in my face, and I don't want to cause a scene in front of smarmy Brett. God, I really hope Mark doesn't take his business advice or his money – I don't fancy having to see him on a regular basis. The way his fringe flops across one eye, like an Eighties popstar, is just one of the things that irritate me. I took an instant dislike to him the moment we met all those years ago. I was possibly too harsh in my judgement. It was mostly because of the way his eyes had swept over me, settling a little too intensely on my face, as though he recognised me. I can still remember the icy chills that rippled over my skin when he later said, 'Good to have met you, Jane . . . oh, sorry, I mean Jen.' Him turning up now, the same time as the dead animals on my doorstep, is unnerving to say the least.

'Jenny?' Mark says again.

'Yeah, just a little tired,' I say, impassively, mesmerised with the wisps of steam drifting upwards from my coffee. I know I can't avoid sitting with them, not when the kids are at the table. I finally plonk myself down and immediately begin speaking to Ella and Alfie to prevent being drawn into a conversation with the men. When there's a gap in conversation, Brett jumps in like he's been waiting for this opportunity. Keen to convey something – or as I fear is the case, to stir up trouble.

'Sorry if we were a bit rowdy coming in last night. You were so kind to let me stay – I hope I haven't offended you.'

I give him a tight smile, and through narrowed eyes, reply with the response I assume is expected of me. 'Not at all. Didn't hear a thing. What time did you roll in?'

'Oh, not late, really. Half eleven?' Mark says, shooting Brett a look, daring him to disagree.

'About that, I guess. Nice local you've got here, Jenny.'

Something in the way he enunciates my name raises the hairs at the base of my skull. I don't know what it is about Brett, but I don't trust him.

The timing of him turning up and snaking his way into our lives is off. I hurry the morning routine along so I can make my escape.

Ella holds my hand tightly as we walk into the playground. It's unlike her, which makes me wonder if things are being said – scary things relating to what's going on. As much as we think we're shielding them from any horrors, I've no doubt she and to a lesser degree Alfie pick up on the unspoken cues – the body language, the hushed conversations just out of earshot. I shouldn't ignore the situation, hope it merely goes away or blends into the murky background of village life. Children are intuitive, Ella especially.

'Are you worried about anything, Ella?' I say, giving her hand a gentle squeeze.

I hear her draw in a sharp breath, and in turn, I hold mine.

'Isabella isn't coming back,' she says. Her head is down, her steps slow and deliberate. I stop walking and duck

113

down in front of her, letting go of Alfie's hand in the process. He says a quick 'bye, Mum, see you later', and hurries off in the direction of his classroom. I'm guessing he'd rather not be involved in any kind of heart-to-heart.

'Why do you think that, sweetie?'

She shrugs.

'Is it what your teacher said?'

'No. It's what Ethan told me.' She tilts her chin up; her eyes focus on mine. 'And he knows because his mummy told him.'

His mum being Willow. I sigh. Why doesn't this surprise me? 'Oh, my darling girl – I'm sure Isabella *will* come back, as will her mummy.' I know I shouldn't have added that bit, because if she doesn't, Ella will remember my words and it'll undermine her trust in me.

'No, you're wrong.' A flicker of fear reflects in her eyes – *my* fear. I swallow hard.

'Why do you think I'm wrong?' Dread shoots through my veins. I'm not sure I'm ready to hear her answer.

'Because her mummy is dead.' Ella pulls away from me and turns, suddenly skipping across the playground as if now she's shared this with me, she's been unburdened. But her words leave me with a heavy feeling, like I've got rocks in my belly. A hot flash rushes to my face and I storm over to the gaggle of gossips, burst through the circle and square up to Willow.

'What the hell have you been saying to your son, Willow? Why would you tell him Olivia's dead for Christ's sake?'

'Excuse me! Don't come tearing over here like some crazed woman yelling at *me*,' she says, her eyes blazing. 'I mean, I know it's your thing to make public accus-ations, but—'

114

'What's that supposed to mean?' I cut in sharply, before realising exactly what she's saying. Heat creeps up my neck. So, people clearly did know about me confronting Olivia last year, maybe they even know about Mark having an affair with her. No one's ever told me to my face. I swallow hard, my throat tight. They're all staring at me, open-mouthed now, and shame burns my cheeks. 'I'm sorry.' I hold my hands up. 'I was wrong to have a go at you. It's just that Ella . . .' My voice cracks. 'Ella has just said Ethan told her Isabella isn't coming back – but more worryingly, she said that Olivia is dead.'

'I can absolutely guarantee she did *not* hear that from my Ethan,' Willow says, her shoulders back, chin up in defiance.

'Okay,' I say, wanting to disagree but knowing it isn't a good idea. 'I suppose she could've heard it anywhere, maybe even overheard the teachers talking or something . . .' I offer an apologetic smile.

'More likely overheard the police asking their questions,' Zari says. 'They're still going door to door.'

With a calm voice now, I offer what'll be considered more acceptable input. 'But it's been days – surely they've moved beyond that stage?' The huddle tightens as we all move closer to continue our private conversation. Thankfully, it appears my outburst has been quickly forgotten as more pressing matters take over. I imagine there are various huddles of parents of children from different year groups all doing something similar.

'Apparently they've not. I suppose not everyone was at home when the police went knocking – they'll have to make second, maybe third visits before speaking with everyone.'

'They can't be asking the entire village – that's a waste of resources. They should be concentrating on searching for her.'

'None of it will be wasted if they get a lead,' Zari says, her eyebrows rising. 'I heard they'd been asking about any suspicious sightings or behaviour in the area during the days prior to Olivia's abduction. My guess is they've got zilch so far, which is why they're still visiting every house in the vicinity in the hope someone saw, or knows, something. Did you watch the televised appeal?'

'No, I didn't. Hadn't realised it was going to be on if I'm honest,' I say.

'They had it on in The Union last night,' Zari says, looking at me pointedly. 'We all watched it together.' The others all murmur something in acknowledgement.

My pulse takes a dive. They were at The Union last night, too. I wonder if Mark and Brett spoke to them. If they watched the appeal along with them. By the looks passing between the women now, the answer to at least one of those is yes.

'Did you learn anything new?' I'm careful to avoid direct eye contact – I don't want them to clock my sudden awkwardness.

'Not really.' Rachel's voice is shaky. 'Was heart-breaking seeing Olivia's parents crying in front of the cameras, though. So mean to put them through it. And wrong if you ask me – you'd have thought Yannis would do it, wouldn't you.'

Willow scoffs. 'Probably afraid to show his face. He'd automatically be branded the abductor – or worse. It's always the husband . . .'

'Yeah,' I say distractedly. My mother said that once.

While we were watching just such an appeal. 'Crocodile tears,' she said. 'Look at 'im. Lying bastard. He did it. It's obvious.' Funnily enough, after Dad was taken, she never said those words again. Never saw it coming, did she? Her own husband turned out to be the murderer of multiple women, yet she never knew. Is it easier to judge others? More obvious seeing their imperfections and flaws? Are you quicker to spot lies if they're being told by someone you don't know? Claire never forgave him for that. She'd trusted him, trusted *in* him, and he'd let her down. Let us all down.

'Your Mark was on fine form,' Frankie says, jolting me from my thoughts. 'Nudge-nudge, wink-wink.' She giggles with the others as she literally nudges Willow with her elbow.

'Meaning?' I force the word through my clenched teeth. I have to resist the urge to simply walk away.

'I know he's always been . . . you know . . . *friendly*, but I was surprised he was so flirty with us, given we're friends with you. It's like him and his mate were out on the pull.'

Each word pelts me as if they were pebbles. 'Bet you didn't rebuff him though, eh, Frankie?' My tone is sharp, caustic. I'm angry with Mark, but even more so with them. An image of them panting around him like bitches on heat pops into my mind. Before I can rationalise it, or make light of it – which would be the preferred option in this situation – I push past Frankie, exiting the huddle. I hurry off, not stopping until I'm out of sight.

In the privacy of my car, I cry.

Chapter 24

JENNY

With tears distorting my vision and adrenaline pumping my heart twice the normal rate, I accelerate the car, speeding through the village. It's a stupid, irresponsible move, not least because of the heavy police presence, but I'm powerless to stop myself. It's like my conscious mind has switched off. Before I know it, I'm on the road leading to the vet practice. The journey, as short is it is, is a complete blur since leaving the school.

Something catches my eye on the road and I slam my feet on the brake and clutch, the tyres screeching on the tarmac as I come to a dramatic halt. The seatbelt snags hard across my chest as I'm propelled forward, then releases as I flop back into my seat. My head bangs against the headrest. I take a deep, steadying breath.

Rubbing my chest, I unclick the belt and lean closer to the windscreen. I spot a rabbit attempting to hop into the hedgerow – but it's badly injured. I whack my hazards on and get out. My legs wobble uncontrollably as I slowly attempt to retrieve the frightened creature. It too is shaking; shocked. Its hind leg is limp and bloody. Poor thing. Someone must have hit it and just driven off. It jerks in my hands as it tries to free itself. He doesn't understand I'm trying to help. Some animals do, I think. They might struggle to start with, then a Zen-like calmness washes over them, like they realise someone is going to look after them, make them better.

I gently place the large, brown wild rabbit in the spare cage I always keep in the boot, then get back behind the wheel and drive, slowly and with care, to the vet clinic. As I take it into the practice, I'm met by Samir, who says he'll take a look at it while I grab a tea. Vanessa takes me by the arm and leads me to the break room. I must look a state for them to be reacting like this. Hopefully, they'll think it's just to do with the rabbit and won't ask any probing questions. They've already wrongly assumed I hit it, and I haven't put them right, because I don't have the energy to speak and it's better they think I'm merely upset over an injured animal than an injured ego.

All I can think of is Mark at the pub with the playground mums last night. The thrum of my heartbeat intensifies as Frankie's words echo in my head: 'It's like him and his mate were out on the pull.' Why is he doing this to me?

The adrenaline from the morning's events takes its time to wear off. Each time I calm down, my mind conjures up images of Mark and the group of mums again. My fight-or-flight hormones flood my body over and over all day. I'm exhausted now and grateful we're coming to the end of surgery hours.

120

'Last client,' I say with a sigh of relief as I lead an excitable Border terrier into my consulting room with Nisha.

'Oh, not according to this,' she says, nodding towards the computer.

I look over her shoulder at the screen. That can't be right. 'That's the diagnostic I thought was first thing tomorrow,' I say, confusion furrowing my brow.

'I'll call reception,' Nisha says, pressing the intercom button that sounds by the desk. I take the dog and lift him onto the table. He belongs to Mrs Harris, an elderly lady in the village. Someone had recommended a Border for some unearthly reason – really not suitable for a woman in her seventies who has debilitating agoraphobia. Her neighbour has dropped him in today because she's worried he's not getting enough exercise and is obese. Giving him the once-over now, as I wait for Nisha, I decide the neighbour is right. I'll get Nisha to make up a diet and exercise plan.

'Nish,' I say. 'Can you work up a plan for Buddy here?'

'Er . . . yeah, sure. And I'm sorry, but the diagnostic *is* here now. In the waiting room.'

'I don't understand,' I say, irritation lending an edge to my tone. I check the wall clock. 'We've literally ten minutes before close. Everyone knows we don't book in diagnostics at this time.'

'It was an oversight, Jenny.' Nisha shrugs.

'I don't see how. Anyway, you finish up here and I'll go and see.'

I'm about to storm out, but Nisha catches my arm. 'Don't be too hard on her – she's still learning the ropes.'

'Ah. I see.' I shake her free and go to reception. The dog for the scan is lying under his owner's chair in the waiting room. Ken Frances, the pub landlord is sitting reading a pet magazine. I slip behind the desk and lean over Abi as she types up notes from the previous consultation. 'You've been here for long enough to know, Abi.' I try and keep my voice low, but in doing so, know it's also coming across harshly. My tone sounds almost threatening even to my ears. But I don't alter it. 'For God's sake – I needed to be away from here on time. Now your screw-up will make me late getting the kids from after-school club.'

'Oh, my God. I'm so sorry.' Abi's face crumples, and I feel a pang of guilt. Mistakes happen – I should know. But for some reason this knowledge doesn't stop me being a bitch, and, despite the awareness I'm taking my anger out on the wrong person, I don't back down.

'Well, it's too late for apologies now, isn't it? I can't exactly turn Mr Frances away, can I?'

'I can explain it's my error,' Abi says, lifting herself up from the chair. I push my hands down on her shoulders, forcing her back in her seat.

'No. I'm not making a client pay for your mistake.' I add with a smile: 'We all make them at one time or another.' As if that'll help smooth it over. Abi's face is aghast and she looks as if she's about to cry. Sometimes I scare myself with how like my mother I can be.

'I could call the school and explain you're going to be late.' Her voice shakes.

'The whole point of the after-school club is so working parents can pick their kids up later than the usual school finish time. Being late to after-school club is really frowned upon.' If Hayley were here, I'd ask her to pick them up for me – she's done it a few times in the past. But she left early for a doctor's appointment, and I don't trust anyone else to do it.

'I'll make sure they realise it's not your fault. I'll ring now, shall I?'

'If you could,' I say, tightly. 'The number is in the family and emergency contact file on the database.' I turn on my heel and plaster a wide smile on my face to greet Ken Frances and his black Lab, Whiskey who runs to lick me as though I'm an old friend.

'Hey, there, boy.' I reach down to rub him behind his ears. My annoyance immediately subsides, like it often does when I'm around animals – they have a great ability to calm and de-stress, hence why we're a nation of animal lovers. On the whole, anyway. My mind flicks to the poor, maimed creatures left on my doorstep and I have to shake my head to rid the images again. 'Okay, follow me through to the x-ray room, Ken. You can help settle him, but then you'll have to wait outside. Don't want to make you radioactive.'

'No, maid, that'll never do. Enough strange goings-on here without that, eh?' By this, I assume he means Olivia's abduction – though 'strange goings-on' isn't how I'd describe the situation. I open my mouth to ask him if he's heard anything new, but then stop myself. If he had, he was the type of person who'd relish in telling me without the need to enquire.

Following completion of the diagnostic imaging of Ken's dog, I rush out the door, shouting over my shoulder to Abi for her to lock up because I haven't got time now I'm over half an hour late. My choice of words likely came across as passive-aggressive, which I didn't really mean, and coupled with not even making eye contact with

Abi, she will think I'm still mad at her. But I'm well aware it's really Olivia, the macabre gifts, the school mums and Mark's juvenile behaviour that are the true cause of my volatile mood. In the car, I tap out a quick text.

Can we have a catch-up? I'm desperate to see a friendly face xx

I could really do with leaning on Roisin, because I can't talk to Mark. And she's the only one who knows what I went through after learning about Mark's 'thing' with Olivia. I have to share all this with the most trustworthy friend I have before I explode. And if the behaviour I've just displayed is anything to go by, that moment isn't far off. I'm appalled and shocked at my outburst – almost as much as it shocked Abi. I need to get a hold of my emotions, because if I don't, I'm not going to need to worry about someone else ruining my life – I'm going to do that all by myself.

Chapter 25

The Painted Lady Killer

Inside the mind of serial killer Paul Slater

Paul Slater's crimes against women all involved a level of violence incongruous with the family man he purported to be. Aggression was a trait at odds with how he came across to others in his community, who up until his arrest had seen him with his wife and daughter on many occasions – although it was widely reported that the majority of those times he'd been observed with just his daughter, Jane. When asked about his relationship with her in particular, Paul Slater has always clammed up. He hasn't spoken about her. He has never divulged any details about his life as a father. Over the years, media attention has tended to focus on his victims and their families, as well as Paul's wife, Claire, and how she was affected by her husband's crimes. But little cover has been given to Jane, who was eight at the time of Slater's arrest.

During his trial in 1988 Paul was questioned repeatedly about his aggressive nature. He answered the prosecution's questions simply, no doubt well rehearsed with his brief. Psychologists offered their take, of course, and together with incidental findings and interviews with neighbours and co-workers, a picture of a man prone to aggressive outbursts was painted. It was as though Paul had two distinct personalities, with some people in the community vouching for his good nature and others saying the opposite. Paul's lawyer was keen to point out how it was only after Paul's arrest, subsequent charge and the continual media attention that these accounts changed.

Within this book, Paul will recount in his own words how this picture was inaccurate and misleading, denying his temper was ever out of control. Conversely, he will explain how every aspect of his life, his actions and behaviour were in fact completely controlled. He'd learned it.

'To do what I did,' he states, 'you not only require a steady hand, but a steady mind.' He admitted that to others it might have appeared as though he was someone who flew off the handle. But rest assured, Paul was – and is – a man who shows what he needs to show; manipulation and coercion were his key mental weapons then, as they are now.

Chapter 26

MARK

The cursor hovers over the news article link. My chest is tight as I finally click on it. The page pops up, Olivia's face filling the screen. I immediately tap the cross to exit the site; I can't look at her flawless skin, her soulful eyes and soft, full lips without a deep sense of regret chipping away at my conscience. Guilt has eaten a hole in me, and it's threatening to devour me entirely.

There haven't been any developments, I'm sure – it would've been on the radio when I drove to the office if there was a major update. I was curious to read the details – the headline of this particular article was: **Was Olivia having an affair?** But, it's proven too much, my stomach too weak. Or maybe it's me, my character, that's too weak.

Standing, I walk to the large window offering a view over Exeter Cathedral and beyond. From this high up, all activity below me seems to be carrying on in silence. Worker ants going about their business, seemingly without a care in the world. Although, I'm sure that probably isn't the case. I imagine if I were aware of their every thought, their worries and concerns, my mind would explode.

I'm certainly worried about multiple things. So many that my brain can't separate them – they're bundled together like a bunch of wires and they're so intertwined I'm afraid I won't ever disentangle the mess. I've brought this on myself. For years I've been happily burying my head in the sand, allowing anything even slightly resembling a problem to be ignored and avoided at all costs. Because it's easier, isn't it? If you ignore the problems, they simply cease to be. They melt away and disappear, leaving me a happy, contented family man.

It's the reason I ignored the most recent issue and the subsequent problem that arose when Jen began asking awkward questions. And now the biggest of them all.

Ignoring the fact I think my wife has harmed Olivia Edwards.

Chapter 27

Do you remember when we took our little trips?

The ones we kept secret from Mum? Yes, I remember.

You used to love collecting things – anything from the ground, whether it was a pinecone, a leaf or a stone – you'd pick it up, pop it in your backpack and take it home and hide it.

And she'd discover each of my hiding places and throw every item away.

I kept your drawings, you know. The ones your mother had allowed you to send. I know why she chose those in particular. They were the ones with the three stick figures – two of them always holding hands, one always placed at the edge of the paper. That person was looking on, not really part of the family. Because the figures were drawn the same size, I naturally assumed it was me on the outskirts – I wasn't the one holding your hand anymore because I'd left you. And that's the reason she allowed it – because she knew I'd think just that, and it would cause hurt. But some years later, I realised I'd been wrong.

So, who do you think that person on the edge was, Dad?

It was her. Your mother was the one on the outside looking in. It was ironic she sent them believing it to be me, thinking she was somehow getting her own back. She was always jealous of us, Princess, because she was never able to penetrate our bubble.

That explains a lot. She hated that when you were gone, she couldn't just step into your shoes. Hated the fact I still didn't love her the way I love you, Dad.

Chapter 28

JENNY

I put my mobile on the worktop and plug in the charger, then go and check on the kids – they've been very quiet since getting in from school. Ella was particularly huffy with me for being so late and didn't utter a word during the drive home. She then disappeared into her room. I watch her now from the doorway – she's sitting at her desk, writing. She covers the notebook with an arm when she realises I'm there, shielding it like you would an exam paper, making sure no one copies. I simply ask if she's okay, and when she responds with a sharp 'yes', I leave her to it and look for Alfie.

Mark is late home. It's happened occasionally before, when he's been engrossed and lost track of the time, but this feels different; purposeful. He was noticeably uncomfortable this morning at breakfast and I'd put that down to Brett's presence. After all, I was awkward because of him too. Now, I'm certain his demeanour was because he was afraid Brett might let it slip that Mark had been 'flirting' with the playground mums. He'll have some excuse when he finally gets home about something important coming up that prevented him leaving on time. Or, it really could be the case that something has come up. It happened to me this afternoon, and I haven't got the monopoly on unexpected events.

I find Alfie in the back garden. He's built a den with the old tent material and is lining up his little soldiers – Mark's old ones he found boxed up in the garage – ready to fight against each other. I stand, leaning against the large sliding patio doorframe and consider that's how I'm feeling. It's what I should be doing: lining up my defences, ready to go forth and do battle. Only, *my* enemies are unknown. I need to change that.

While the kids are occupied, and without Mark here to see or question it, I go into the garage and rummage in the packing container marked *Relics*. There are still numerous containers we haven't sorted through despite having lived in this house for six years. I come across Mark's old school yearbooks and almost go down a rabbit hole by flicking through the pages, but stop myself. There's no time. I keep digging for what I'm looking for, and with a dart of triumph, I pull it out. Our old video camera. I root around some more for the charger, and feel a swoop of relief when I find it tangled at the bottom of the box. Now, I'll set it up on the balcony overlooking the driveway.

By some miracle it still works. I've had to plug it in, as the battery will take ages to charge fully, but the lead is long enough to position the camera on the table I've dragged outside to the balcony. Before I go to sleep, I'll start recording. It doesn't have night vision, so I'll switch the security lights from motion sensor to on. There's a chance that might put off whoever is leaving the bin liners, but it being on sensor hasn't stopped them, so I hope it won't make a difference. As long as Mark doesn't switch it back, of course.

Mark finally comes through the door at eight-thirty. His face is taut, eyes dull with tiredness as he slopes into the kitchen muttering a brief apology before disappearing upstairs to change. The kids are already fed and settled, so it's only the two of us to eat. When Mark returns, dressed in jogging bottoms and sweatshirt, I silently dish up the reheated beef hotpot. Tension clips our words as we exchange blunt, perfunctory appraisal of the food, but nothing else. Not even the usual 'how was your day', conversation. It's like we're both afraid to be the first to mention the elephant in the room, so it's a stalemate. Later, we watch Netflix, to avoid seeing anything on the news about Olivia. While it's likely we're both keen to know if there've been any developments, neither of us wants to see her face on the screen or acknowledge our increasing fear that comes with each day she's not found alive.

We fall into bed at eleven, and after a peck on the lips to say goodnight, we turn away from each other. The distance between us is stretching, and with that realisation, a deep ache radiates through my insides. I roll onto my back and wrap my own arms around my belly, cradling myself while hot tears bubble on my lower lids. They tip over, spilling onto my nose and down my cheek, as I turn towards Mark and stare at the back of his head in the darkness. Moving one hand, I reach to touch his shoulder, but pull back before I make contact. Is there any coming back from this?

While I lie awake, my pillow damp against my face, I listen to Mark's guttural snores. My mind drifts to the video recorder on the balcony.

Chapter 29

JENNY

Saturday

I'm on the kitchen floor when I come to. The second time this week, I think with dismay.

Getting to my feet quickly, I give myself the once-over. I'm in my pyjamas – the hems of both legs are damp and the white material is now brown. God. I've been outside. Casting my eyes around the kitchen, I don't note anything out of place and the back patio doors are shut. I have no recollection of opening or closing them. I check if they're locked. No. In which case, it's likely I'd gone in and out of them as Mark or I always check the locks of every door before going to bed.

A dull thud sounds and I dart upstairs in case someone is up, careful not to make a noise; I don't want to be caught out like this. It must have been one of the kids dropping a toy from their bed, because all is quiet as I reach the landing. I let out a shuddering sigh.

After creeping into our bedroom and swapping my dirty pyjamas for clean ones – remembering this time not to put them in the hamper – I walk across the landing to the access point of the balcony. Again, this is always locked as I don't want to risk the children going out there. I've heard some real horror stories of children falling from balconies and so right from the off, when we got this place, we made sure the children were well versed in the safety aspects and also kept the key high up out of their reach. I stretch up to retrieve the key from the brass hook and quietly open the door and go to the table.

The camera has stopped recording, but it looks as though it's captured a fair few hours' worth. Nerve endings tingle, sending waves of tiny electrical pulses over my skin, as I press the rewind button. The tape is taking forever to come to a stop, the whirring noise a reminder of technology when I was growing up. I'm scared to see if it's captured anything. If it weren't for my jitteriness, I could have checked the front doorstep before coming upstairs – if there's nothing there, I'd have saved myself this stress. Finally, it clicks. Right. This is it. The moment of truth.

I take the camera and balance it on my lap as I sit down on a patio chair on the balcony. It jiggles with the shaking of my legs. It's chilly in the fresh, crisp morning air, but my skin is hot; clammy. Tension pulls my muscles taut. I press play and wait for the wobbly, grey, grainy picture to settle. For a moment, I think it's completely blank and I've wasted my time, but then I make out the two parked cars and the sweeping driveway. Yes! It's worked.

I watch for a few minutes, seeing the time tick by in the bottom right corner, then I fast-forward the tape. It's unlikely the person will make an appearance before midnight. I stop and start it several times and am about to give up for now, thinking I'll be caught out here if I stay much longer. Plus, cold has seeped through the thin material of my silk pyjamas and I'm violently shivering.

And then I catch a shadow on the screen. It's moving. I peer more closely and my heart leaps.

The figure is a woman – I'm sure from the stature and movement, and she's wearing what appear to be white pyjamas.

'Noooo,' I whisper. I don't believe it.

It's me.

I've captured myself while experiencing a blackout.

I hit the stop button and slump back in the chair, disappointment sapping all energy. I'd so hoped I was about to unveil the culprit. My breath clouds in front of me as large puffs of air escape my mouth. Then, with a jolt, I realise what this means. My blackouts, and what I do during them, have always been a mystery. Although I've been made aware of some things because of the nature of what I'd done in my trance-like state, I've never seen myself – never had first-hand evidence. Now, I have the opportunity to actually witness an episode. I sit forwards and press start again. With my face inches from the screen, I stare intently as I follow my journey from the back door, presumably, as I've only just come into sight from that direction, to the driveway. I observe my surprisingly quick progression down it, where I then disappear from view.

Where on earth am I going?

I shift in the plastic patio chair to relieve my cramping muscles. And I wait. The clock continues counting: two minutes pass, then three, four, five. What could I possibly be doing for all that time? On foot, it would take about that to get into the centre of the village. But surely I'm not wandering the streets of Coleton Combe in my bloody nightclothes. How embarrassing it'll be if someone saw me and says something. I'll be forced into coming clean and admitting I sleepwalk. I cringe at the thought. I've kept these things to myself since I was eight years old – only my mother, and Mark, know I suffer with blackouts. Oh, and now Brett of course, if I overheard the late-night conversation correctly. But, I'd be mortified if everyone finds out and I become the village entertainment.

After more fast-forwarding, finally I see myself returning. It's been eleven minutes. I'm walking more slowly now, I note. And as the image becomes slightly clearer, I can see I'm carrying something in my arms.

My heart hammers erratically against my ribs. I can't make it out – the picture quality is too poor – but I'm holding something that appears to have some weight to it, and the bundle is darker against my light pyjamas.

Am *I* the one leaving the bin liners? Why in God's name would I do this to myself?

But then I watch as I veer to the left, and lose sight of myself completely. I don't think I went towards the doorstep. I guess it's possible I might've walked underneath the balcony, though. I rewind and watch more carefully. It looks more like I headed to the side of the house – leading to the bins.

Unplugging the camera, I take it and rush to the spare room. I place it under the old dressing table – the one I was meant to have refurbished at least six years ago when I thought I'd take it up as a hobby when Shabby Chic was popular. Then I slide on some sandals and head to the back door.

138

Outside, I visually sweep the area before walking to the bins. I don't know why, really – am I expecting someone to be there? Observing me from their hiding place? With some trepidation, I lift the lid of the wheelie bin.

Nothing.

Confusion clouds my mind. If I didn't put whatever I'd been carrying into the bin, then where is it?

My pulse pounding, I rush around to the front door.

There's a new bin liner on the doorstep.

I freeze to the spot, tears springing to my eyes.

There was no one else in sight on the camera recording – no one approached the house from the driveway. Only me. But I was so sure that I went around the back. So, if it wasn't me leaving the bin liner . . .

It had to be someone from inside the house.

To have not been captured on the video, the person would've simply had to open the front door and pop the bin liner on the step.

And the only other person who could do that is Mark. Isn't it?

Chapter 30

The Painted Lady Killer

Inside the mind of serial killer Paul Slater

According to records – those supplied by the police and what the papers reported – Paul Slater's first victim was Harriet Jennings, whom he raped and murdered in 1975. But Paul has subsequently divulged further details and now, exclusively revealed in this book, Paul shares how his illicit behaviour began much earlier in his childhood – in 1968 when Paul was eleven – and that in fact, his first victim was aged just ten.

Raised single-handedly by his mother, Paul never knew his father – instead, he became accustomed to a string of different men coming and going from his home because that's how his mother made her money. Paul shared that on a daily basis from the age of five, he was shoved into a wardrobe and threatened with a beating if he so much as 'made a peep' while his mother 'entertained' her gentlemen friends.

As the years went by, he came to realise this meant while she had sexual intercourse with them. He spoke of a memory when he'd been in the wardrobe for six hours straight, with just a glass of water. He'd had to use the same glass to urinate in. His lack of nourishment and outright neglect led to him struggling at school. He was bullied. He fell asleep in class. He failed in every subject. His way of dealing with it all was to become introverted. And in his head, he began to plan how to hurt others so he could be the one in control for a change.

His first victim, he revealed, was a girl in the class below him. Despite being younger, she'd taunted him, made him feel inadequate and he'd seen how she flirted with all the boys, gaining their attention at every break time. He'd watched as she'd taken different boys around the back of the bike shed, observed her kissing them. He'd waited weeks until she was finally on her own walking home. He knew her route, knew the point in the field near the quarry where it was quiet – she took it as a short cut, so he knew this would be his best opportunity. By age eleven he'd witnessed his mother having sex with strangers – but at that time, he hadn't wanted to do that. He did want to hurt this girl, though.

He attacked her from behind, jumping on her back and pushing her to the ground, face down in the mud. Then he hit her on the back of her head, and she stopped moving. He spoke about how he'd felt in that moment, and while he admitted it made him feel powerful, he explained it was more than that. It was the release of pent-up anger, shame and hurt that was the key result.

With the victim still and silent, he tore her shirt off and flipped her over onto her front. He traced his finger across the smooth skin of her belly, and he described how an immense sense of calm came over him. As if to cement his thoughts of the act being beautiful and serene, a butterfly landed on her and he watched, mesmerised. Then, without conscious thought, he slowly moved his hand above it, and with a swift slap, he brought it down onto the butterfly, squashing it perfectly flat against her belly.

He said he relived that moment time and time again – it was the most peaceful his mind had ever been: it was as still as both she and the butterfly had been.

Of course, we know this victim didn't report the attack on her. Nor did she come to further harm at the hands of Paul Slater. Not in the way his later victims would.

Because, I can exclusively reveal that this victim was Claire Woods.

And fifteen years later, she became Paul's wife.

Chapter 31

JENNY

After snatching the bin liner from the step, I march back around to the wheelie bin and, without looking at its contents, throw it in, slamming the lid closed with as much force as I can muster. It might wake everyone up, but in this moment, I don't care. My mind is reeling at seeing myself on the video. I was so desperate to capture the detestable person who's doing this to me on camera, I hadn't considered I'd be the one caught. And it certainly didn't cross my mind before now that Mark could've possibly left the macabre packages. A burning sensation is building up in my stomach as I consider it.

I'm not quiet when I return to our bedroom and stomp into the en suite, noisily clattering around, crashing open the shower screen, whacking the shower on, lifting body wash, shampoo and conditioner bottles one by one, then slamming them back down again. I huff and puff loudly and, when I'm done, I exit the en suite, banging the door behind me.

Mark isn't in bed, which I'm glad about. At least he didn't witness my childish tantrum. Or, maybe he has only just left the bedroom because of it. I stay, wallowing in my own self-pity for another twenty minutes, until the frustration has seeped out of my body and I feel calm. Or calm enough to face the day, at any rate.

If it's not my turn to attend the practice for emergency consultations, Saturdays are reserved for family fun. Swimming, adventure parks, cycling are our go-to activities.

But not today it seems.

Mark is lying on the sofa, arms crossed under his head, feet hanging over the armrest, watching Saturday sport. I passed the kids on my way down the stairs. Both are in their rooms – Alfie is playing with his Hot Wheels cars and Ella is deeply engrossed in reading a book. I'm discombobulated – a deep sense of disconnect makes me feel I'm teetering on a cliff edge.

Mark doesn't hear my approach, so I take a moment before making myself known, leaning against the doorframe watching him. This thing with Olivia has brought all of my insecurities rushing back. And being subjected to the playground mums' jibes yesterday added fuel to the already blazing fire. I felt as though I was being taunted. Ridiculed. I'm a strong, successful woman – I won't be made to feel a fool. Yet, as I look at Mark, then consider he might be the one placing the bin liners of dead animals on the step, I realise that's precisely what he's doing – making a fool out of me.

But why?

Maybe he wants to leave me. For Olivia. What if they both want a long-term relationship, not merely a fling? In my jumbled mind it suddenly makes sense. They've come up with this plan together – if they pin her abduction on me, get me out of the picture, then they can be together without interference from the woman scorned. Could be the perfect plan. Let's face it, more bizarre things have been known to happen in real life. But, of course, she'd have to be 'found' and then I'd be off the hook, so it wouldn't really work.

Unless they disappeared together: new names, new identities, new lives. It's what I did, so I know it's doable. But I didn't have children then; it was so much easier to start afresh. Dragging Ella and Alfie around the country – trying to begin again with them in tow – would be much more complicated. And Mark would never, ever leave his kids. I'd bet my life on that.

I force my paranoid theories from my mind, and walk into the lounge, bending to kiss Mark on his forehead. He jumps.

'Didn't hear you come in.' He swings his legs around and sits up. 'Morning.'

'Hey,' I say. 'Aren't we going out today?'

'Do you *want* to? I assumed, you know . . . given the *thing* . . .' He looks sheepishly at me. God, are we not even able to utter her name now? She's become 'the thing'?

'It might take our minds off the situation. To be honest, I could do with getting out of the village – it's become claustrophobic. Seeing police here every day, news crews and journalists, it's like living in a soap opera.'

'Yeah, good point. Shall we take the bikes, go to Haldon Forest?'

There's not a hint of concern on his face, in his voice. If he *had* been the one to leave the bin liner this morning – or at any other time – wouldn't I spot something in his body language? See guilt or betrayal in his eyes? I'm sure I'd seen it last year, when the mention of an affair came up and I assumed he was going to leave me immediately. Then, he'd spent days trying to convince me he had no intention of leaving and his slip with Olivia was a one-off. Over time, I believed him. Or, on the surface I did. I'm coming to realise deep down, the mistrust remained and even though he never outright admitted it, and nor did she, I feel certain it was more than a one-night stand. I think he so desperately tried to convince me it was nothing serious that he ended up believing it himself.

'Sure,' I say. 'I'm not exactly brimming with energy, but if we did the easy route . . .' Not brimming with energy is an understatement. I'm running on fumes. It's my default, though and has been for years. Insomnia is a killer – no wonder sleep deprivation is used as a form of torture.

Mark gets up. 'I'll get the bikes from the garage and load them on your car. You want to get the kids ready? We can grab some breakfast on the way.'

I watch him leave, then run upstairs, shouting to the kids to be ready in five minutes. They're keen to get a McDonald's brekkie but I would rather eat my own toenails than consume that. I suggest getting something from the shack at Haldon instead and am met with disappointment. They'll get over it by the time they're in the car.

Within ten minutes, we're all strapped in. Mark's driving at my request – I hate it when the rack is loaded top and back – I never can judge the length and height well and fear I'll crash us into a hedge. Over the years, since Mark first met me after having done just that, my driving skills have been the butt of many jokes.

'We'll have to pop in for petrol,' Mark says, swinging into the Texaco garage. 'Mummy's left it on empty *again*.' He smiles as he berates me. But I lean across to check the dial. I swear I had at least quarter of a tank. It's not as if I drive very far and I only put twenty quid in last week.

'That's weird,' I say. 'You been using my car?'

'Er . . . how would I do that? You've had it at the vets' every day.'

'Oh, yeah.' I frown, and get out. 'You two want a drink from here?' I mouth through the window. They shake their heads, so I check the petrol pump number and go inside ready to pay once Mark's filled up.

'Morning, Jennifer,' Kam says when I reach the desk. I've tried and failed to get him to call me Jen or Jenny, but he has at least dropped the formality of 'Mrs Johnson' each time I come in now.

'Hiya. You good?' I hover at the till, glancing out the window at Mark as I wait for him to replace the pump.

'Ah, you know. I have my good days and my bad ones,' he says. His eyes are sad and I don't want to press him on the reasons. I'm aware he and his wife have been struggling with the village garage for some years – the price of fuel, the rival garages at the supermarkets, all putting pressure on them. 'Nyra's mum is ill and she's been spending more and more time at hers to help. I think she'll have to move in with us. Just not ideal, you know, living over the garage – not for an elderly lady with mobility issues.'

'Oh, Kam – I'm so sorry to hear that. Maybe social services can help – put a care package in place for her?'

'Everything takes so long. Paperwork.' He shakes his head.

I hear the ding, indicating that Mark has finished filling the car. 'How much has my husband cost me?' I laugh, but it catches in my throat as I see a woman approach Mark on the forecourt. Kam follows my gaze and his eyes widen.

'That woman has been speaking to every one of my customers,' he says with a deep sigh.

'Why?'

'Reporter, I think. Trying to get the scoop on Olivia.'

My blood runs cold. 'Really? Can't you tell her to leave?'

He shrugs. 'She's on her own at least, not like the village shops – they're teeming with them.'

'Awful isn't it? Olivia's life has suddenly become public property.'

'Indeed. But I guess at least it means they'll uncover useful information – enable them to find her. And the monster who took her.'

'Have the police done any updates? They got any leads do you think?'

'Well, your nurse was in this morning – Nisha. And she said she saw police at Mrs Brewer's place. A pair of them.' Kam's voice takes on a different pitch, bordering on excitement, and I realise he's as capable of gossip as the next person.

'Caroline Brewer's?'

'The one with the camera on the front of her house, yes. And apparently, it didn't look like the typical door-step chat they've been conducting so far – they actually went inside.'

I let this sink in. This is an escalation. Up until now police have been going door to door and that's literally it – standing conducting their brief questions on the doorstep. If they went in, it had to be for a good reason. They must have wanted access to her CCTV footage.

'You all right, Jen?' I snap out of my thoughts at the sound of Mark's voice behind me.

'Oh, yeah – sorry. Just having a chat with Kam. I've paid.'

'We'd best get going, then,' he says. 'Oh, actually, I'll just grab some bottles of water.'

I say goodbye to Kam and leave, careful not to make eye contact with the reporter, who I can tell is eyeing me. She'd better not approach me. I jog to the car and get in, quickly shutting the door and turning around to speak with the kids. If the woman has a camera, I don't want her capturing my face. Not that she has reason to photograph us anyway. Better safe than sorry though. Mark gets back in the car, handing me the bottles. I bend to place them in the footwell so I can remain out of sight. I wait until Mark has exited the forecourt, then sit up, and ask him what the reporter wanted.

'Oh, the usual, you know.'

'Well, actually, no, Mark. I don't. Not like this kind of thing is common here, is it.'

'She asked if I knew Olivia—'

'And what did you say?'

He shoots me a withering look. 'If you let me finish . . .'

'Sorry. Go on.'

'I said I knew of her, and that we'd had a conversation or two in the past.'

'Why would you tell her that? Are you stupid?' I hiss.

'Calm down, Jenny.' He gives a sideways glance in the rear-view mirror, checking to see whether the kids

151

are picking up on the tension no doubt. He hates having cross words with me in front of them. As do I.

'You shouldn't have uttered a single word,' I say harshly, before flipping straight back into Mum mode and starting up the Johnson family sing-song we always have on car journeys, to lift the mood.

Internally, I'm screaming.

Giving these hacks even the tiniest scrap of information is tantamount to giving them an exclusive. And Mark has voluntarily offered enough to ensure they keep digging. If he was going to say anything, it should've been that he didn't know Olivia at all. With the way I acted, avoiding her and then keeping my face turned away, alarm bells would no doubt have rung. Seasoned reporters must be intuitive, having witnessed a range of human behaviour. Now she'll use what Mark, and by proxy me, gave her and will start dropping it into conversation with the other poor saps she catches.

Before we know it, she'll have found out about my altercation with Olivia and it'll mean the press, and police, will realise both me *and* Mark have a possible motive for harming her.

Chapter 32

JENNY

Haldon Forest car park is busy, as usual – but the cycle route we choose, the easiest, is the least congested. Mark leads, Ella and Alfie are next, with me bringing up the rear. We've found it's the safest formation as I'm slower than Mark and also more observant: I can spot a fall before it even happens. We're both acting as though nothing is different from last week's family fun day, despite both knowing everything is.

Before Tuesday night's blackout, and then learning about Olivia's abduction, our life had been ticking along. It was by no means perfect – things have been a little off kilter since last year's 'bump in the road', as I prefer to think of it. But I really felt we were managing to move on. There was hope we could get back to a firm footing and I could rebuild my trust in him. I'm not so sure now whether Mark is even worthy of that trust. I find myself questioning where we can go from here. Life without Mark is unimaginable, but I don't know that our marriage can survive. Will we make it through this as a couple?

I stare at the back of him as he cycles ahead of me – watch his muscular legs pumping away, and the thought I had earlier returns. When the video hadn't captured anyone leaving the bin liner, but I found one anyway, my immediate conclusion had been it was Mark who'd left it.

Since the lies my mother told came to light, and I realised how she and my father let me down, trust became the hardest thing for me to give. Like building a structure with matchsticks, when I met Mark, I began placing one, then another on top, carefully gluing them together as I went until, years later, my building was near completion. I *almost* finished it. Only the roof remained to be built. Then, last year, the structure was damaged. The roof is unfinished and now it's raining, the roof leaking.

There is no real, firm evidence – at least yet – to prevent getting the last matchsticks required to make the building secure, watertight. The only thing stopping me from getting them and gluing them on, is me. Mark did wrong, risking our happy family unit for what was, he said, a slip – a lapse in judgement. But he did *admit* it. He had to confront a difficult situation and now I should do the same. My past is hindering my ability to trust Mark enough to tell him what I should've before I even married him. I'm allowing the fact I'm the daughter of a killer to dictate my life. After over twenty years of being proactive and building my life, my career, my family, I'm now being weak and submissive. If I come clean to Mark, I take the perceived control my father and my mother have on me, *away* from them.

To get over this new bump in the road, I need to flatten it once and for all.

The trees become denser, the wind rattling the branches and causing leaves to come free. They float down around us as we cycle through – and I look up, breathing in the fresh air. I feel as light as they are. Like a weight has been lifted. It's time to strip away the lies and alter the narrative. Tonight, I'm going to tell Mark everything.

Once, he told me he'd always catch me if I fell. I hope against all hope he will now.

We've been home for two hours following our long bike ride through the forest and I've already fed us all, got the kids bathed and settled in bed. My plan is to make sure they're asleep, then pour Mark and me a glass of wine and sit him down and tell him I've something important to share. Nausea overwhelms me. What if this blows up in my face? I'm expecting him to understand, support and love me after eleven years of deceiving him. After making such a big issue of *his* breach of trust last year. I have no way of telling how he'll react to finding out my father is a serial killer, let alone the fact I've kept this from him for our entire marriage. It'll make a mockery of our vows, our life together up until this point. It's likely to make him angry and resentful about how I treated him over the night he spent with Olivia.

I could be about to make the biggest mistake of my life. Second to the mistake of not confessing in the first place, of course.

I lick my lips – they're dry and cracking with lack of moisture. I'm going to have to have a drink first to summon the courage to go through with this. I hear him coming down the stairs – he's been in to check Alfie and Ella, kiss them goodnight as he does every evening. I rush into the kitchen, open the fridge and neck wine straight from the bottle. Then I fill two large wine glasses. For good measure, I gulp down half my glass and refill it before taking them into the lounge and setting them on the white, high-gloss coffee table, the liquid slopping up the sides of the glasses because my hands are shaking so much.

Mark looks up at me, his eyes narrowing. 'What's this in aid of?'

'It's the weekend,' I say. My pulse races; I can feel it banging hard in my throat.

Now. Do it now.

I grab my glass and take another gulp.

'Jen . . .' Mark's voice is filled with concern. 'What's the matter?'

'I need to tell you something,' I say. My chest heaves, my breathing shallow.

Mark sits forward, sensing this is serious. 'Okay. I'm listening.' He seems calm, but I know he's dreading this every bit as much as I am, only he doesn't know quite why yet. I put my glass back on the table, afraid my tight grip will shatter it.

I take a deep breath.

Three firm knocks at the front door make me pause. For a second, we both stare at each other, unmoving. Then, another three knocks propel me into action. I stand quickly, the blood rushing away from my head the same time as alcohol floods it. Mark throws out a hand to steady me.

'I'll get it,' he says.

'No, it's fine. You stay there – I'll get rid of whoever it is.' I don't want him to move. I have to get back to this conversation quickly before I bottle it.

I open the front door, ready to swiftly dismiss who-ever's there.

Two police officers with clipboards are standing side by side and it's as though my life flashes before my eyes in an instant: a visual rerun of my past shoots through my mind like I'm watching an Instagram reel.

'Hi, can I help?' My voice is tight, my words slurred, but I keep eye contact.

'Yes, sorry to bother you, er . . .' The younger man gazes down at the clipboard in his hand, then raises his eyes to mine. 'Mrs Jennifer Johnson?'

I swallow before acknowledging that I am, and I wait for his next line.

'Are you aware that on Tuesday evening at approximately 11.45 p.m. a woman – Olivia Edwards – was abducted from Slade Lane while walking home?'

As if there's a single person in the village that doesn't know by now. 'Yes, I'm aware,' I say, then add: 'It's so shocking to think something like that could happen in Coleton Combe.' I speak the truth, here – I never imagined the peaceful, quaint village would be the location of such a crime.

'Shock and disbelief are the overriding reactions we're getting from the community, and everyone is being co-operative, trying to do their best to offer insight so that we may find Olivia safe and well, and bring the perpetrator to justice.'

'Of course,' I say, giving a nod. His words sound scripted, but I'm guessing this is his umpteenth time saying them.

'Jen?' I hear Mark calling me from across the hallway.

'Sorry,' I tell the officer as I turn my head to shout back to Mark that I'm speaking to the police. 'Do carry on.'

I give a weak smile towards the officers as I hear Mark's footsteps coming up behind me. I realise the policemen haven't shown me any ID or even stated their names. I also note there are two of them, when I know from those who've already had a visit that only one officer conducted each doorstep inquiry. Kam mentioned earlier how two had gone into Caroline Brewer's place, but that was the first time as far as I'm aware.

Which leads me to think they're here for a reason – not just to ask the brief set of questions they've been asking everyone else – but for something more specific.

Shit. I bet it was that reporter woman from the garage earlier. Was I right to suspect what would happen next? If the police are here, it's because she found out about the argument between Olivia and me over her affair with Mark and passed that nugget of information on to the investigating team. My fear from earlier is being realised. The police are here because they believe I have a motive for taking Olivia.

Chapter 33

MARK

Each day since Olivia's abduction, I've been expecting this. The door-to-door inquiries have been the talk of the village and now, finally it's our turn. They've taken their time to get to our house because it's further from the centre – from the location Olivia was last known to be. From what I've been told, the questions are the same for each household, run-of-the-mill, what you'd expect for a crime of this nature. Still, a sense of unease sits in my stomach. I want this over with. Not least because it's clear, to me anyway, that Jen is tipsy. I'll have to make sure it's me who does the talking here.

The questions are basic to begin with: who we are, how long we've lived here, who exactly lives in this property and then they move on to what we were doing the night Olivia was taken, if we noticed anything out of the ordinary prior to that day and on that day. I've managed to speak the most, with Jen offering the odd yes or no and nodding in agreement with what I say. But then the focus changes and they direct questions to Jen, virtually blocking me from answering.

'And you're sure you didn't leave the house at all that evening, or later that night? Not even to nip to the shop, or to go for a walk?'

'No, I'm sure,' she says.

'Neither of you?' He looks from Jen to me.

'We were here from our return from work, all night, until we both left for work the following morning,' I say, confidently.

Then the next question steals the breath from my lungs.

'Have you ever been to Olivia Edwards' house, Mrs Johnson?'

Oh, no. Why would they ask her this? I know it's not on their list of questions because I watched the other copper tick them all off as they were asked. There are no remaining boxes to tick on his clipboard. This question, asked by the man who appears to be the superior, came from him alone. And he's got his own electronic notebook, which his stylus is now poised over, awaiting Jen's response. I sense her hesitation and swear I feel her muscles tense. Last year, she *did* visit Olivia – seething with anger at her 'stealing' me and calling her all the names under the sun. Or that's what Olivia later told me – Jen never owned up to all of it.

'Once, I think. Last year sometime,' she said, vaguely. I'm glad she didn't lie – I have the feeling they might already be armed with the fact.

'But not recently? Are you sure about that?'

There's a long pause while Jen makes out that she's carefully considering it.

'I don't believe so. Sometimes I walk past her place on the way to the primary school – our children, Ella and—'

160

'Alfie, yes we know your children attend Coleton Combe.'

I gape stupidly, taken aback. One, that they appear to have done their homework – surely they haven't done background investigations on every bloody house in the village. Why on us? And two, that Jen said she *walks* past with the kids to school. I don't even recall the last time they walked; she always drives them because otherwise she wouldn't get to work on time.

'Okay, thank you for your co-operation. Someone from the team will be in touch.'

Again, I'm pretty sure that isn't what everyone is being told.

They know something.

Jen heads back to the lounge as I close the door to the police and rest my head against it, attempting to gather my thoughts. I agreed when Jen said she'd been in bed all night, but I know it's not entirely correct. I found the muddy clothes. She'd had a blackout and had clearly been outside. Her wedding ring had been thrown to the floor. Now, with police asking specifically if she'd been out at all the evening of Olivia's abduction and whether she'd ever been to Olivia's house, alarm bells are ringing. All of it points to trouble.

And what was Jen about to tell me? It was serious; I could tell that much as she'd downed several drinks before even broaching the subject – which must mean whatever she was about to say was bad. She was *afraid* to tell me.

'Are you coming back in?' Jen calls.

I don't want to. If I can delay this conversation for as long as possible – forever would be preferable – then I can continue hiding the facts deep in my brain and not have to face them. People who know me often comment on how laid-back I am, but truth be known, I'm just cowardly. Avoidance has worked well for me – it's something I'm good at. Why rock the boat?

But it's precisely this thinking that has led us here. More specifically it has led me to question my own wife. Had I faced facts a while ago, confronted her over certain events, I'd have a clear picture of who she is. But no. I didn't question the things that needed questioning – why she left her hometown and never returned, why she never visited her parents, why she has such bad night terrors – I didn't confront her at all because it was easier not to.

But I can't avoid the events unfolding now. With what the police hinted at, and given the blackout, I add two and two together and the result is disastrous. A flash of memory from last year hits me: Jen, standing in Olivia's garden in her nightclothes, holding a rock in her hand as she stared through the window. I shut my eyes tightly to squeeze the image out. And then there's the new mutilated animal I found in the bin. Why didn't she mention it? Disgusted by my find, I merely buried it beneath some rubbish and waited for her to tell me how and why it was there. Nothing. Not a whisper. She's been acting strangely and now I'm thinking it's because she's afraid of what she's been doing during the blackouts.

Did my wife take Olivia?

It's a question I can no longer put to the back of my mind. I must face it; deal with it. My priority is to protect my family. But to do that, does it mean keeping us together as a unit, even though I suspect my own wife of harming another human being – or does it mean protecting my kids *from* her?

Jen calls out my name again, then appears beside me. She lays a hand on my shoulder, but I don't turn around.

'Mark, are you okay?'

'Not really, no.'

She leans against my back, the heat of her offering familiarity, some comfort. Her arms wrap around my middle and she grasps her hands together in front of my stomach. I reach mine down, covering hers. I love her with all my heart. How can I think this kind, loving woman is capable of such a despicable crime? Muddy clothes and weird behaviour don't make her a *criminal*. Suspecting the woman I've been with for eleven years, the mother of my children, is such a huge leap. What kind of a man does it make me if I'm capable of even considering it?

I lie on my back next to her, knowing she's also awake because her breathing isn't in a settled pattern. We're both silent, though. Probably each going over the events. I try to think about the evidence as objectively as I can, taking any emotion out of my analysis. What I have is Jen's history of blackouts and past behaviour during them – and the specific blackout that occurred the night of Olivia's abduction. Jen's reaction to Olivia following the uncovering of the 'affair' as she insists on calling it despite my objections, in which Jen displayed anger, and more importantly a desire to confront Olivia – which she did. Aside from the midnight wandering, she'd stormed to Olivia's house in broad daylight, accusing her of being a marriage wrecker and a slut. At the time, I remember being shocked at her level of aggression, never having seen it before, or since.

Then, there are the muddy clothes I found in the hamper, and her somewhat erratic behaviour. Most of this *could* be explained away. In fairness, if it hadn't been for the blackout, I'd never have given a second thought to her being involved in any way. And isn't it my guilt that's making me question her? If I hadn't given her reason to mistrust me, none of this would've ever come up.

I owe it to her to give her the benefit of the doubt.

Unless real, hard evidence comes to light, I'll back Jen. Because, if it comes to it, and the police suddenly question me, I need Jen to back me up, too. I'll need her to say I was also in bed the entire night. Because since that night when I got drunk and believed I'd been asleep until morning – a horrible realisation has come to me. I *did* drink far more than I recalled. When I panicked after finding the dead animal and hid it in the wheelie bin, I found the evidence at the same time. Two empty vodka bottles. And I did get out of bed that night. It was me who turned my alarm off – that memory also came back to me.

What I haven't been able to remember, though, is exactly what I *did* do while I was out of bed.

Chapter 34

JENNY

Sunday

When I finally drifted off, I dreamed of dead animals coming back to life and rising out from the earth like a scene from a Stephen King film. The location was our house – the back garden – and it was so real I felt the damp ground on my bare feet as I made my way towards the shed. Before I could make it, something snagged my ankle. I looked down in time to see it was a muddied hand, erupting from the rose garden. It dragged me beneath the ground to join the rotting corpse of Olivia Edwards. Her lips – tight and crispy, almost as though she'd been burned – were retracted, revealing her teeth, which chattered together like a zombie about to attack.

I tried in vain to release her hand from my ankle so I could climb back out. In the end I had to snap it from the wrist to escape. When I came out of the ground, I was still holding her silver bracelet, the charms shining in the moonlight. I awoke, gasping for air. *Had* I been outside? I check my pyjamas, then my feet for evidence of mud, sinking back into bed with relief when I was certain it had been a nightmare, not real.

After the visit from the police, I didn't have the guts to carry out my plan to tell Mark about my childhood – about my controlling, manipulative mother and killer father. The timing was too bad. I feared he wouldn't believe I had nothing to do with Olivia's abduction if he were armed with that knowledge. Especially as I know he knows I wasn't in bed the entire night; that I'd experienced another blackout.

I received a text from Roisin before I went to bed. We arranged to meet today, after lunch. She suggested we meet in town, but I would rather have total privacy, so I said I'd like to come to hers. Mark will take the kids to visit his mum and dad, so I have some time before I need to leave to attend to the issue of the bracelet, which I don't feel is safe in the shed anymore. It's too easy to find there. I think that's what my dream was trying to tell me. That, or I really did have something to do with Olivia's abduction. If they find her body, charred and buried, I'm going to have a heart attack.

I drive to Roisin's place in Topsham. It's a stunning house right by the River Exe and every time I visit, I'm reluctant to leave. I love my house, don't get me wrong, but I'm drawn to the spectacular river views and of Haldon Hills in the distance. We sit in the decked garden, which, with its south-west aspect creating a little suntrap, is bright and warm. I lift my head to the sun, taking a moment to imagine everything in my life is fine.

'So, what's up?' Roisin breaks the spell. 'I mean, I'm assuming you have something you need to get off your chest?' For a split second, I think I hear annoyance in her voice, then realise it's concern. The last time I invited myself over was when I was in bits about Mark's affair. Usually, I wait for an invite, or we meet up in town, have a coffee and catch up and, occasionally, the four of us – her and her partner, Harry, and Mark and me – go out for a meal.

I take a long, slow breath in, then release it. I do this twice.

Roisin slips her sunglasses up onto her head and glares at me, her amber eyes wide. 'I guess I'd best prepare myself for something monumental, then,' she says with an awkward laugh.

'Sorry. I feel awful dropping this on you.' I lean forward, grasping my hands together on the glass patio table.

'No, no – come on, it's fine. But should I top up my wine before you give me it with both barrels?'

I smile at her and nod. 'Might be wise,' I say.

She goes to the sliding back door, disappearing for a few seconds before returning with the bottle. She fills her glass and reaches across to top mine up. I shoot a hand across it.

'Best not. One is enough – I'm driving remember.'

'Course, sorry. You're just making me nervous.' She takes a large gulp of her drink and keeps it in her hands, eyeing me across the table. 'Right, go.'

'You heard about the missing woman from my village,' I say, knowing she has because we'd spoken about it in our texts. 'Did you click who she is?'

Roisin sits back, her mouth opening. She stutters,

then shakes her head. 'I hadn't. But I have now. Shit. It's *that* woman.'

'Indeed it is.' I raise my eyebrows and await Roisin's next response.

'The news said she was abducted, Jen! Thank God it didn't happen after the time you had a go at her for sleeping with Mark, or . . .' Her eyes narrow. 'Hang on. I know this is terrible and all, but why are you freaked out enough to come here to talk about it?'

It's as though she knows already. Can feel in her bones there's more to this than meets the eye.

'Well, mainly because I'm worried the police will start digging and uncover the history – and we'll somehow be under the microscope . . .' I twist the stem of my glass, turning it around and around on the table, not daring to look Roisin in the eye.

'Oh, Christ. I was being flippant. I'm sorry,' she says. I hear a deep intake of breath before she continues. 'Okay, well, it shouldn't matter, though? Just because you found out about their affair that doesn't mean you have a motive for abducting her, Jen – that's mad. And it was last year – it's all over and done with now. Plus . . .' She leans forward, putting her hand over mine, stopping me from twisting the glass and forcing me to make eye contact with her. 'She was taken from the street, mate. Late at night. I'm assuming you and Mark were at home, safely tucked up in your beds, so even if the police do find out about it neither of you will come under the microscope because neither of you were in the vicinity of her abduction. Right?' She pauses, shaking my hand to elicit a response. 'Right? Jen?' Her voice is imploring, desperate for me to agree. But I can't. I stay silent.

'For fuck's sake, Jen – tell me you weren't anywhere near her that night?'

'I need a friend, Ro,' I say. 'Please will you listen and not jump in when I tell you this?'

Her face pales and she draws her hand away from mine. I see her swallow, then purse her lips. She's considering whether she wants to hear what I'm about to say. I don't blame her. By telling her this, I'm dragging her into my problem. Involving her. I'll be asking her not to repeat a word of it. In effect, I'm asking her to lie for me. I'm stretching the bonds of our friendship here. But I don't have a choice – Roisin is all I have. But, telling her about Olivia, the mutilated animals I've been receiving, the bracelet – I'm only divulging half a story. By excluding who my father is, I'm giving only part of the equation. How can I expect her to help me if she isn't armed with the full story?

Maybe I shouldn't be so selfish. By unburdening myself, I'm saddling her. And that's not fair. It could also be the worst decision I ever make. She's my closest friend – my only friend. By exposing my past, who I really am, I'm risking it all. Once she finds out, she could distance herself from me entirely, tell me she doesn't want anything more to do with me. Or, worse, she could tell others and I'd be outed. I'm sure, at this point in time anyway, the police would be very interested in me if they were to realise I was the daughter of *The Painted Lady Killer*. He might be safely behind bars, unable to commit further atrocities, but given Olivia fits his victim typology would they look to me and think I'd carried on where my father left off?

Ultimately, it comes down to this. Do I trust Roisin with my fate?

Chapter 35

The Painted Lady Killer

Inside the mind of serial killer Paul Slater

He thinks the printed extracts I've allowed him to see are going to be part of the final manuscript for his book, due to be published in eighteen months' time. He thinks I'm going to show him the completed manuscript prior to sending it off to my editor.

But I don't have an editor . . .

And I'm not really writing his bloody book.

When I first visited the prison to meet the man the media had dubbed The Painted Lady Killer, he was sitting, confidently upright, his shoulders back, arms loosely folded on the table in front of him. The one that separated us, keeping him at a safe distance from me (although, thinking about it now, a small table didn't really offer protection.

Had he wanted to reach across and grab me, he could've. Having prison officers close by had put me at ease – he couldn't have done any real damage even if he'd lunged at me – could he?).

I'd been nervous of the in-person visit – having only conversed via letter and more recently spoken on the phone – it was also the first time I'd ever set foot in a prison. Unsurprisingly, though, Paul had quickly put me at ease – keen to assert his dominance, yet also to ensure I felt comfortable in his presence. Given the topic of our previous communications, I think he wanted to get across his eagerness to tell his story, but wanted to be in control of it – of me – and how it was told. What I included. What should be omitted.

It was fine. I wanted him to believe he had the upper hand, that he was in charge. I mean, he was, in any case – he would only tell me what he wanted me to know, after all. But I was the one who decided what was written down, how, and what I then did with the information. I'm going to show him bits and pieces of what I'm writing – enough to make it look as though I'm doing a professional job. He seemed happy with the opening – I'd reiterated I'd be showing the final MS to my editor, as discussed and agreed. He thinks I'm doing this for love.

And I *am*, in a roundabout way.

Chapter 36

JENNY

Monday

This morning, my head is less clogged, my body less tense as I shower. I even find myself humming the earworm song that was playing when my phone alarm went off earlier while I make everyone breakfast. Maybe speaking to Roisin yesterday helped. In the end, I'd given her a pared-down version – leaving out the vital part about my father being a serial killer, and instead, repeating the lie my mother had told me when he'd first been taken by the police: he'd committed fraud.

I did, however, go into detail about my life with my mum following his imprisonment, how I'd basically been kept prisoner in my own home and how I'd escaped her and then changed my name so she couldn't find me. Dad and I had that in common – both of us were denied our freedom. I shared my fear that she'd found me and was looking to destroy my life all over again. Telling Roisin this allowed me to then ask the favour I'd been desperate to ask since the mutilated animals with the butterflies attached began showing up on my doorstep.

The stunned expression on Roisin's face had remained while I told my story, her mouth slack, and when I finished, tears had made tracks down her cheeks. After another glass of wine to "recover" she gave me a hug, saying she was upset because of how I'd been treated, and because I hadn't felt able to talk to her about it all before. She covered any hurt she was feeling well, and was so understanding and comforting I wished I had disclosed it earlier. She agreed to keep my true identity to herself, and more importantly, she said she'd pay my mother a visit and do some digging. Even though recent developments no longer point directly to her leaving the macabre doorstep gifts, a niggling suspicion still lurks in my mind that she's somehow involved and I can't shake the feeling she might've found out where I'm living.

Given how light I feel this morning, I can only imagine how much better I'd be feeling had I been able to come clean to Mark about it all. Although, as I'd intended to give him the full, no-holds-barred, undiluted version, I know it would've also been far harder to tell him.

'Mum, can you leave me at the gate this morning, not come in?' Ella says. I'm tidying away the breakfast dishes. Mark has left the table and gone upstairs to help Alfie, barely uttering a word to me, so it's just us. I shoot Ella a quizzical glance.

'Oh? How come?' She's never asked me to just drop and go before – something is up.

She shrugs, trying to come across as nonchalant, but her eyes tell me otherwise. 'I'm not Alfie. I don't need you to come in with me. I'm older now.'

While on the surface this appears as a perfectly reasonable request for a valid reason, I sense she has ulterior motives for keeping me out of the playground. Every day the mums have congregated to discuss Olivia's abduction and any developments. This must be unsettling for the kids, especially with Isabella still being kept off school. They must be wondering what's going on.

'Is there something you're worried about, Ella?'

'No,' she snaps, her brow furrowed.

'Okay, well, I still have to take Alfie in, love, so . . .'

She huffs. 'Let me go in first, then. And you can go in the other entrance.'

Clearly she wants me to avoid the junior end of the school. Now I know there's an issue. What doesn't she want me to see? My mind flits back to how I'd previously thought she might be being bullied – a worry that's been overshadowed by recent events; casually put aside due to my own anxieties. I feel terrible. How could I have put myself before my daughter? Other kids could be picking on her and she's ashamed to tell me. And now, she's afraid I'll see and . . . do what? Confront them? I know it's embarrassing when a parent intervenes so publicly – I recall the absolute horror and humiliation on Ethan's face when Willow stepped in on an argument between him and one of his mates. I suppose Ella would be equally mortified if I did something similar.

I nod in agreement and Ella, appearing satisfied, skips out of the kitchen and I hear her run up the stairs. I'll go straight to the other end of the school, but I'll make sure to keep my eyes peeled. I need to know if my girl is being bullied, because if she is, I'll be having strong words with the head teacher. A passing thought that this is what my own mother would've been going through when my father was arrested crosses my mind. I'd hated her for taking me out of school, believing her actions to be selfish, not in the slightest way altruistic. Maybe I hadn't been entirely correct in my assumption; there's a likelihood she really was trying to protect me. I push this thought back in its box and squirrel it away deep inside my mind.

Mark hurries down the stairs, immediately heading for the door.

'Oh, bye, then,' I say. 'Have a good day.'

I hear his footsteps halt, before he saunters back in and comes across to where I'm standing. 'Sorry, my mind . . . it's all over the place.' He kisses me on the cheek, and I let out a sigh.

'We've resorted to this, have we?' I look into his eyes – or try to, but he's making it difficult by looking anywhere else but at me. A guilty conscience?

'I'm struggling a bit, if I'm being honest,' he says, quietly.

'Right. Well, that makes two of us.' My face burns. It takes all my willpower not to take this opportunity to confront him about his inappropriate and hurtful flirting with the school mums at the pub. Not up for the fallout now though, I instead bring the topic around to the children. 'And you know, Ella isn't herself either. We really need to keep things . . .'

'Normal?' Mark finishes for me. Then, he finally looks me in the eye. 'I'm not sure I know what that even is anymore, Jen.'

'Well, you not really speaking to me isn't helping matters.' I drop my gaze.

'Nor is you disappearing in the dead of night.'

I snap my head up. 'I didn't disappear. I just . . .' Just what? What did I do the other night? 'I was only down here, in the kitchen—'

'I'm not talking about last Tuesday,' he says, sharply. 'I mean last night, the night before that, and whatever other night. I'm losing track of your night-time antics, Jen.'

'What are you talking about?' I stare at him, genuinely taken aback. What is he trying to tell me? But he shakes his head, turns and leaves without answering, leaving me confused, my cheerful demeanour a distant memory.

After taking an age to find a spot in one of the side roads near school, I park up. The parking issue is at a level where it's only a matter of time before there's a crash, or worse, a child gets hit. I grab Alfie's and Ella's hands tightly and cross the road. I feel Ella tug loose once we get to the other side, so I do as she'd asked. I let her go off one way as I head to the lower entrance. I give her a wave goodbye as she strides confidently to the other gate. I watch to make sure she walks in, then continue to Alfie's class. As usual, he walks in happily – thankfully he, at least, appears to be unaffected by the events of this past week. One less thing for me to worry about. Because after what Mark said just now, I've got enough to occupy my mind.

Why did he think I had a blackout last night? Maybe he really is confusing the nights because he *did* falter – saying it was 'last night, the night before that, and whatever other night', so he must be mixing it up. Of course, it might be Friday night he was referring to, bearing in mind I saw myself on the video footage. There was no evidence of me having ventured from the bedroom during the last two nights. I had that nightmare, but I checked, and my pyjamas were clean, no sign of having been outside. He must be mistaken.

As I'm leaving, I gaze around the playground, hoping to see Ella. I glimpse a small group of children over by the far fence and squint to check if she is among them. I take a few steps closer. She is there, but after watching for a few moments I don't notice anything untoward going on. In fact, she seems to be very animated; in charge, even. I smile, my concern about her being bullied melting away.

Turning, I spot the usual group of mums in their huddle and, despite my better judgement, walk over to them. It's been a bit awkward since their joyous retelling of the evening at the pub when Mark had been flirtatious, and so I'm keen to show I'm not bothered. It's important they don't realise how much it affected me.

'Morning, ladies,' I say, smiling. 'What's the low-down today?'

'Still nothing,' Rachel says. 'Honestly, it's ridiculous. How can someone disappear without trace? In Coleton Combe for Christ's sake. She's been gone almost a week and no leads?'

'Perhaps she wasn't abducted,' I say. All heads turn my way, frowns on each face. I lift my shoulders in a slow shrug. 'What? Come on, think about it. The police don't appear to have any real suspects, no one has been arrested or, unless I'm mistaken, even hauled in for questioning. Isn't that odd? Maybe she left of her own accord and doesn't want to be found.' I raise my eyebrows for dramatic effect. It's a theory I've been praying could be right. That way, I'm off the hook. If they find she's simply gone AWOL, I'll know for sure I did nothing weird during my blackout on Tuesday night into the early hours of Wednesday. Alarm bells ring at this thinking – a voice in my head immediately contradicts it: *But you've got Olivia's bracelet and you yourself might be the one who left it on the doorstep.*

'No. I don't think you're right, Jenny,' Frankie says. 'Her parents did an appeal, there's been a heavy police presence since the start, and they're still around this area. I don't think they'd use all those resources for an adult who has decided to up and leave, do you? They must have found some evidence of an abduction and she'd never have left without Isabella.'

These are fair points, so I don't push my theory any further, instead listening intently to their musings. The fact of the matter is, it's extremely unlikely Olivia decided, at the point of leaving the pub late at night, to simply abscond. Not go home. To leave her daughter with her boyfriend and go off with someone else of her own free will is too far-fetched.

'Have we all had the police visit now?' Zari asks.

Everyone nods, including me.

'Do you think that's it then? They've covered the whole village now?' Rachel says.

I want to ask if anyone else had the two-police-officer treatment, without actually disclosing the fact we had, so take this opportunity to slide it into the conversation. 'They've doubled up I see, so maybe that means they're coming to the end as it was only one per door at the beginning.' *Nicely done, Jen.*

'What do you mean, doubled up?' Willow widens her eyes at me. 'Only one officer came to my door.' The others all murmur in agreement. This is disconcerting. I'd hoped for a different response.

'The only time I've known two officers questioning someone was at Caroline Brewer's and that's because of her camera,' Willow says.

My stomach drops. I definitely don't want to mention that two officers came to ours now – or that they said someone from the team would 'be in touch'. But I am curious to find out what else Willow knows about the camera, so I keep the topic of conversation on that.

'Kam, from the garage, told me about that, too,' I say. 'Do you know if they found anything of interest?'

'Caroline told me they took the recording from the week previous right up to that day, so about eight days' worth of footage. I guess they'll be scouring it, watching for anything suspicious seeing as the camera angle included the road outside Olivia's.'

'By the look of it, I reckon it shows her front garden too,' Zari says.

Rachel shakes her head. 'No, I don't think it shows that much. I remember the fuss the residents opposite Caroline's made when she first put it up. They asked her to angle it differently because they didn't like the thought she could see what they were doing. There's rules and stuff about privacy.' Rachel isn't the only one who remembers that, but I keep quiet as I don't want the conversation to go off on a tangent. I have a feeling Caroline did as they asked to begin with, but then manoeuvred it slightly because she couldn't see up the road far enough to catch the oncoming lorries in time to get outside otherwise. Which meant some gardens *were* visible on her camera. And Olivia's garden could easily be one of those.

'Yes, that's true. But I suppose the road and pathway to Olivia's might've offered something of interest,' Zari says.

The police officer's question about whether I'd ever been to Olivia's house slams into my mind and I take a wobbly few steps, backing away from the group. When did I last go along her road? I told the police that I walked the children past her place to get to school sometimes, but I've driven to school for the best part of this year.

'You okay, Jenny?'

'Yeah, fine,' I manage. 'Late though, best rush.' I turn and walk out of the playground, my head pounding.

Chapter 37

MARK

Once I'm sure Jen's left to take the kids to school, I double back on myself, swinging the car around to the side of the house so it can't be seen from the lane if she were to drive past home on the way to the vets'. I'm pretty sure she exits the village at the opposite end, but who knows what she'll do with what's going through her mind at the moment.

I head straight upstairs and walk across the bedroom to search the drawers of Jen's bedside table. After rummaging through them for a minute or so, it becomes obvious I'm not going to find anything of interest; it's not as though she'd keep something in there she wanted to hide. I move towards the wardrobe, my foot finding a wobbly floorboard as I reach for the top shelf. There's nothing here either. I don't know what I'm looking for, what I think I might find. I'm driving myself nuts thinking Jen had something to do with Olivia's abduction and trying to find things that just aren't there. My heart feels heavy. Jenny is a good person, she loves our kids to bits, helps animals, is caring – while I'm just a terrible husband. Why am I even doing this?

I back away from the wardrobe and turn to leave the bedroom.

But something tugs at my consciousness. I hover by the doorway, leaning against the frame. I'm missing something.

The wobbly floorboard.

Darting back in, I drop to my hands and knees and fan my hands out, swiping them over the carpet in the area I'd walked. There's a loose board beside Jen's bedside table. For all I know, it could've been this way since we moved in, but it was a new-build, so I doubt it. I focus my attention on the carpet's edge and my heart judders. It's frayed, like it's been pulled away from the carpet gripper more than once. Slowly, I pick at it until it comes away. Pulling it back to expose the floorboards, I then kneel on it to keep it from flopping back. The loose board has a bigger gap between it and its neighbouring board than any of the others. This one has definitely been removed before.

Aware that once I lift it, uncovering what's beneath, there's no going back, I pause. I chew on my lower lip, while running through the pros and cons of pulling up the board, pulling my marriage, our lives apart. I could put the carpet back now, never look again and carry on as before, blissfully unaware of what Jen could be hiding there. But things are already different; strained. And while I try and tell myself I'm 'blissfully unaware', that's not entirely true. I've had doubts, questions, worries, for a while. Maybe I'm merely acting cowardly, again. Because if I do find something untoward, that means I'll have to do something – take action. Not avoid the situation as I have been doing.

In a fit of anger at myself, and my lack of courage, I lean forward and dig my nails into the gap, grappling it with my fingertips until I manage to lift the edge. I should've got a knife or pair of scissors to use as a lever, but it's like I'm glued to the spot, unable to leave this floorboard until I've got it free.

About a foot of the wooden board comes free. I lay it to one side as I stare into the darkness, hoping against all hope the space is just that – a hollow space. Nothing in it. And then I can replace the board and take a long hard look at myself and why I don't trust my wife.

But there *is* something there.

Taking a breath and holding it, I reach a hand into the underfloor space. It's deeper than I imagined. My fingers touch what feels like a bundle of paper and I withdraw my hand, placing a pile of letters, secured together with string, beside me and delve my hand back in. I feel around, and hopeful that's all there is, am about to withdraw my hand when I brush against another bundle. This time, it's plastic I feel. I pull out a small item that's wrapped inside a black bin liner.

My stomach clenches and bile rises into my mouth. I swallow a few times and sit back against the bed with the item on my lap, staring at it, debating what to do. Fear grips me. What am I afraid of?

I'm being pathetic. Yet, in my gut I know this is bad. I don't have time to consider all the consequences, to be nostalgic and allow my memory to recall the wonderful parts of my marriage, or even to consider what my next action will mean for our children; our family. It's simple, really. I have to know.

I unwrap the bin liner and tip it up so that whatever's inside will drop onto the carpet.

There's a gentle thud as it lands.

I can hear my own, rapid breathing, the air being forcefully blown through my nostrils, and at the same time, tears sting my eyes. I put my elbows on my knees, and lower my head into my balled-up hands.

Why has Jen got Olivia's bracelet?

I rake through my memories and try to visualise Olivia the last time I saw her. Was she wearing this bracelet then? She'd often worn it, but I honestly couldn't say with certainty that she *always* wore it. There's a reasonable explanation for my find. There has to be.

It's hidden under the floorboards. What reasonable explanation can there be for Christ's sake?

Maybe she stole it. That, while still not great, would be better than the alternative. Jen was hurt, upset, angry when she first suspected I'd had an affair. There's a possibility this was done then, that Jen wanted to punish Olivia in some way.

Yes, that has to be it. The bag is a bit dusty; it might've been there for some time.

Reassured with this thinking, I relax a little. Although, I know I'm going to have to confront Jen about it. I can't just pop it back under the floor and forget about it. I will have to face this and not avoid it as I'd like to. I bag it back up, unconsciously using the bin liner to grasp the bracelet, not touching it with my fingertips. Then my attention turns to the letters.

Taking the edge of the top letter, I slip it out from the

rest and turn it over in my hands, frowning. They aren't addressed to Jenny. Was I wrong? Thinking about it, maybe none of what I've found is anything to do with her. I've jumped to the wrong conclusion. This bundle of letters and the bracelet were already here, put under the floorboards by the previous owner. Relief floods through me and I laugh. What an idiot. I've tortured myself for nothing.

If the letters aren't Jenny's, and weren't put there by her, then the bracelet is unlikely to have been either. It must just be similar to Olivia's – it's a coincidence. A horrible one, but one all the same. Curiosity burning, though, I take the folded paper from the envelope and begin reading.

Chapter 38

JENNY

'Hayley's off sick.' The high-pitched, panicky tone greets me as soon as I walk through the reception door.

'Oh, morning, Abi,' I say. 'I'm sorry to hear that. Arthritis flare-up?'

'Yes, she left a message.' Abi points to the phone. 'It means I'm on my own.'

Her anxious tone makes sense now. I give Abi a reassuring smile. 'You'll be absolutely fine, Abi. Try to see it as an opportunity to put into practice everything you've learned. You'll smash it.'

'I appreciate your confidence,' she says, her eyes wide. 'I think it might be misplaced. I haven't done anything without Hayley's say-so, or without her looking over my shoulder—'

'Breathe, Abi. Breathe. Take it slowly – you really can't mess anything up.' As I say this, I realise I'm the one who has likely made her panic after giving her an earful for booking in the dog last week at the end of the day. 'And if you do, I promise not to shout this time.' I place my hand on her arm. 'I was out of order before. I'm so sorry. There's no excuse, I've just had a lot going on . . .' I don't want to share more, so leave it there.

'Okay. I don't want to let you down. I am a little sensitive to being shouted at, I know. I need to toughen up. It just reminds me of when my mum takes great joy in telling me I'm useless, and not nearly as good as my sister.'

'You are as good as your sister . . .'

'Well, to be fair, you don't know that.' She gives a short laugh. 'I can't possibly compare, really. Trust me, I have tried continually my whole life.'

I shrink a little inside, hearing Abi's lack of confidence and self-deprecation – I added to that and bearing in mind I can relate to it, I feel a terrible person. I don't usually show a lot of emotion in work. Being an employer means ensuring certain boundaries, but at this moment, it feels the right thing to do. I put an arm around Abi's shoulders and draw her in, giving her a tight hug.

'Please forgive me for being an awful boss. You're doing really well here, Abi, and I'm so grateful for all your hard work. You will do a good job on reception today, and actually, I think it'll be good for you to have a break from Hayley breathing down your neck. You've got this. Okay?'

'Okay. Yes. I've got this. Thanks, Jenny. And you're not an awful boss. I'd be chuffed to bits if I were to become as popular and successful as you. I bet your mum is proud of you,' she says. Her face immediately flushes red. 'Oh, er . . . sorry. I . . .' she mumbles. 'I forgot what you said.'

'It's fine,' I say. I don't continue the conversation. It's not like I expected her to remember what I'd said about not having spoken to my mum for years. And the fact my mum *wouldn't* be at all proud of me remains unspoken. As far as Claire was concerned, I wasn't intelligent enough to make anything of myself – she'd just say becoming a vet was a fluke. Or, she'd simply turn it around and say it was somehow thanks to her. My stomach knots as I remember the time I'd dared share my dream job with her. 'You're not clever enough, Jane,' she'd said, her bony hands gripping my shoulders as she stared me straight in the eye. And when I'd retorted that perhaps she should send me back to school then, her nostrils had flared and she shot away from me like I'd given her an electric shock. 'Jane, you know Mummy is protecting you. I've sacrificed everything to make sure you're safe and I'm doing everything a teacher would. Don't be so ungrateful.' The tears had started then, and I'd had to apologise and give her a hug.

I blink the memory away. 'Right, let's begin the day, shall we?'

Before going to my consulting room, I pop in to the others to check everyone is in, and I have a quick catch-up with Samir – we're going to have a meeting tomorrow to ensure we're up to date with everything. On a whim, I decide to go to the waste room. I haven't been to the animal-by-product area since going there to drop the bin liners. I'm surprised to see Nisha is in there, labelling a yellow tub.

'Morning, Nisha. Everything set for surgery?'

'Oh, bloody hell.' Nisha swings around to face me, a hand on her chest. 'Didn't hear you come in.'

'Sorry. Early morning jump-scares not your thing?'

'God, no. Heart's jittering all over now,' she says, laughing. She quickly pushes the tub she had in her hand to the side of the worktop and takes another. 'And yes, all ready. Did you need me to do anything?'

'I could do with you printing off the next few weeks' surgery lists please,' I say, moving closer. Nisha gives a nod, trying to look at me at the same time as writing on the disposal labels.

'Yep, will do. And I see Hayley is off today. Do you need me to fill in on reception later? Help Abi?'

'No, actually. Thanks though, but I think it'll be good for Abi to give it a go on her own today. Boost her confidence a bit . . .' As I say this, I realise Nisha has stuck a high-risk label on the yellow tub, but we haven't had an animal with a disease classed as harmful to humans. 'Ooh, careful, that's the wrong one,' I say, quickly. 'Sorry, I'm messing with your concentration.'

'Oh, is it?' She looks down, then stares at the label and back at the yellow tub. 'Damn. So it is.' She grimaces and rips off the label, balling it up and binning it. 'Sorry. Rubbish at multi-tasking.' She scores a line through the waste register.

'Right, well we don't want to be mixing stuff up out here. All sorts of rules and regulations as you know.' If a diseased animal gets mislabelled and ends up low risk and doesn't go for correct disposal, that's problematic, but conversely, if an animal was to be labelled as high risk by mistake . . . it wouldn't go down well that a much-loved pet didn't receive the cremation the owner expected. I smile to cover my sudden annoyance at her lack of care, then realise there shouldn't even be anything in the fridges left to label. 'Haven't all the animal by-products already been taken?'

'Sorry, I missed this one,' she says, nodding to the one

in front of her. 'Think I need one more coffee to properly wake up,' Nisha says, sticking on the new, correct label and popping the tub into the large fridge. 'Don't want to slip up during surgery now, do I?'

With my mind being elsewhere lately, have I been missing instances where best practice hasn't been followed? I'm to blame, I should be keeping a closer eye on things. Perhaps my staff need a refresher of the procedures. Tension pulls on my shoulders. All of us are a little distracted at the moment. 'Could certainly do without a negligence lawsuit or anything right now, that's for sure,' I say, rubbing my temples.

'No. The village is in the news quite enough.' Nisha's shoulders slump as she turns to face me. 'I feel so sorry for Olivia's mum and dad. Seriously, they look like they've aged another twenty years over this past week. I honestly can't believe police haven't got any good leads still.'

'We might not know even if they have.'

'True.' Nisha shrugs. 'People are in and out of their place all the time. I don't know how they even cope with that amount of attention. My mum said Mrs Edwards hasn't left the house at all, and Mr Edwards spends hours in the shed at the end of the back garden by all accounts.'

Nisha's slip of concentration is forgotten as I wonder if she knows anything about Caroline Brewer's CCTV. I'm about to ask but realise the time is rushing along and if I start the list late, I'll be playing catch-up all day, so I round off the conversation and finally head to my consulting room. Vanessa is waiting for me, an animal already on the table, an IV in place. As I begin operating, a thought crosses my mind. If police are checking known CCTV or security camera footage in the village, might they come looking here? The activity in the surrounding fields suggests it's an area of interest, so it seems likely they will seek out all available vantage points. With the vets' CCTV pointing in the direction of the road and field to the right of the building, it could offer an angle they have yet to check.

The sudden need to view the CCTV recordings overwhelms me – if I was captured bringing in the bin liners on Thursday afternoon, I'll have to make sure it gets wiped. Not that it makes me look guilty of anything, but I don't want to bring attention to myself in any way, and that's something they may well question me about. I'm not sure I could give a good reason why I was bringing stuff *into* the vets' to incinerate when usually all the animal by-products originate from inside. Once I finish up here, I'll leave Vanessa doing the post-op checks and sneak out to the desk.

It's a good job Hayley isn't here as it turns out. She'd immediately have cottoned on to something being off if she saw me searching through the computer files for the CCTV recordings, but with Abi being fairly new and naive, she doesn't question my reasons for checking the footage. And even if she does ask me about it, I'm confident I can offer a satisfactory explanation.

'Abi, don't suppose you fancy making me a cuppa, do you?' I say, sitting down at the computer on the far side of the desk, the one that faces away. If anyone comes in, I can quickly change the screen without them seeing what I'm looking at.

'You not coming for lunch in the break room?' She scoots her chair back and stands.

'In a bit. I've some admin to catch up on first.'

'Oh, can I help? I don't mind doing it, save you—'

'That's kind, but it's stuff I can't delegate, sadly,' I say, with exaggerated exasperation.

'Sure. Did you want tea?'

'Yes, thanks,' I say without thought. I don't much like tea. I wait for her to walk around the desk, then click on the icon for the CCTV. I know the bit I'm searching for, and find a file with the right date stamp. Then, after fast-forwarding to roughly the right time, I stop it, my fingers trembling. I watch for about ten seconds before I see anything. Then, my Volvo is clearly visible driving into the car park. Even though I parked outside its scope, I knew I wouldn't have avoided detection entirely. Then I watch myself walking to the back door, a bin liner in my arms. I squirm as I see myself looking up to check the camera, giving a suspicious glance before entering. I select this part of the footage and press delete. Then do the same for the part where I walk back out.

If anyone has reason to check, the few missing minutes might well be noticed. But hopefully, as it's not a day or time particularly relevant to their inquiries, the police won't even look. With some relief, I'm about to close the file, when I see a thumbnail relating to last night's recording – it goes from 10 p.m. last night until 10 a.m. this morning. Mark's words come back to me, and curiosity makes me click on it. I keep the cursor on the fast-forward icon, but the slow one: x2, so I don't miss anything. Frame by frame I watch the dark shadows sweep across the camera, foxes, rabbits and other nocturnal life dart about, until the clock reads 02.55.

My heart plummets.

I press stop, then rewind it a little.

I check the date stamp again.

It's 02.55 hours. This morning.

There's no way this can be right. I go through the recording for a third time, rewinding, then stopping at exactly the same time stamp. It's not a mistake.

The beginning of a tension headache throbs at my temples, and I press my fingers to them as my mind whirls. This footage captures my car again, and there's no doubt because the end of the number plate reads EZS. I sit back hard. I can't have been here in the early hours of *this* morning – I woke up in bed with no evidence of anything untoward having happened – no strange flashbacks, no mind fog, no unexplained bruising or marks on me, no wet or muddy clothes. Mark's comment this morning, though – despite his apparent confusion about which nights he believed me to have had blackouts, he had talked of last night, the night before . . .

And even I can't argue with the evidence right in front of my eyes. I check around me before I continue watching, frame by frame, my face now inches from the monitor, my eyes squinting, afraid I'll miss something vital. What am I doing here, at the practice? I can't see any movement; the back doors to the building are the only ones visible. I see the car jiggle, as though someone has got out – the weight causing the car to rock slightly. I watch intently but don't see myself come closer to the practice building.

Which means what? I've headed for the fields?

A cramping pain grips my stomach. There's no good reason to be going to the fields. There's no good reason for me to have driven to the vets' either though, so this thinking isn't helpful. I need to know why I came here and exactly where I went.

Sixteen minutes and thirty-three seconds later, I see the car judder again. I must finally be getting back in. Then it drives off.

With my pulse banging, I delete the file. That's two recordings I've deleted now. I feel sick, and click off the CCTV file, leaning back and crossing my arms around myself. I rock gently in the chair, my mind clouding . . . and panicking.

What did I do?

Abi walks back to the desk, placing a mug in front of me. 'Jenny, are you okay?'

'Oh, er . . . thanks. Sorry, though. Something's come up. I have to go.'

'Nothing serious, I hope?' Abi's expression is filled with concern.

'I . . . I'm not sure. Sorry. Can you tell Samir and the girls that I'm . . .' I try to think of a plausible reason I'd be rushing off. I go with a version of the truth. 'It's a personal matter,' I say.

Then I get my bag, leave through the back door and rush to my car.

I drive out, down the lane, then out of the village. And I keep driving.

Chapter 39

You might not believe me when I say this, but I have always tried to protect you from it all.

Like when you woke me in the dead of night and tried to get us out of the house before the police arrested you? That seems like it was more a case of saving your own skin.

I judged it badly, I know. I really did have your best interests in mind. I didn't want you to have to suffer for the person I was. You're my little princess, always will be, no matter how old you are. The times I spent with you were the most precious – the memories of them keep me going during the darkest times here.

It's a shame my memories of you – of us – are ruined because of what you did; who you are. They don't keep me going in the darkest days – they drag me down, make me feel worse. Make me question who I am.

I never talk about you because I don't want anyone to use what I say against you somehow. You're the one thing I keep private no matter how hard psychologists, fellow inmates, journalists and the like, press me for details. They try their underhand tactics to trick me into divulging what we did together – how we spent our time. They want me to tell them that you saw something, that you were involved in some way. They're hateful. No matter what I tell them, they twist it.

Twist it how? I didn't see anything. I had no clue what you were doing. How could I have?

No wonder you suffer with night terrors. My poor princess. I'm so, so sorry. I wish I could help you.

Chapter 40

MARK

It's ten o'clock and all impetus to get to work has vanished now. With my legs sprawled, letters scattered around me on the floor, I lean back against the bed, my energy drained. Despite all the problems Jen and I have faced in our marriage over the past year, I never considered a life without her. My momentary flight of fancy with Olivia was just that. A fleeting desire. I'm not stupid – I know all marriages take work. I'm well aware it's unlikely that just because you've betrothed yourself to one person for the rest of your life, you aren't ever going to find another human being attractive; be attracted to them – physically or emotionally. Olivia being the former. Or, that's what I tell myself.

Now, as I contemplate where to go from here – from this floor, with my concerns and suspicions all around me – I feel flat. Numb. My mind is awash with doubts. About me, Jen, our future. Olivia . . .

'God, Olivia. Where the fuck are you?' I bury my head

in my hands. Something needs to happen – I must take some form of action to either confirm or dispute my findings. With sudden vigour, I leap up from the floor. If these letters – and the bracelet – belong to the previous owner, then it won't take much to find them. Or, at least find someone who knows them and where they moved to. Without digging out paperwork, which could be anywhere, I can't even recall their names right now.

The village post office is my best bet – the postmistress has been there years; her whole life, I think. I dart down the stairs, fling on a jacket, grab my keys and head out. I glance at the car but move past it, deciding the walk will help clear my head. Plus, parking in the centre of the village is always problematic, let alone now there's increased activity. As I walk, I go over what questions I'm going to ask. And also how I might steer the conversation towards Olivia. If I can get a sense of what's going on with her case, too, that'll be a bonus.

To get to the post office I need to walk by Olivia's house. Unless I literally go the long way around and come at it from the opposite direction. That seems ridiculous – and if anyone sees that's what I've done, they'll think I'm purposely trying to avoid her road, which will draw attention to me. Now, would a usual person – as in a normal villager with nothing at all to hide – look at Olivia's house as they walk past? Knowing that it's the subject of the biggest news story the village has ever had, most people would be curious, wouldn't they? If I walk past, not even glancing at it, won't that look suspicious? Overthinking has become my new preoccupation.

But I remember watching a true-life crime documentary once about police homing in on their murder suspect, a police helicopter tracking him as he walked through the village. And I distinctly recall the policeman's comment when the man in question doesn't look up, just keeps his head down and continues walking. He said, 'Most people, hearing a helicopter above their heads, automatically look up to see it.' And the fact he didn't led them to believe he was definitely their man. So, with this in mind, as I walk past Olivia's, I do glance up at it, then I shake my head gently. If anyone were to be watching, they'd merely think I was sad about her having not been found yet, just like everyone else in Coleton Combe.

I wonder if Jenny has been past here and done the exact same.

'Morning, Teresa,' I say, entering the post office and slipping a newspaper off the shelf. I look at it briefly, then take it to the desk.

'Don't usually see you about this time of day,' she says. 'Day off?'

'Sort of. Decided to work from home today.'

'Not much working though,' she says with a chuckle, pointing to the paper.

'Ah, break time. Needed some fresh air and a smiley face, so thought I'd pop in and see my favourite post-mistress.'

'Ah, flattery will get you everywhere.' Teresa winks. She's in her late sixties, will be here until she's physically unable. She inherited the post office from her father – it's third generation now. Unfortunately, it ends with Teresa. She and her late husband never had children. She used to muse about what would happen to the place when she left, hoping the villagers themselves would take it over. It's always been the hub of Coleton Combe; it would be awful to lose it. Thinking about it, it might be an interesting project to take on.

My mind has digressed – I must remember why I'm here.

'Teresa, you'll know,' I say.

A look of excitement crosses her face. 'Probably.' She laughs. 'I know everything.' Her statement makes me pause, a cold shiver running up my spine. Does she know about me and Olivia? About Jenny finding out? I shake the feeling and continue.

'For the life of me, I can't remember the name of the couple who lived in our house before us. Can you?'

Teresa puts a hand to her face, pausing to think. I wait in anticipation for her furrowed brow to unfurrow, giving a sign she has remembered.

'Do you know,' she says finally, 'they kept themselves to themselves – never really got involved in the community. They had an odd name, if I recall . . . something to do with food.'

I watch Teresa intently as the cogs in her brain turn. If she can't help, I'm sure one of the local councillors will. The new house was opposed by a number of villagers. They're bound to have details on record. Doesn't mean they'll have the names of the buyers though. I'm going to have to go through the solicitors who handled the sale – get the deeds. I really hoped Teresa would be a quicker route.

'Never mind, Teresa. It'll come to you in the middle of the night, no doubt; these things often do.'

'Is that why Jenny goes off wandering the streets at night in her pyjamas is it? Because she's remembered something?' She says it in good humour, but I can't keep the shock from my expression. I had no clue anyone else had seen her during one of these 'events'. I stutter and fumble over my words in response, failing to string a sentence together.

'Oh, don't worry, dear. My Harold suffered too. Terrible business – used to scream the house down some nights, and I'd often catch him leaving the house, naked!'

'Oh, did he?' I'm not sure how to play this now. I'd no idea Jenny had been seen in *public* during her late-night antics.

As I'm leaving, Teresa shouts, 'Butternut.' She looks triumphant. 'Knew it was food-related.'

I go back to the desk. 'Good going,' I say. It's not the surname on the envelope to the letters, though. 'Did they have children?'

'Not that I remember, no,' Teresa says. 'The villagers wondered why they'd want such a large house being it was just the two of them.'

'Maybe that's why they didn't stay long. They might've only bought the property to sell on at a profit.'

'Damn outsiders,' Teresa mutters. 'We were so pleased when you and Jenny got the place. At least you have history here, with your sister and all.'

'I'm pleased too.' I smile. 'Don't suppose a first name popped into your head too, did it?'

'Think it was a short name . . . traditional, you know?'

I don't want to put names into her head by guessing, so stay quiet while she thinks.

'Joan . . . no, that's not right. Jean, maybe? Sorry, Mark. I think I've overstretched the old brain cells with the surname.'

'Hah! No problem. You've been very helpful, thank you. Have a good day now,' I say, giving her a nod and leaving. The surname may not have matched, but the names that Teresa was giving for the first name are at least similar. A possibility the letters – and bracelet – belong to the previous owner is still on the cards.

I walk partway up Olivia's road before stopping dead. There's a car outside her house, parked on the double-yellow lines. Something tells me it's an unmarked police vehicle. I stand and watch as two people emerge from her front door. A woman dressed in a grey trouser suit and a man in a dark suit walk slowly towards the parked car. Detectives. The woman gives a casual glance around before sliding into the passenger seat and for a split second our eyes meet. I swallow hard but don't look away – that would make me appear suspicious. She turns to her partner and they seem to chat for a little while before he pulls away. I swear I feel her eyes on me as they drive past. The car performs a U-turn and comes back past me a second time before heading up the hill and disappearing from view.

Might they have just imparted bad news to Olivia's partner?

Could they now be looking for a murderer?

Chapter 41

Reading the investigating police statements and accounts of the murder of Paul Slater's first victim from court transcripts leaves out the emotion; the psychology of his actions. The details are stated simply – the lead-up to Harriet Jennings' abduction are merely bullet points and the way in which he killed her denoted in terms of the post-mortem report. Cold, hard facts. The way Paul Slater describes this first kill is very different.

'I'd watched her for some time,' he told me. 'I had heard about her, how she prostituted herself, leaving her kid at home alone while she spread her legs for anyone with a fat wallet. She disgusted me. The kid needed saving, a mother like that was not going to give him a good life. So, I took her. She was nothing special, see – just an over-made-up woman with no self-esteem. I felt sorry for her, really. I made her better. When I finished with her, she was prettier. Cleaner. Purer. I did her a favour.

* * *

Paul seemed happy with the new excerpt I showed him – I called it my WIP, short for 'work in progress'. I've looked up a lot about writing so I'm trying to use the correct language – things to make me sound as though I know what I'm doing. I did explain I was new to it, though, to cover up any gaps in my knowledge in case he asked me something I couldn't answer. He asked if I could tweak the part about his first victim. I agreed. Obviously, I won't. By the time he thinks I've finished the first draft I'll have got what I needed from him so it won't matter.

It took a year researching, planning this part, wondering how I was going to get a serial killer to open up to me. I wasn't part of a media outlet; I wasn't a journalist or a writer. I was, however, an attractive female and Paul Slater had been incarcerated for thirty-three years. I figured he must be lonely; he had no visitors – I'd found that out easily enough – he'd surely jump at the chance to get to know me.

My initial way in was via becoming a love interest. The very notion both disgusted and excited me. Whilst obviously I was in no way interested in the man in that way, I was safe in the knowledge I never had to 'do anything' with him. He wasn't getting out of prison and, thankfully, conjugal visits aren't a thing in the UK. I could fake it in letters, phone calls if I had to. Even face to face I could come across as interested; being flirtatious was a skill I picked up long ago to get what I wanted. If I dressed provocatively, too, I knew that would help.

Psychologists believed, had he not been caught, that Paul Slater might've continued to kill, but think his latest victim marked a change in preferred target. It was one of the things I was keen to discuss with him – for the purposes of 'the book', of course.

However, when it came to it, sitting face to face with the man was more nerve-racking than I'd anticipated, and it took me two visits before I had gained enough confidence – was sure there was no recognition on his face, no hint of mistrust – to begin asking the questions I needed answers to. It's a tedious process, having to write everything down as he says it – for obvious reasons, I can't take any equipment into the prison to record our conversations. I know I miss some things. As soon as I'm back at home, I write up a transcript from my notes and from memory, trying to get everything down on paper as closely worded to his as I can.

After today's visit, I was able to tick one of the key questions off my list. I marked today down as a win. A breakthrough. I think he's really beginning to trust me. Hopefully it won't be long before I can plan my next move.

Chapter 42

JENNY

There's another vehicle parked next to Mark's Audi when I pull into the driveway so I park behind Mark's to ensure this other one has room to swing around and drive out rather than reverse. The lane is quite narrow; backing into it isn't advised. The blue Vauxhall isn't a car I recognise, and there's no one on the doorstep, which means its owner must be inside my house.

'Come on then, kids. Inside and straight up to your rooms to do homework, please.'

'I need help with my maths,' Alfie says.

'Have a go yourself first, love.' I pull out the backpacks, and hand them to Ella and Alfie.

'I don't have any homework,' Ella says, stubbornly.

'Fine. Then do some reading.' I'm aware I'm being short, but a heavy, nervous feeling in the pit of my stomach is a warning that something is up. Gut feelings are usually right. I approach the front door slowly, almost afraid of who's inside. At this point I'd even be happy to see that it's Brett. The unknown is far more anxiety-inducing.

As I enter the hallway, I discern several distinct voices coming from the kitchen. One is Mark, the others – one male, one female – aren't ones I know. The kids rush towards the sounds, clearly keen to see their daddy. I sigh at their immediate disregard for my instructions moments before. I don't rush to join them, instead, attempting to decipher what the topic of conversation is. But now the kids have run on in, whatever was being discussed has paused anyway.

I hesitate, my feet reluctant to move, but I don't have a choice. I have to go into the kitchen.

The woman, dressed in a grey suit, an ochre blouse beneath the open jacket and sensible-heeled court shoes, leans against the worktop. Her eyes fly to me as I enter and she pushes off the worktop, standing poker-straight like her superior has just walked into the room. Her hand instantly juts out towards me as she takes a few confident steps forward.

'Detective Sergeant Davis.' Her terse manner makes my stomach flip. Her grip is firm, her dark-brown eyes lock onto mine. We're of the same height and build, but she looks a good few years younger than me, her olive complexion radiant and clear, the creases around her eyes at nowhere near the same level as mine. 'We were just telling your husband here that we're following up on the original house call our team made on Saturday,' she says, her wide smile too easy; too practised. Part of her repertoire no doubt. It's the kind of smile I can still recall from when I was young and it causes me to shudder – not unlike those I also remember experiencing back then. I shoot Mark a nervous glance, but he merely shrugs.

'Jennifer Johnson,' I say, with a confidence I don't feel.

'I'm Detective Constable Bishop,' the man says. He

doesn't offer a handshake, just remains seated at my table. He's shiny-faced, no hint of stubble. Probably not long out of his teens. His suit, which seems a size larger than required, looks as though it's come from Next. The fact he hasn't stood to greet me leads me to believe he's either relatively new, or that he's plain ignorant.

'How can we help?' I look to Mark again, for backup, or reassurance, or merely for him to say something in agreement, like, 'Yes, detectives, can we assist in any way?' But he leaves me floundering, instead just staring right through me. I wonder how long they've been here – whether they've had a lengthy conversation prior to my arrival. The thought dries my mouth and I struggle to swallow. Has Mark told them about my blackouts? How I might well have been wandering the village the night Olivia was taken?

'Yes, I very much hope you can,' DS Davis says. I can't place her accent; it certainly doesn't sound local. 'As you're aware, the police force have been conducting door-to-door inquiries, and one of those visits threw up something . . . interesting. We're here to follow it up.'

Her voice is drowned out by the whooshing blood in my ears. This is to do with Caroline Brewer's camera, has to be. 'Right, sure. Has my husband offered you a drink, detectives?' It's a play for time, but also what I assume to be the right thing to do in this situation. It's what I remember my mother doing when police called in. Christ. Do these detectives know who I am?

'No need, thanks,' DS Davis says. 'This won't take long.'

A fleeting optimism blooms. I smile and await the question.

'Where were you on the . . .' She pauses, getting an electronic notebook from her pocket. In that pause, my mind has already filled in the blanks. Where was I the night of Olivia's abduction. But they know this because I told the officers on Saturday.

'The night of Friday, August 12th.' DS Davis concentrates her gaze back onto me.

'Oh, I don't know,' I say, genuinely puzzled. I was fully expecting them to ask about the night she was taken, not days beforehand. 'That was a couple of weeks ago.'

'Yes, maybe you keep a diary? Or you have something on your mobile?' she offers, helpfully, then waits while I check. I don't have anything written down for that day or evening but I get the feeling it would be bad for me to admit that.

'Nothing in my phone, but I'm afraid I don't make use of the calendar app.' It's the truth, so she can't read anything into that.

'What about you, Mr Johnson?' DC Bishop says. He's still seated, but has his notebook out on the table, his expression more serious now. 'Maybe *you* have something recorded for that evening?'

There's a brief moment of hesitation before Mark gives his answer. In that minuscule of timeframes I realise he isn't even going to try and help me out. And he doesn't. With a conviction in his voice that sends a shiver down my spine, he simply states, 'No. I have nothing in my calendar for Jenny. There's a mark against the date, though – but I believe that's in relation to something else. A meeting, or something, I think.'

'An evening meeting?'

'I'm really not sure, sorry. I can't remember.' *Now* he decides to be vague. My disappointment must be plain to see on my face because Mark looks at me, narrowing his

214

eyes slightly. I sense he's trying to send me a silent apology, but that's no good to me. My insides feel like they're on fire. I'm all alone right now. My husband has just landed me in the shit.

'Okay, well, maybe you could find out. It would be helpful to our investigation.'

'Yes, of course,' Mark says.

DS Davis turns her attention back to me. 'Mrs Johnson. Jennifer.' She smiles sweetly. The prelude to the sting that's about to come. 'We have some footage, from a camera situated opposite Olivia Edwards' house, which has captured a female fitting your description lurking outside.'

The way she says 'lurking' is filled with menace and my legs suddenly feel weak, like they won't hold me up any longer. Sitting down now would look bad, though, so I lock my knees in the hope I won't collapse in a heap on my kitchen floor. I need to play this carefully. The realisation I should probably not say anything at all hits me. I should have a solicitor present, or something, because this line of inquiry is more than gathering information. They're trying to place me at the scene of the victim's house prior to her abduction. They're attempting to trick me. Like they tricked my father. He was known to say how the coppers were gunning for him, that they manipulated him and my mother into telling them stuff that put him in a poor light. Poorer than the serial killing light he was already in seemed unlikely, but his lawyer, who eventually had some evidence thrown out because of the way in which it was obtained, stated my father might have been cleared of some of the murders had the police executed the interviews above board and to the book.

Yes, my father murdered multiple women – but he

could've got away with some of them had his lawyer been present at the early interviews. While he clearly *was* responsible for every killing he was accused of, the fact of the matter was that, legally, he probably shouldn't have gone down for them all.

However, if I say I'm not talking without a solicitor present, I'm drawing attention to myself. I may as well have an arrow pointing at my head saying 'guilty'. *Be vague*. Until I know more about the footage, I don't want to categorically say I was, or wasn't there and play right into their hands.

'Fitting my description?' I cock my head to one side. 'What do you mean?'

I catch a look pass between the two detectives. 'About your height, slim build, shoulder-length copper-blonde hair,' Davis says. 'You seem to walk past Olivia Edwards' house first, then back up a little, loitering for a few moments before entering the garden.'

'You mean *the person in the footage* appears to do those things. You don't know that it was me, Detective.' The calmness in my voice is not reflected in my body. My pulse crashes and my lungs burn. How dare she word it that way. I want to tell them to leave.

'Yes, of course. The person in the footage,' she repeats. 'So, do you have any recollection of being at Olivia's house at the time stated?'

'No, I have no recollection of it. I don't see why I would be loitering outside her place, nor do I have a clue why I'd be in her garden.'

'You and the victim weren't friends?'

I shrug. 'Not really, no. We didn't socialise together.' I'm losing my patience for this now. I'm going to have to

216

suggest if they want to question me further that they do so at the station. And that maybe they should caution me. But it's as though they've read my mind. DC Bishop pushes his chair back and stands.

'Thanks for your time, Jennifer,' he says.

I open my mouth to speak, but think better of it. Hopefully, their bit of digging hasn't worked – I haven't inadvertently given them what they came for. They'll have to work harder for it.

When they've left, I turn to Mark. 'Thanks for your support.'

'Look, I didn't know what to say. I'm sorry. I could've made the whole situation worse had I said anything.'

'Worse how, Mark? They clearly believe I was the one in Olivia's garden a week before her abduction. They think I might have had something to do with it. You not even backing me up looks really good, doesn't it? Or were you the one who suggested it could be me?' Anger drenches my words as I practically spit them out. 'Let's face it, as soon as the police asked about it on Saturday, you thought I must've been seen at Olivia's.'

'That's not fair, Jen. And actually, while we're being accusatory, maybe I do believe it was you on that footage. Because it wouldn't have been the first time and even Teresa at the post office has witnessed you wandering around in your pyjamas late at night during your supposed blackouts.'

'*Supposed blackouts?* Oh, right. I see. Now it's all coming out, isn't it?'

'Well, you tell me, Jen. You seem to be the one holding back information here.'

Hot tears bubble and run down my face, anger and fear a potent mixture.

'Mummy?' The little voice sounds behind me and I whirl around to see Alfie, his astonished face wide-eyed. 'Why are you shouting?'

'Yes, Jen,' Mark hisses. He comes up close to me and bends down. 'Why are you shouting?' His breath whispers against my ear. 'Is it because I hit a nerve?'

I pull back, glaring at him.

'You know nothing about me,' I say.

'That, we agree on.' He pushes past me and takes Alfie's hand. I hear him talking softly to our son as he leads him upstairs, leaving me alone and suddenly feeling very vulnerable.

Chapter 43

JENNY

His hands, though large, were gentle as he painstakingly spread and separated the wings, pinning them carefully, symmetrically. She watched, mesmerised, in awe of her father's care and attention to detail. She loved the expression on his face as he worked: peaceful, calm. The way he looked at her sometimes. As she backed away from the door, her elbow caught the doorjamb and she yelped in pain. She covered her mouth quickly with her hand, but it was too late. Her father's expression changed in an instant. His lips snarled back, like the neighbour's dog always did when she walked past the gate, and his cheeks turned red. His hands slammed down hard on the table, knocking the butterfly to the floor.

'Now look what you've *done*.'

Jane's eyes immediately filled with tears and she backed up, afraid to take her eyes off her daddy. 'I'm sorry, I'm sorry, I just wanted to see.'

As though a switch was flicked, his face softened. 'I guess

there's nothing wrong with curiosity,' he said. 'Come here.'
He smiled as he beckoned her. Relaxing again now, Jane
stepped closer. 'Want to see how it's done?'

'Yes, please.'

'We'll have to get another specimen; this one is ruined
now. Fetch your coat. But be quiet. Don't let your mother
hear you or see you. Understand?'

'Yes, Daddy.'

She returned, her coat on and buttoned up. 'It'll be one
of our secrets?'

'Yes, my princess. It will.'

Cold seeps through the flimsy material, bringing me to
consciousness.

I'm in the garden shed.

Why am I here? I've woken on the kitchen floor the
last few times, but with no recollection of where I've been
during the blackout. I wonder if the shed is where I've
been coming when I've left the house. I cast my eyes
around in the dim glow of light offered by the moon. It
looks the same as usual as far as I can tell – everything
is in its place. My eyes fall upon a black ceramic cat
ornament poking out from beneath the wooden bench. I
don't immediately recognise it – but maybe Mark put it
here. Frowning, I crawl across and pick it up. In that
moment, I'm jolted by a flash of memory – the weight in
my hands familiar. Do I collect random objects from
people's gardens during a blackout? My mind is too weary
to contemplate this further so I replace it and stand up.

I'm assuming I've had this latest episode because of the
police visit and Mark's less than supportive attitude. His
bitter words, the way his face hardened when he looked

at me, played on my mind while I lay awake next to him. Even during the problems we had following his affair, he didn't act that way towards me. Something has snapped; broken. I'm not sure we'll recover from this. We might still be sleeping in the same bed, but we couldn't be more distant from one another. I'm betting the sleeping arrangements won't last, either. This is the worst state my marriage has ever been in and I can't see a way forward. Even if I now come clean about the reasons for my recent behaviour, it won't turn things around; probably just make it worse. Kill our suffocating marriage dead.

My body is heavy, as though I'm literally weighed down. I shuffle to the window. I see the silhouette of the house against the dark-blue sky. Still night, then – or at least, very early morning. My concept of time has gone. Checking myself over, I find scratches on my arms – they sting as I run my fingertips over them. Fresh: tiny spots of blood punctuate them, but they're superficial. And, as far as I can tell, not made by human nails. I suck in a slow breath. That's something. Still, I've managed to get these somehow and the fact they're not human-made means an animal has inflicted these on me. So, the question is, what did I do to deserve it and what happened to said animal?

There's no evidence of an animal having been in the shed. I look all around me and feel certain. In fact, everything is neat and tidy; I haven't disturbed anything. Time to sneak back inside. This is getting more challenging with each new blackout and as they're becoming more frequent, I'm having to deal with the difficulties they throw up more often. I should have some kind of kit bag, ready in the shed – a change of nightwear, wet wipes to clean myself up, a pair of shoes so my feet don't become muddy again. That would at least help save time, and I wouldn't be spending ages in the bathroom at weird times of the night. I make a mental note to do this as I tiptoe across the cold, damp grass and let myself in the back patio door. It's open, as it's been every time I've found myself outside, so this must be the way I leave the house on each occasion.

My bare feet make gentle slapping sounds as I make my way over the marbled floor towards the stairs. I've no phone with me, so no light – I can't afford to switch on the main one leading up the staircase, so I keep a hand on the wall as I feel my way back to the bedroom.

As I reach the top stair, light blinds me.

'Where've you been this time?' Mark's voice, deep and abrupt, gives me a fright.

'Shit, Mark. What are you doing?'

'I asked you first,' he says, angling his mobile phone torch into my face.

I put a hand up to shield my eyes, blinking rapidly. 'Can you move that thing?' I carry on past him, my eyes squinted, but he pulls my arm, swinging me around to face him.

'We have to talk. Now.' He drags me back towards the stairs and I fumble my way after him, my feet almost tripping over each other.

'Can you stop?' Tears prick my eyes. He's never been heavy-handed with me before. This is scaring me, his anger palpable. I really feel in this moment that he hates me. He takes my hand in his as we reach the hallway, pulling me in the direction of the lounge.

'Right, sit there,' Mark says, pushing me roughly so I

collapse onto the sofa. 'And we're not moving until you tell me everything.'

'I don't know what you mean?'

'Don't play dumb, Jen. You know damn well what I mean. You've had another blackout. Where did you wake up?'

I contemplate my answer. I could be honest, because I know there's no longer anything incriminating in the shed. I need to weigh up the consequences of each of my answers as I know I'm about to be grilled to the level of a police interrogation. 'In the shed,' I say, simply.

'Really?' His tone is incredulous. I shake my head, staring into his face and seeing nothing but contempt.

'Yes. Really. So, no need to worry, eh?' I snap at him.

'You have been seen in the village, you know – which means you go much further afield than you let on.'

My jaw slackens and I try to hide my surprise by going on the defensive. 'Let on? You know I have no clue where I've been during a blackout but it's not like I'm lying to you when I say I've been in the shed – that's all I can recall.'

'No.' Mark begins pacing the lounge. 'I don't think it is. You're keeping stuff from me, Jen. I know it. Why don't you trust me enough to tell me?'

'Well, if you're going to bring up the trust issue—'

'Enough!' He hurtles towards me, shouting in my face, spittle hitting my skin. 'Stop doing that. Stop trying to make this all about me, about a one-off mistake that you can't let go of. This is about *you*. And about whether or not I feel my kids are safe in this house.'

Shock pushes me back; he may as well have hit me. What is he talking about? 'Our kids are, and always have been, *safe*, Mark,' I hiss the words slowly, quietly. How dare he question their safety.

'I'm sorry, Jen. I disagree. And as you don't seem capable of telling the truth, I'm going to have to be the one to safeguard them.'

I jump up from the sofa and square up to him. I want to argue the point, but realise he's got the upper hand. Without divulging everything right here and now, I can't even come up with a counter-argument. 'I need your support, Mark,' I whisper, my eyes imploring his. 'The blackouts are scary – finding myself on the kitchen floor or in the garden, my clothes dirty, sometimes an hour has passed – it's the worst experience. But I have never put our kids in danger. Only myself.'

His face has softened slightly, though his anger is still filling the room. He's a good man, not prone to flying off the handle or being confrontational, so I know he's scared too. The detectives being here has rattled him and he's trying to deal with his emotions as well as dealing with me. I need to remember that.

'I don't know how to help you, though,' he says. 'And, given the intensity of the blackouts, the fact you don't know what you've done during them . . . I'm . . . well, I'm . . .' His face crumples and my stomach cramps.

'You're what?' I coax.

'I'm wondering if you did something to Olivia during one. The night she disappeared, you had a blackout. And as Teresa's spotted you before in the early hours of the morning wandering the village, you could've done it that night too.'

'Okay, I realise this looks bad. But, think about it, Mark. Think.' I stab a finger into my temple. 'How could I – in

224

my trance state, and in only my pjs – have overpowered a woman? And, even if I'd managed that, then what? Physically drag her through the village to a location where the police haven't been able to find her? It's impossible, isn't it?'

Mark stares at me, saying nothing. I continue on the same trajectory.

'To be able to abduct her, I would've needed a plan – an escape route – and on foot that would be really challenging. Whoever abducted Olivia must've had use of a car. If police have seen CCTV and all they've picked up is me in Olivia's garden days beforehand, then that means nothing.'

'That's the only thing they've *divulged*, Jen. You know they aren't going to tell people everything.'

'If they had more, they'd have arrested me.'

Mark looks thoughtful for a moment, his face relaxing. 'Yes, that's true.'

'I'm experiencing more blackouts due to stress, love.' I go up to Mark and wrap my arms around his middle, laying my face against his chest. 'If you help me, stop being so accusatory, I might stop having them. Then you won't need to worry about the kids.'

'I'm sorry,' he says. He circles his fingertips in my hair, then kisses the top of my head.

'Can we go back to bed, now, please?' I ask. Mark gives an awkward half-smile. For now, I think I've brought him around. Planted the seed of doubt into his mind, made him feel guilty for even suggesting I had something to do with Olivia's abduction. The similarities between the gaslighting my mother used and what I'm doing now dawn on me. Am I like her? I can't worry about that now, though

– and besides, I may need to use these tactics again because his suspicions of me will no doubt resurface. He's clearly questioning so much more than he's done before. How much time do I have? As we pass the front door, the illumination of the streetlamp snakes through the glass, spreading a beam of light up the first few stairs. 'Our guiding light,' I say.

Mark stops dead, his head turning towards the door. I feel his arm loosen from around my shoulders and he takes a step away from me. I freeze. What's he doing?

'Come on, love,' I say, reaching out to him. 'The kids will be up soon and we'll feel like crap. Let's grab a couple of hours at least before facing the day ahead.'

He hesitates, paused between me and the front door.

'Sure,' he says, finally. He takes a big breath in, and he comes back to the foot of the stairs. He looks into my eyes for a split second before taking my hand, and we go back to bed.

Chapter 44

MARK

I wait until I hear steady, rhythmic breaths before sliding out of bed again. After gently stepping across the bedroom, I leave and head to the balcony window. I can get a clear view of the driveway from there. It was Jen's mention of Olivia's abductor having to have use of a car that made me remember it. Once, last year, I'd got up to leave for work in the morning and her car was blocking mine. She always parks next to me – there's plenty of room for her to do that. You can park three cars side by side in front of the house. But that time, her Volvo was skewed, the front end encroaching on the back of mine enough to make it difficult for me to swing it around and drive out. At the time, she gave an explanation that seemed plausible. But now, I'm questioning it because thinking back, it had occurred following a blackout.

With my breath held, I approach the window, slowly peeking out, praying I'll see the Volvo neatly parked next to my car.

My heart drops.

The Volvo is haphazardly parked sideways-on behind my Audi.

It most definitely wasn't like that when we went to bed. Jen must drive during her blackouts.

Chapter 45

JENNY

Tuesday

Breakfast is filled with awkward silences. As has become the norm, Mark barely makes eye contact with me. His face, much like my own, is drawn; tired – the early morning discussion, imprinted on him. To get past this, I know I must be the one to make the move. Again.

'We should have a night out,' I say, observing him over my coffee mug to gauge his reaction. His expression remains neutral as he shrugs and takes another bite of toast.

'Your mum and dad would love to babysit, I'm sure,' I plough on, despite no enthusiasm from Mark.

'Go ahead and make the plans then,' he says, his voice monotone.

I get up, taking my mug and rinsing it under the tap, keeping my back to Mark and the kids as my eyes cloud with tears. I should eat, but I've zero appetite. Turning back, I reflect on my family, sitting around the kitchen table the same as every day. It was such a normal routine thing not long ago. So much has changed and for the moment, I can only see the changes that are for the worst.

'When are you taking us to school, Daddy? You promised ages ago,' Ella says suddenly.

'I did, didn't I?' Mark leans towards Ella, his smile wide for our daughter. 'How about today?'

'Really?' Alfie says, jiggling in his chair.

'Yass!' Ella pumps her fist in the air. Where has she picked that up from?

'Oh, well . . . er,' I mumble, suddenly aware of being out of the loop. 'Daddy should leave early, really, to get to work on—'

'No.' Mark puts a hand up to me, still not looking at me. 'I want to take my angels to school today. Work can wait.'

I note his use of 'my' angels and all my muscles tense. After the conversation about him not thinking the kids were safe with me, this is bad timing as far as I'm concerned.

'Of course—' he finally turns to face me '—you're going to have to move your car first, Jen. Seeing as you seem to have abandoned it, blocking me in.' He smiles sarcastically as his words cut through the atmosphere. I feel their impact.

Shit. I used the car during a blackout again. And now, Mark knows it. I have nowhere else to go. I'm trapped, like an animal caught in a snare.

I leave, without speaking, and go to the stand in the hallway, where we keep the car keys hung on a hook above. Mine aren't there. I freeze, panic sweeping through me. Where are they? Maybe they're still in the ignition. As I

230

unlock the front door and take a step outside, a black bin liner catches my eye. Can this day get any worse?

Before hiding the bin liner out back, I peek inside. The stiff tabby cat looks familiar. Oh, God – please don't be the neighbour's cat. Is there a butterfly attached? Not this time, it seems. But there is something, sticking to the cat's matted fur. Looks like paper. My pulse soars – it could be a note. I might finally find out who's doing this to me. I duck down, between the wheelie bins, and careful not to touch the cat with my bare hands, manipulate the bin liner so I can get a good look at the poor animal and what's attached.

Disappointment washes over me. It's not a note. It's just part of a label. However, this too looks familiar. It's like the ones we use at the vet practice for the toxic waste: the animal by-products. I fall against the wheelie bin, my legs giving way. This isn't the neighbour's cat. It's from the vets' – it was one Samir euthanised, I'm certain of it. Am *I* the one driving to the vets' and taking the dead animals? It's bizarre – why would I be doing that in my trance states? But, I *have* seen the evidence myself – my car pulling up in the vet car park in the early hours. What other explanation could there be? A memory of my father in his shed crashes into my mind, my seven-year-old self, watching on in amazement.

'Come,' he said, beckoning Jane with his finger. She took a tentative step forward, her eyes wide.

'It won't bite, Princess. It's long past that stage. Come on.'

Jane peeped at the animal on the workbench, then took a few more steps closer, keen to see what her father was doing to it. 'Is it a cat?'

'Yes, he belonged to the Sampsons next door.'

'What happened to it?'

'Got hit by a car I suspect. Stupid thing was always sitting in the middle of the road, not a care in the world. It was inevitable it would be struck one day.'

Jane cocked her head to one side as she looked the cat up and down. 'It's not squashed.'

'No, it's still perfect, isn't it? Well, apart from the fact it's a common tabby that is.'

'Common tabby?'

'Yes, they're two-a-penny round here. Not unique in any way. Not yet, anyway.'

'What are you doing to it?'

'Making it special,' her father said, taking a scalpel to its belly.

Jane snapped her head away as the knife sliced through the fur and skin, but then curiosity won over, and she turned back. Her dad smiled.

'That's my girl,' he said. 'After this, I'll show you something even better.'

I wipe the tears with the back of my hand. I should've written down each time I experienced a blackout and the timings of the bin liners, because right now I can't think if they arrived after every episode. Could I really be the one leaving them on my own doorstep? Since finding out about the horrific crimes my father committed, I've felt huge guilt and spent my life trying to outrun my past. There's the possibility I still feel responsible, somehow, and want to punish myself. It's the only reason I can think of as to why I'd do this: my subconscious is trying to make me suffer. If it's not me, then who?

I need to catch up with Roisin to check if she's found

any evidence to the contrary, but the theory of it being my mother is getting lower down my list. Realistically I'm left with the person who abducted Olivia as being the culprit.

Or Mark.

It had crossed my mind when I found the other liner in the wheelie bin, but I dismissed it. But, thinking about it, what a perfect way to drive me mad – to make me out to be a bad person; a bad mother. Perhaps Mark's plan all along has been to push me out, ensure I leave so he can have custody of Ella and Alfie. A coward's way of going about things, but then, he's always been a bit like that – the easy option, the path of least resistance is how he works.

Chapter 46

JENNY

I'm filled with a queasy feeling as I drive the short distance to work; uneasy knowing Mark is now at the school, probably chatting away with the gossipy group of mums and they'll be flirty and attentive, keen to keep Mark talking. But I do have other, more pressing things I should be worrying about at this moment. I need to check the vets' CCTV for last night – if I can see myself driving into the car park again, I'll have absolute proof I'm the one doing this to myself. The wider issue, the more troubling, is whether it also means I'm responsible for Olivia's abduction. I can only suppress this question for so long. I have to know what I'm up against. What I'm capable of.

'Jen, are we having that meeting to catch up today?' Samir asks the second I walk through the reception, stopping me from checking the computer for the CCTV footage.

'Can do,' I say. I don't recall making the arrangement for today, but I should try and keep things running smoothly here.

'Is everything all right?' His forehead creases with concern. 'Only, you've not been yourself lately.'

'Oh, really? Well, I'm fine, honest. Just not sleeping well.'

Abi walks into reception and joins us at the desk. 'Morning, all,' she says, brightly. I want to sigh, knowing I definitely can't search the footage now – I'll have to do it later.

'Morning, Abs. Lovely to see a smiley face,' Samir says, pointedly looking at me.

'I love mornings – they're my favourite time of day.' Abi flashes Samir a wide smile.

'Good to hear. Right, I'd best set up. See you at lunch for the meeting, Jen?'

Damn, lunchtime was likely my only chance to get to the desk and search the files in peace. 'Er . . . Yeah. Unless you want to do it after the first surgery slot?'

Samir makes a face like he's contemplating the suggestion. 'We'll see how the morning goes.' And with that, he leaves. Samir pointing out that I've not been myself strikes me as a little ironic given he's not altogether his usual, chirpy self either. The last week he's been uncharacteristically abrupt, avoiding getting into conversations, and his demeanour has been off.

'Are you all right?' Abi says. 'You look tired.'

'Oh, I never really sleep. I'm used to functioning on a couple of hours. Although, I must look even worse than normal for you to have noticed.' I give a brief, disingenuous laugh.

'You should try lavender oil. Or hypnosis maybe?'

'Thanks, Abi. I've tried everything over the years.'

Vanessa bursts through the door, her face set, her posture

236

stiff. Internally, I deflate; it feels like everything is falling apart. 'What's up, Vanessa?' I ask.

'Nish is so insensitive,' she says, gesticulating towards the entrance. Nisha follows in behind, also with a face like thunder.

'No, Vanessa. I'm not *in*sensitive, you're just *over*sensitive. It was a comment, that's all. Christ, everyone is coming up with Olivia theories. You gonna have a go at all of them too?'

'What's going on, girls? Come on, let's not fall out with each other – there's enough going on. We need to stick together,' I say.

'Shall I make us all a cuppa before surgery starts?' Abi asks, helpfully. I'm glad at least one of us is in a good mood and can help defuse this situation.

'Thanks, Abi, that seems a good idea.'

'There must be something in the water,' Abi says. 'Everyone seems a bit on the grumpy side today.' She smiles and goes to walk around Vanessa and Nisha, who are blocking the doorway. I catch the look of annoyance on Nisha's face as Abi approaches her, but she steps aside to let her through.

'Maybe we're all having trouble sleeping since Olivia's disappearance,' I say. The atmosphere in here is tense, almost as bad as being at home. I can't have that. I need something in my life to be positive – somewhere I can feel comfortable and be myself. 'Are either of you due any time off soon?'

'I've got a week off next month,' Nisha says. She looks keen to leave the conversation and get to her own treatment room, her gaze drifting to the door.

'Nope,' Vanessa says. 'Nothing for me until October.

237

Not bothered, though – I'd rather be here, working. Not much else going on in my life.'

'Sometimes a little distance between work and home is good, even if you haven't got plans.'

'If you've got family, maybe. And *friends*.' She narrows her eyes at Nisha. This is going nowhere. Perhaps they just need a bit of distance from each other for the time being.

Abi returns with a tray of mugs. Both Vanessa and Nisha take one, then silently retreat and go into separate treatment rooms. I wonder what it was that Nisha said to spark Vanessa's anger like that. It's so unlike them; they're usually sociable at work and I know their friendship extends to outside the practice hours too. It seems unlikely Nisha would be insensitive, given she is living next to Olivia's parents. Although, thinking about it, she did enthusiastically put forward suspects when we first discussed Olivia's abduction in the break room.

Abi's voice penetrates my thoughts. She's been talking and I haven't been listening. '. . . need to let your hair down. Fancy a quick drink after work?' she says.

'Oh, erm . . . I can't, really – kids to pick up, dinner to cook. But thanks for the offer.'

'Ah, okay. Easy for me with no strings. But to be honest, I just need to get out of the flat. It's so noisy – kids stomping above my head, music blaring below. I'm sandwiched between the neighbours from hell. I tend not to spend time at home – I'm out as much as possible. If you change your mind, here's my mobile number.'

'Oh, I've already got it, thanks,' I say.

'It's my new one,' Abi says, holding up a Post-it Note with digits scrawled on it. 'Dropped the other, cracked the screen to bits, can't see a thing.'

As Abi's hand extends with the Post-it, I notice new cuts and some bruising on the inside of her wrist. Guilt surges through me as I consider how my treatment of her last week might well have been a contributing factor. I wonder if I should bring up my suspicion of her self-harm. I could be wrong, but my gut tells me I'm not.

'Thanks,' I say, taking it from her. 'I'll update it on our records, too.'

Our gazes linger on each other, then she turns to start work. 'Actually,' I say, deciding in this moment to do the right thing. 'Stuff it. Can you make it seven-thirty? The kids will be tucked up in bed by then and Mark'll only be lounging in front of the telly – he had a night out recently; it's my turn.'

Her face beams. 'That would be fab, yes.'

'Sorted. Shall we meet at The Union? Do you know where it is?'

'Yes, I pass it to go to Kelly's Bakery often enough,' she says with a burst of laughter, placing her hand on her belly as if to say she's gained weight. 'But, are you sure you want to go there?'

I contemplate it for a split second before confirming that, yes, I do want to go to The Union. I might find out some vital information about Olivia's abduction – it's bound to be a topic of conversation in the bar and I'm sure I could get the landlord, Ken, talking. Abi appears genuinely happy I've agreed. At least I've pleased one person today.

When I reach my consulting room, Vanessa is busy sorting instrument packs.

'Are you okay, love?' I say.

'Yeah, sorry for that. So unprofessional,' she says, her

face sullen. 'Honestly, I didn't mean for it to turn into an argument. She just rubbed me up the wrong way, that's all.'

'What on earth did she say?'

Vanessa shrugs, and I assume she's not going to say more. Then, her expression hardens, and she lets rip. 'She's being so . . . *voyeuristic*. She's lapping it all up, enjoying the buzz Olivia's abduction has created – the influx of media and stuff, you know? And actually, despite us all joining in the conversation about possible suspects, even then it was Nisha who instigated all that.' Vanessa takes a breath but continues before I can respond. 'Anyway, as we were walking in this morning, she started chatting shit about Mr Edwards, that he was acting all weird. She said he was always disappearing into his shed, as well as avoiding media and even the police, according to her – so she's decided he must've had something to do with his own daughter's disappearance. She's taken it too far, Jenny – her interest in it is verging on obsessive. She literally sits at her bedroom window every night, lights off, spying on Olivia's parents' back garden – practically stalking poor Mr Edwards. So, yeah – I lost it a bit and told her I thought she was insensitive.'

My phone vibrates in my bag. I rummage inside to find it, while keeping eye contact with Vanessa, who's red in the face from ranting, but is still in full swing. I glance down at the notification. It's from Roisin.

Call me.

My pulse pounds. Has she found something?

My attention drifts from what Vanessa's saying and instead the possible reasons for Roisin wanting me to call her swirl around my head. It's not until I'm aware the room is quiet, that I realise Vanessa is waiting for me to respond.

'Oh, sorry, Vanessa – I was trying to take it all in. I agree, Nisha's obsession does seem to be on another level.'

'You know what they say about perpetrators inserting themselves into the investigation somehow, going to the scene and stuff. Maybe *she* knows more than she's telling us.' Vanessa flounces out of the room; I hear her calling for our first client.

While I know Vanessa is right with her assertion about perpetrators of crime returning to the scene, or ensuring they're involved in the resulting investigation in some way, suggesting Nisha could be doing this – that she might be responsible for Olivia's abduction – is way over the top. I'll have to take them both aside, try and sort this out before it becomes a real problem.

The morning flies by – the planned surgery has gone well and despite my fear about the Vanessa and Nisha spat getting out of hand, there've been no further dramas. Although, if there's going to be another scene, it's more likely to occur at lunchtime in the staffroom. I wonder if Samir is aware of what's going on – I've not set eyes on him again since first thing. I'll go find him; he should be made aware of the current situation. He might even put off our meeting if I emphasise how worried I am that things will kick off if one of us isn't there to keep the peace.

Luckily, Samir agrees and says he'll sit in the staffroom, which gives me my much-needed opportunity to check the CCTV footage. I listen at the staffroom door for a minute to check everyone is in there, then go to the reception. I lean over the keyboard and click onto the file containing the recorded footage. As I'm about to open last night's file, I'm startled by the reception door banging. I quickly minimise the screen, just as someone speaks. I turn, immediately taking a sharp intake of breath.

'You frightened me,' I say.

'I can see that,' Hayley says. 'Looks as though I've caught you with your hand in the cookie jar. So to speak.' She gives a nod towards the computer.

'Hah! If only I had real cookies as opposed to online ones! I do miss yours. How are you feeling? We've missed you.'

'Oh, not brilliant, if I'm honest. Been back and forth to the GP but I'm told there's nothing much they can do. Have to get on with it – you know how it is. Keep on keeping on,' she says, sighing.

'I'm so sorry, Hayley. Must be so frustrating. Is there anything we can do here to make life easier for you?'

'That's why I'm here. Just come to do some research if that's okay. I know I'm officially off sick, but I'm trying to find some more ergo-whatsit stuff – better equipment, for me to use here. I don't want to let you down being off sick longer than needed.'

'Oh, please don't think that. We're coping just fine, really. Abi is stepping up to the mark marvellously.' I catch Hayley's alarmed expression and a bit too late realise I've said the wrong thing – basically implying we can get by without her now. 'Obviously,' I whisper behind my hand like a child, 'she doesn't hold a candle to you.' I smile, hoping I've averted disaster. The entire team will be at loggerheads if things carry on like this. It's like stepping on eggshells.

'I'm glad she's finding her feet; I had my concerns.' Hayley returns the smile and sits behind the desk, commencing her 'research'. Clearly, I'm not going to get the opportunity to check the footage now.

'I'll leave you to it,' I say, heading outside. If I can't complete one task, I'll just move on to the next. Ensuring I'm well out of earshot of any windows, I call Roisin.

'Claire comes and goes early mornings,' Roisin tells me when I ask what my mother's routine is. 'But while I was watching she didn't drive out of town. She did meet with someone in a park, though. Couldn't get close, but looked like another woman – the conversation appeared heated.'

'Well, doesn't that sound just like my mother,' I say, sarcasm dripping from each word. The feeling I get merely thinking about her makes my skin itch, but giving her headspace, actually talking about her, fills me with a hot anger I struggle to control. 'Could it be someone she's paying to deliver the dead animals?'

'It's a possibility. I'm sorry I didn't get anything definitive . . .'

'Don't be sorry. Thanks so much for doing this, Ro. I really appreciate it. I have no one else I can turn to.'

'Should I have followed the mystery woman?'

I ponder this. It might be helpful, but I feel guilty enough dragging Roisin into this. I can't ask more of her. 'It's likely nothing – just a friend she meets or something. I assume she has made *some* friends since I left twenty years ago.'

'Do you ever have contact with your dad?'

Roisin's question throws me off-guard; I stumble before blurting: 'What? God, no.'

I hadn't thought this all through. Giving Roisin details about my mother, where I lived and grew up, is basically arming her with all she needs to find out about his serial killer status. The fact she's asked this leads me to suspect she knows. Before she can ask a follow-up question, I make my excuses to leave the conversation.

My father isn't someone I'm ready to discuss with her.

Chapter 47

I'm back from another visit, buzzing with what Paul's told me today. I wrote the key points down as he spoke them, but there was so much information that I couldn't keep up. I tried to retain the details in my head, then dictated as much of the conversation as possible into my phone as soon as I got back to the car.

I'd watched her for some time. It became an obsession. I suppose you could say it was a bit like a sport – observing the target, planning the how, where and when; executing the plan. The build-up was often the most exciting part – the anticipation, like a drug, made me high. For a long time after that first encounter, the feeling sustained me without needing to act further. Then, as the 'drug' wore off, the excitement and the anticipation of it all lessened. So I had to go one step further to achieve the high. That's when I started taking them.

It wasn't until I had abducted three women that I realised

I required something extra. A more intense high. I needed to take bigger risks. Letting them go wasn't satisfactory.

I had to kill.

And when even the act of killing began to lose its shine, well, things took a turn. That's when I made the mistake. It wasn't enough to stalk, abduct and murder. I had to make them better – prettier, more unique. It stopped being like a sport.

Instead, I came to think of myself as a creator. An artist. And art needs to be seen to be appreciated.

Chapter 48

MARK

The kids are excitable as I drive them to school – it's rare for me to take them, so they're both in high spirits. It's good to see Ella this way – she's been distant of late. After some high-speed chatter, they calm down and before I can have any real conversation with them, we arrive. Parking is shocking. I've heard Jen say it many times before, but experiencing it first-hand is an eye-opener. I don't feel I'm in a position to complain given we live less than a ten-minute walk away and really shouldn't use the car for such a short journey. Talk about adding to our carbon footprint – what sort of example am I setting my children?

'You know, kids – we should really try harder to walk to school. Sometimes, at least.'

'Mummy says the same,' Alfie says, with a huge sigh.

'Then says we don't have time to walk,' Ella adds.

'Yes, well, I think there might be changes afoot,' I say, quietly as I climb out the car, while thinking: *And I don't think Mummy will be happy about any of them*. I suck in a large lungful of air, but all that accomplishes is disturbing the butterflies in my stomach. I focus on my surroundings. I've forgotten how noisy and chaotic a school playground first thing in the morning can be. I wish I had just half of some of these kids' energy levels. I gaze about, at a bit of a loss because I can't even recall where I should be headed.

'You go that way,' Ella says, both hands pushing me away. 'I'm too old to be taken in, but Mummy always takes Alfie.'

'Oh, okay, sweetheart. Then, I'll see you later. Have a good day.' As I bend to kiss her, she backs away. 'Not *here*, Daddy!'

I guess the days of being able to hug and kiss my little girl goodbye are well gone. A sensation, close to loss, pulls at my guts. She's only eight; I didn't expect this yet. I thought I had a while before she no longer wanted physical affection from me. Maybe it's a good thing; the right thing. These days children should have the power and control to decide if they get hugs and kisses from family members. I look at Alfie as he lifts his face.

'You can give *me* a hug, Dad. I'm not too old.'

My heart melts and I do just that. 'Right, let's get you inside,' I say, holding back my emotion.

After Alfie shows me where he hangs his coat, and proudly points out his art project that's been put up on the classroom wall, I walk back out into the playground. I spot a huddle of women in the centre and, recognising them, head over. Frankie clocks me approaching and the circle breaks.

'Mark,' she calls. 'Nice to see you here for a change.' She shoots me a beaming smile as I join the circle. It closes around me. It's as if I've been swallowed up.

248

'Good morning, ladies,' I say, returning the smiles. 'How do you all look so stunning this early in the morning?'

'Oh, *you*,' Willow gushes, brushing her hand down my arm. 'Always the charmer.'

As if I'm now one of them, they continue whatever conversation they were having and as suspected, it's about Olivia. Her parents. How devastated they are. About her daughter who has returned to school today – what a tough time it must be for her. I need to try to shoehorn in a mention of Olivia's bracelet. They might know if she wore it all the time.

'Now I have the attention of Jen's friends,' I venture, 'I wondered if you could help with a gift choice for Jenny. It's our anniversary soon, and I thought about a silver bracelet, but something with stones, or charms. Something like the one Olivia wore.' It's an awkward attempt and I sense immediate suspicion. I feel my face flush as they stare open-mouthed at me. God, how do I get out of this now? 'Maybe now's not the time,' I mutter before quickly changing tack and asking about the woman who lived in our house before us – now I have a name.

'Do you know anything about the Butternuts?' I realise that's too much of an open question and might result in a load of non-specific information, so quickly add: 'Whether they had a relative or friend staying with them at any point?' Must keep the topic focused so I get what I'm after now I've messed up my first opportunity.

All four faces look thoughtful, but no one offers a single piece of information. I'm going to have to prompt.

'I think there was someone named Jane living with them?'

'Do you have a surname?' Rachel asks.

For some reason, I'm reluctant to disclose everything. But a surname could spark a memory more than just 'Jane'. 'Slater, I believe.' I cast my eyes around the circle, hoping to catch a hint of recognition in their faces. But nothing.

'No. Sorry, really can't remember anyone other than the pair of them at the house. They kept themselves to themselves,' Willow says.

'Never mind. I'm sure someone will know.' I make my excuses to leave, but Zari grabs the arm of my coat.

'Have you Googled it?' she says.

'Oh, hah! Never thought of that.'

'You being an IT whizz, too.' She giggles.

'I know. Madness. But I went straight to the village oracle, thinking that Teresa was my best bet. Local knowledge is often better than any internet search.'

'Yes, true. Teresa knows an awful lot, that's for sure. And, I mean, it's a common name, so Google might not yield much I suppose. Worth a try though. Why are you trying to find her?'

'Oh, I found an item I think must belong to her at the house and want to make sure she gets it,' I say, then briskly walk off, out of the playground, eager to be alone so I can begin my search.

Once in my car, I take my mobile out and scroll through the mass of hits.

One stands out.

Heat rises up inside me; panic swelling. I pull at my tie, loosening it, trying to catch my breath.

Then, I throw the phone on the passenger seat, push the gearstick into first and head back home.

I reread one of the letters and in light of my new knowledge, it sends chills up my spine.

You might not believe me when I say this, but I have always tried to protect you from it all.

I judged it badly, I know. I really did have your best interests in mind. I didn't want you to have to suffer for the person I was. You're my little princess, always will be, no matter how old you are. The times I spent with you were the most precious – the memories of them keep me going during the darkest times here.

I never talk about you because I don't want anyone to use what I say against you somehow. You're the one thing I keep private no matter how hard psychologists, fellow inmates, journalists and the like press me for details. They try their underhand tactics to trick me into divulging what we did together – how we spent our time. They want me to tell them that you saw something, that you were involved in some way. They're hateful. No matter what I tell them, they twist it.

No wonder you suffer with night terrors. My poor princess. I'm so sorry. I wish I could help you.

Love, as ever, Dad xx

With my car keys in one hand, I hesitate at the front door. My eyes are drawn to the framed family portrait, and I run my fingertips over the faces of Ella and Alfie. Their beautiful, innocent faces blur and a sob escapes my lips. How did it come to this? I could ignore it all, pretend none of it is real. Put it in a box. Like I did with the uni 'prank', with what Brett did to Hannah. Taking her to the woods that night was meant to be a harmless bit of fun – an initiation of sorts. My gut twists now at the thought of our utter immaturity. *My* naivety. Blindfolding her, tying her hands, like some pathetic game of Blind

Man's Buff, then leaving her to stumble through the woods trying to find us. It was idiotic. That was the least of it, though. I remember my attack of conscience, a sudden realisation of how dangerous it was, so had doubled-back. That's when I saw Brett, seemingly luring Hannah to the edge of a steep drop – the rushing ravine about ten feet below. I watched on in horror, afraid he was going to let her fall. It wasn't until the last second I saw his hand reach out to grab her. But she'd slipped. Of course, afterwards, Brett had toned down the seriousness of it, saying it was just a prank that got out of hand. An accident. And I went along with it.

Brett was so keen to point out that I was a wuss back then. And I had been weak. I always let him take charge and convince me his games were harmless. It was just a broken bone and a few bruises, he'd said. Christ. We were so lucky she hadn't been killed. Hannah believed it was an accident, but something deep inside me couldn't quite believe it and I've lived with the guilt since. I'm not going to be that person now; I can't brush this under the carpet. *This* time, I must do the right thing and act before it's too late.

With the package on the passenger seat inside my car, I dial the number. And while waiting for it to connect, I cry.

Following a very brief conversation, I turn the ignition and swing the car around, the tyres crunching the gravel. At the end of the driveway, I turn left, go up the hill and out of Coleton Combe to drive into town.

After today, everything will be different. I'm leaving our home as one person and I'll be returning as another.

I have no choice.

Chapter 49

JENNY

There's a knock on my consulting room door, and before I've had chance to respond, Abi enters. I stop what I'm doing – just a regular check-up on a chihuahua, thankfully – and give her a questioning glance.

'Sorry to interrupt,' she says. 'I . . . er . . .' She opens her eyes wide at me, like I'm supposed to get what she's trying to say. 'You're needed, a moment . . . in reception. Please.'

I frown. She's flustered, sheepish. Now what's she done? 'Just a sec,' I say. I really hope she hasn't booked a late appointment again or something – I need to leave sharpish today because I want as much time alone with the kids before Mark gets back. 'I'll be right back, little one,' I tell Tony, giving him a rub behind his ears. 'Sorry, Emily,' I turn to Tony's owner. 'Can you stay in here just while I sort this out? I won't be long, then I'll finish his annual check and you can be on your way.'

'Sure,' Emily says, coming to hold on to Tony.

I push open the double doors into reception a little too forcefully – one bangs against the wall and I flinch. Then I see the look on Abi's face and clock the two detectives standing with their backs to me at the desk.

Fight or flight.

For a split second, I consider retreating and escaping out the back door. But it's already too late for that – my noisy entrance has alerted them to my presence and simultaneously, they both turn to face me.

'Ah,' DS Davis says. 'Hello, Jennifer. So sorry to bother you at work.' She offers a smile, though it's not exactly friendly, merely polite. DC Bishop gives me a curt nod.

I don't trust my voice – the fact my throat feels as though it's just closed over makes me fear it'll come out as a squeak – but I can't stand here mute, so decide on a simple, 'Hi.'

Davis jerks her head towards the door, in a fashion that implies 'follow me' before she walks that way. I look to Bishop, to check I haven't misread the situation.

'Do you mind?' he says, holding out one arm and indicating the door.

I give a furtive glance around the waiting room. I'm glad there are only two witnesses to this. But the look of concern, or maybe it's curiosity, on Abi's face is enough to give rise to panic. Had the detectives been grilling her before she came to get me? Has she allowed them to look at the CCTV? God, I wish I could talk to her before having to go outside with these two. I attempt to give Abi a reassuring smile as I walk by, but doubt I succeeded. The detectives asking for me specifically isn't good news.

Pulling me outside, away from anyone else – well, that's even more concerning.

My legs shake as I follow Bishop. The sun glares into my eyes and I lift a hand to shield them. I see Davis standing by her car, leaning up against it, nonchalant. Okay, she looks relaxed, that's a good sign. But, as I'm thinking this might not be as bad as I imagined, she opens the back door and flicks her hand to tell me to get inside.

What is this?

I do as instructed, the door banging closed the second I'm inside. Then they both climb into the front seats. Davis swivels in the driver's seat to look at me.

'Didn't want to make a fuss at your workplace,' she says. 'But we'd really appreciate you coming to the station to help with our inquiries.'

Oh, my, God. I swallow hard, fighting to stop tears, but all the emotions inside me threaten to cause overload. 'I . . . I don't understand.'

'There are a few questions, things we could do with . . .' Davis looks up to her right, as if trying to find the right phrase. 'Clearing up,' she says. I'm not sure if it's intended, but her voice is menacing.

My first thought is I've left a client in my consulting room, waiting for my return. And Samir doesn't even know I've left the premises. Although, I guess by now, Abi has told him. Everyone. I wonder if Davis and Bishop had already informed them of their intention to take me to the station – and that's why Abi looked so concerned.

'When we reach the station, you may call your solicitor if you wish – if you'd like counsel while we ask questions.'

'Am I under *arrest*?'

'No, Jennifer,' Bishop says. 'Not at this time; you're assisting voluntarily. But we are going to caution you.' He looks back to Davis and I see her draw breath, readying herself. My jaw slackens as she speaks the words I've heard so many times on crime shows. She reiterates I'm free to leave at any point and that I have the right to free and independent legal advice. My mind races to think who I could call. I don't have a solicitor. I pick at my lower lip, trying to think. But, if I'm not under arrest, why would I need one?

Then, the horrific thought hits me. Do they know who I am? I raise my eyes to meet Davis's. 'It's fine,' I say, confidently. 'I don't require a solicitor. But I'm going to need to arrange someone to pick up my children from school if this is going to take more than an hour.'

'Your husband will be collecting your children, so no need to worry on that front.'

My heartbeat increases, thundering along, banging against my ribs.

I clearly need to worry on every other front, though.

Chapter 50

JENNY

'Could you take a look at these, please?' DS Davis pushes three photographs across the table towards me. We're in the police station in town, in a stuffy room that by the smell of it isn't regularly used. Both Davis and Bishop are sitting in front of me, rigid and serious-looking. I mirror this, my chest tight, my muscles sore from holding myself so stiffly. I have to keep reminding myself to breathe.

I drag one photo closer, squinting at it. It's dark, grainy, but I immediately realise what, and where, it is. I say nothing as I look at the other two in turn, silently taking in the detail, giving myself thinking time. The voice in my head screams: *Ask for a solicitor now!*

After regarding the photos for as long as appears natural, I look up, straight into DS Davis's deep-brown eyes and hold her gaze. I wait for her to speak – despite knowing where they're going with this, I'm not going to jump in before I know their exact thinking.

'Can you tell me what you see in those photos?' DC Bishop asks.

I don't take my eyes from Davis when I answer. 'I see a dark image with poor detail,' I say. Davis smiles and nods.

'What about the person seen in all three photos?' she says.

'What about them?'

Out the corner of my eye, I see Bishop shift in his chair. But Davis remains inert.

'It would be really helpful to our investigation if you co-operate, Jennifer,' she says.

'I *am* co-operating. I came with you here and I'm looking at the photos you've put in front of me. I just don't understand what you want from me. I can't see anything in these.' I push the photos back towards Davis. I catch a brief expression of frustration on her face before she ploughs on.

'We believe the person in these images is you, Jennifer.'

'Well, I don't,' I say.

'Look again.' Bishop takes the photos, slamming them down one by one in front of me for a second time. I do as he asks.

'I don't see it. All I can tell from these is that there appears to be a figure, male or female, I can't tell, seemingly standing – with their *back* to the camera – outside a house.'

DS Davis purses her lips and leans back heavily in her chair. 'Analysis of the photos indicates the figure is female. Her hair colour and style matches that of your own. And she appears to be wearing pyjamas.'

Although my heart crashes wildly, I keep my calm, repeating the words: *They have nothing, they have nothing*, in my head. I shrug, gently shaking my head. 'So?'

The smile that spreads across Davis's face makes my insides shake. I get the impression that's a smile of someone who has something else up their sleeve. I clench my hands beneath the table.

'This camera footage was shot on the night of 12th August. We've taken these stills from the actual footage. There is more.'

I swallow hard. For some reason it hadn't crossed my mind they were only showing me part of the whole. Of course, while these photos might not be too clear, the video footage may well give more detail. Have I fallen into their trap? Because despite the grainy images, they are right – from the back, this person does look a lot like me, just like they told me yesterday. Mark's words fly through my mind. 'Teresa says she's witnessed you wandering around in your pyjamas late at night.'

Shit, shit, shit, shit.

Bishop opens the file that's been on the table in front of him. He slowly extracts a piece of paper. Good – at least there are no more photos. He leans his upper body over the table and begins reading from the paper.

'I've seen Mrs Johnson a number of times late into the night, or early hours of the morning. It's weird – why would anyone wander around alone in the dead of night in their nightwear?' Bishop eyes me over the top of the paper. 'There's more, but I won't bore you with the rest,' he says.

'The witness puts you in the centre of the village the same evening the camera caught you in Olivia's garden,' DS Davis says. For some reason, I don't think the witness they're quoting is Teresa – she doesn't speak that way. Which means other villagers have potentially seen me.

'What is it that you're getting at, DS Davis?' I say.

'Our belief is, you were the person in the garden days before the abduction of the victim. And we'd like to know why you were there. What were you doing, Jennifer?'

The time has come.

'I'd like to contact a solicitor now, please.'

'Are you sure? We're only asking a few questions. It will delay you here if we have to wait for—'

'As you informed me, my husband is picking up my children, so I have plenty of time to wait. Thank you.' I shoot Davis a sarcastic smile. This isn't a friendly chat – they are trying to pin this all on me. Their nicey-nicey approach isn't fooling me. Davis and Bishop stand, then beckon to me to do the same. I follow them out of the room and they ask me to wait in the main reception area of the station. Davis walks over to the duty sergeant and says something in hushed tones. He glances at me, nodding to Davis. Then Davis and Bishop disappear into a different room along the corridor and the duty sergeant calls me to the desk.

'You have the number of a solicitor? Or do you need us to provide you with one?'

My mind blanks. I can't think of anyone to call. 'Er . . . I have someone, but I can't recall the number. Can I phone the person who knows them to obtain it?'

'Yes, sure.' He hands me the phone.

As I dial, I pray she answers.

'Oh, thank God. Roisin, I need your help. Have you got the number of the solicitor Harry uses?'

'Christ, Jen. Why do you need it?'

'I'm at the police station in town. I've not been arrested, but . . .'

'Okay. You've done the right thing. Hang on a sec.'

The line is silent for a few moments, then I hear Roisin's breathing – it's rapid, like she's been running. 'Got it. She's called Harper Underhill.' Roisin rattles off her number. 'I'll call Mark, and—'

'He already knows. He's going to pick the kids up.'

'Okay. Anyone else I should contact?'

'Samir, please. He's probably already in the loop, but I kind of upped and left the practice, so . . .'

'Sure, darling – I'm so sorry. Try not to worry. They can't know . . . you know, the thing.' She trails off.

So, she did find out about my father, then. That was confirmation. 'No. Hopefully not.' The duty sergeant gives me a look that says hurry up. I end the call with Roisin and tell him I have the number I need.

Then I make the call to Harper.

Chapter 51

JENNY

I'm immediately reassured by the way Harper Underhill – tall and elegant, dressed in a cream trouser suit – sweeps in and without waiting to be approached, strides up to the duty sergeant and demands to speak with the detectives. She then turns her attention to me, giving me a cool, confident smile while loudly declaring, 'You'll be out of here in two minutes.'

DS Davis saunters towards Harper, her pinched expression suggesting she's anticipating the inevitable.

'My client is here voluntarily?' Harper says before Davis even opens her mouth to speak. Davis's chest heaves.

'Yes.'

'So, unless you're arresting her, she's leaving.' Harper swivels on her stiletto heel and ushers me out of the station door, leaving DS Davis standing limply in the corridor. Harper Underhill was true to her word: the entire episode lasted just two minutes.

* * *

I get a taxi to the vet practice to pick up my car. I'm relieved to have escaped arrest, but Harper explained it might only be temporary. I'm now a person of interest.

'They'll be watching you closely,' were her parting words to me. She said they'll be working to gain enough evidence to arrest me as they clearly believe I've something to do with Olivia's abduction. Neither Davis nor Bishop brought up anything relating to my father and I didn't mention it to Harper. It's possible they *are* aware – holding this back for a later grilling. I should mentally prepare for it.

I should also get rid of the letters I keep under the bedroom floor.

God, and the bracelet, and the latest dead animal in the bin. If they find those . . .

My nerves tingle as I swing the car into the drive. What's Mark going to say about all this? I visualise his face, filled with worry and despair. Me being dragged into the station for questioning adds weight to his own suspicions of me and I'm not sure how I can reverse them; how I can convince him I'm completely innocent.

I don't even know if I'm innocent.

His car isn't in the driveway. I guess he didn't know how long I'd be. If I was even coming home tonight. Perhaps he's taken the kids out for something to eat, to keep them occupied. Stop them asking too many awkward questions about where Mummy is. If I'm quick, I can get rid of the letters before they get home.

I haphazardly park the car and rush inside, taking the stairs two at a time.

After grabbing the scissors from my bedside table, I drop to my knees and pull back the edge of the carpet and prise the floorboard up. I dip my hand inside the gap, feeling around. My heart judders. I can't find the bundle of letters. I sweep my hand around further, but the cavity is empty. I pull my hand back out and collapse against the bed.

'No, no, no.'

It's not only the letters that have gone. The bag containing the bracelet isn't there either. I clasp my hands to my mouth, stifling a scream. How could he? How could my own husband do this?

He's the one. He went to the police with the letters and bracelet. He must've. That's why they questioned me. And now, thinking about it, when I was concerned about how long it would take, they said it was fine because Mark was picking up the kids. Because he already knew. He took the 'evidence' to Davis and Bishop.

So why wasn't I actually arrested? While the letters aren't evidence I'm involved in any way, the bracelet surely is.

I think Harper was right. They're waiting until they have firm evidence. Which might mean they're waiting on forensics to prove it was Olivia's bracelet – and to confirm there are fingerprints on it. Once they get that, they'll arrest me, take my fingerprints to see if they're a match.

Then, I'm screwed.

I push up from the floor and make it to the en suite just in time to vomit into the toilet.

Chapter 52

MARK

'What have you done?'

Her voice is a whisper, filled with pain and anguish. Betrayal. I'm glad I can't see her face.

'Why did you lie to me?' I counter, without answering her question. I did what I had to do so I'm not really the one who's at fault here. Not this time.

'Why didn't you speak to me first?' she hisses down the phone.

'Where are you?' I assume she's no longer at the station. I wonder what's happened, how it's been left. DS Talia Davis talked me through how it was likely to go. They didn't want to arrest her at this point; they knew after twenty-four hours they'd have to let her go without charge because there wasn't enough evidence that the CPS would allow them to bring charges. Not yet. Talia was confident they would get it, though. Although she obviously didn't disclose exactly what they had, I'm aware there is CCTV footage of a person whom they believed to be Jenny in

Olivia's garden days prior to her abduction. I'd been asked about Jen's argument with Olivia because Jen's name had come up during door-to-door inquiries. Probably from Olivia's neighbours who heard the accusations Jen was screaming at Olivia. Mostly circumstantial, Talia agreed, before I handed in the bracelet I'd found along with the letters.

Talia was delighted with the finding – her eyes lighting up. There was an air of excitement in the station when I left, like I'd handed them the golden ticket. She was also particularly interested in the letters from Jen's serial killer father. She'd asked if I believed she was still in contact with him as the letters appeared old. I couldn't tell her anything as I knew nothing about him up until today. As I'd driven away from the station, my entire body felt heavy. I'd just handed my wife to them on a platter.

The shock is still raw. I'm numb.

'Mark? Are you still there?' Jen's voice penetrates my thoughts.

'Yeah, I'm here.'

'And where is here?' she asks.

For a split second I'm afraid to tell her. Jesus. What do I imagine she'll do? Come after me? Kill me? I sigh. 'At my parents'.'

'Right. I see.'

The line goes quiet.

'I wasn't sure . . . you know . . . when you would be back.'

'Or *if*,' she says. 'I assume you thought I'd be arrested and held?'

'No, no. I didn't. I knew you would just be questioned. But I didn't know how long for, and I didn't want the kids to be worried, so I brought them here. For Nanna and Grandad to spoil them. Make a fuss over them.'

'You didn't answer my question.' Her tone is flat; cold. 'Why didn't you speak to me before going to the police?'

I grip the phone tight in my hand. 'You didn't answer mine either. Why did you lie to me?'

'I never *lied*, Mark. I told you I had a complex and unhappy childhood. I think that about covers it, don't you? Not disclosing the fact my father is a serial killer doesn't make me a liar.'

'Doesn't make you an open and honest person either.'

'Says the man who lied about his relationship with another woman, then tried to cover it all up. The same man who believed his wife to be an abductor, possibly murderer, but rather than discuss it, went behind her back to tell tales to the police.'

'Touché,' I say, not knowing where else to go with this conversation. 'We're staying here for a bit, Jen. Until things are cleared up.'

'Cleared up? You mean until the police realise I had nothing to do with it and move their attention onto another suspect?'

'Something like that.'

'I want to be with *my* children. You have no right to take them.'

'I think I do. I'm sorry, Jen.'

I hang up and wipe the tears from my cheeks.

Chapter 53

JENNY

'Arrrrrghhhhh,' I scream, throwing my mobile across the room. It lands with a dull thud on the sofa cushions. Rushing across the lounge, I grab each of the cushions and hit them against the sofa, pummelling my fists into them, crying, until I collapse, spent and exhausted.

This is the first time I've been totally alone in this house – I don't know what to do with myself. Then, I remember. I find my phone, buried beneath cushions, and go to contacts.

'Abi, hi,' I say.

'Oh, my God. Are you okay? I was so worried. Where are you?'

'Back at home. I'm fine,' I say. 'Well, no. Not fine, really.'

'I'm not doing anything, as ever – if you want, I can come over? Oh, sorry, that's stupid of me to say. I'm sure you'd rather be alone with your husband after a traumatic day!'

'Actually, no. I would much rather be out,' I say, not wanting to tell her my husband has upped and left, taking our children with him. 'Still up for our pub night?'

'Well, yeah, sure. If you're feeling up to it.'

'Good, I'll meet you there in half an hour, then?'

'Excellent. Can't wait to escape this hellhole,' she says.

Snap, I think.

I haven't walked into a pub alone in years. I can't recall the last time I was in *this* pub. The smell hits me as I open the door – a mix of stale alcohol and warm bodies. Following a quick glance around I realise Abi's not here yet, so I grab the closest table and sit down. I don't want to walk through the entire bar, past the usual crowd, to find another option. Close to the door is fine for now – I'll easily see Abi enter, too. I'll wait for her to arrive before ordering drinks. A few heads turned my way as I walked in, but after a quick nod to acknowledge them, they returned their attention to their conversations, or beer.

I tot up how many people are in here. I can see ten this side of the pub. The low hum of chatter coming from the restaurant part in the next room implies it's quite busy. I wonder if the topic of conversation at every table is Olivia, or whether she's already become old news.

'Beat me to it.' The voice startles me.

'Oh, hi, Abi – where did you come from?' She's dressed up – proper 'going-out clothes' – a gorgeous floral bell-sleeve dress with plunging neckline and she has full make-up on. The opposite to me – I dragged on a pair of jeans, threw on a leopard-print top and applied a layer of the first lipstick I came across loose in my handbag.

'I popped to the loo as soon as I got here,' she says, sitting down. She immediately jumps back up again when she clocks the empty table. 'I'll get the first ones in, shall I?'

'No, no,' I say, getting up. 'My shout. What are you having?'

'G&T please – slimline tonic.'

I order two double G&Ts from Ken at the bar. He tells me it's nice to see me out for a change. 'On your own tonight?' he asks. I'm not sure if it's out of concern, given the Olivia situation, or if he's being nosy.

'With my friend,' I say, indicating behind me, at the table where Abi's sitting.

'Oh, yeah.' He winks. 'Girls' night out without the fellas in tow.'

I smile. 'Something like that.'

'Your turn, I guess – I see your Mark was out last week.'

'Yes, one day we'll get out together,' I say, giving a forced laugh.

'You should! Poor bloke was practically mobbed by the ladies – they do seem to like him.'

'Hmmm. Such a flirt.'

'To be fair, he doesn't need to do much of that. Even Olivia was singing his praises.'

'Oh? When?' My muscles tense.

'The night she was taken. Can you believe it was a week ago tonight? Poor lass.' Ken shakes his head. My heart tumbles in my chest. I hadn't thought about it being exactly a week ago that Olivia was taken, right after leaving this very pub. I'm stunned for a moment, then Ken's voice brings me back. 'I mean, I'm not gossiping or anything,' he says, 'but, well, in here, you always hear things, you know?'

I do know. 'I'm not sure what you're getting at, Ken.'

'Olivia was saying how she'd thought a lot of Mark. Until . . .'

'Until?'

'She said he was mean to her. Pushed her away when she asked for his help, saying she was a nuisance. I'm not judging your fella – as I say, I watched the women swarm around him. I'm sure he was only trying to fend off Olivia's attention. She was, well . . . *known* for it, like.'

'Known for it?'

Ken casts his gaze around, then leans across the bar. 'She'd tried it on with a few locals in here,' he says, his voice low. 'Some people said she was desperate for it.'

'That's awful,' I say. Even though I'm not a fan of her, it's wrong that people are spreading shit like that. 'Being flirty doesn't make you desperate, Ken. I'm sure people wouldn't be so quick to say that if a bloke was flirting, would they? I mean, obviously Mark was – is – a married man, yet you haven't said that about him.'

'Okay, okay.' He holds his hands up. 'Was just making an observation, no need to get full-on feminist on me.'

I want to carry on the conversation, or argument, as it's more likely to be, and find out if he knows anything else. But I'll have to save it until I've at least spent time with Abi. I can't leave her on her own while I extract information. 'I'll catch up with you in a bit, Ken, yeah?'

'Sure, love. Enjoy your evening.' He wanders off to serve someone else, unconcerned by my reaction. Skin as thick as a rhino.

I join Abi and we settle into a comfortable chat before moving on to the serious stuff. After giving her my edited version of the events following being taken to the police station and questioned under caution, and knocking back another round of double gins, we touch on the subject of families. I haven't disclosed the fact Mark was the one who took evidence to the police, or that he's taken my children to stay at his parents' place – I washed over almost all of those details, and instead of telling her my father is in prison, I say he left us when I was young, going off with a new woman.

'We have such a lot in common,' she says. I frown, wondering how she's come to that conclusion from all I've spoken about. Apart from the fact we both have nightmare mothers, by all accounts, I can't see any further similarities. She must catch my puzzled look because she goes on to explain: 'We both come from broken homes, find it hard to live up to others' expectations, yet we're both driven. Keen to make a difference in the world.'

I ponder this. She's right, now I think of it. 'Well, cheers to that,' I say, clinking my glass against hers. 'Another?'

After several more drinks, I find I'm relaxing, the horrors of the day blending into the background. Abi tells me about her boyfriend who she's been with since school. It seems he's one of the few people she doesn't feel the need to uphold expectations – she can be herself with him. It's wonderful hearing about love that's working out. Although, she does seem sad that he's not close by. I wonder why he didn't move to Devon with her, but won't ask – I don't want to dampen her mood. It's unfair to bring her down to my level.

The conversation flows easily with Abi; it's like she's my age, not twenty-odd years my junior. She's more mature than I'd realised. And far more observant, too. Although she quietly gets on at work, seemingly disinterested in getting involved with gossip and hasn't, as far as I can tell, particularly bonded with the other staff – she's been taking everything in. And now, several more G&Ts later, she's opening up and giving her opinion on the latest workplace issue.

'I was shocked when Vanessa and Nisha had that argument,' she says. I raise my eyebrows, letting her continue. 'But to be honest, not wishing to speak out of turn, of course, I'm going to have to side with Vanessa.'

'Oh, really?' I'm surprised Abi's coming down on a side – I'd taken her as an 'on the fence' kind of person, trying to please everyone.

'Yeah, I think Nisha's been really weird since Olivia's abduction – like she's enjoying it, just like Vanessa said. And she's pretty distracted.' Abi turns her glass, her fingertips twizzling the stem. 'Although, I guess we all have been, really. It's probably a bit unfair of me to single her out.'

'When you say "distracted"?'

'I don't want to get her into trouble.'

'It's fine, it'll stay between us.' I wave a hand, dismissing her concerns. 'I'll likely forget you've told me – I'm useless after a few drinks.' I laugh, trying to encourage her to tell me. She draws a deep breath.

'Just that the other day, she was all flustered because there'd been a mix-up of some kind, she wouldn't tell me what exactly. But a client was asking her about the arrangements for her cat that had passed. You remember – the beautiful tabby? Poor thing had been hit by a car, looked perfect on the outside, but you'd said it had massive internal bleeding.'

'Yes, I remember.' The tabby. A pain shoots through my chest; my heart bangs wildly. I rack my brain – do the timings fit with me getting the tabby in the bin liner? A sick feeling kneads at my stomach. I wonder if Nisha knows I took it and tried to cover for me.

'Well, Nisha couldn't find the cat. Apparently. She said it had already been sent for cremation. The client made her call them while she was there, and Nisha said all was in hand. But afterwards, I asked about it, and Nisha was really evasive. So . . .' Abi looks awkward.

'It's okay. Go on,' I say.

'So, when they'd left reception, *I* called the crem. They never received the cat, Jenny. I think Nisha must've mislabelled it or something but was afraid to come clean.'

The image of Nisha mislabelling the yellow tub on an animal by-product comes to mind. If she was aware of me taking the animals, why hasn't she said anything? I won't mention this to Abi now though.

'And the client hasn't been back to complain?'

'Not yet. But maybe she's still in the dark. This was only last week.'

'That's so unlike Nisha.'

My thoughts swirl in my slightly drunk mind. Nisha might not have said anything to me about it, but what if she spoke to the police? 'When the detectives came today . . . did Nisha appear shocked? Did they speak with her at all?'

'Jenny, she literally stayed out of everyone's way. Never said a word to us about it once the police drove you off. But when we all left for the day, she looked drawn. Haunted.'

'Like she was feeling guilty?'

'Certainly looked that way to me.'

Chapter 54

Paul has finally begun to open up about what I truly came for.

I didn't mean to harm her. I loved her so much. She was my princess.

His words still echo in my head.

I'm wrestling with the fact he loved her deeply yet didn't seem to mind at the time whether he was harming her psychologically. His need to show off his 'art' to someone who loved him unconditionally who was too naive to judge or to realise how wrong it was – what an evil man he was – outweighed his conscience.

I'd always believed Jane had seen things. Her relationship with Paul was too close, too intense for her not to have been dragged into the horrors at some point. At first, when he hinted at it, I thought he'd slipped up, that he hadn't meant to share the information with me. But he knew what he was saying. No doubt he'd planned how to say it, too. He looked me dead in the eyes as he whispered:

'I took my princess to the place I was planning to leave the woman. The latest was still alive at that point; I hadn't finished with her yet. There was something . . . spiritual . . . about it. I felt a deep connection with my little girl. She wasn't scared, you know. Just curious.'

Although I pressed him further, he didn't divulge if Jane had been present during the final moments – when he took the woman's life. Which makes me think she was. She'd seen it all. No wonder she suffered with night terrors. Paul shared how she still suffered. He told me he thought she had PTSD because of what she'd seen, and then because of the night he was arrested. She'd collapsed, he said. Claire had informed him some weeks later, through his solicitor, that Jane had experienced a blackout. An affliction that continued into her teenage years. Probably she still suffers. *It's the price she's paying for loving me,* he'd said.

She's paying a much higher price than he realises.

Chapter 55

JENNY

Wednesday

Jane was cold. She shivered.

Forcing her eyes open, she saw a shadowy figure looming above her.

'Shhh . . .' The hand cupped over her mouth. 'It's okay, Princess, it's okay. Daddy's here.'

Both of her hands pulled at his, trying to tear them away because all she wanted to do was scream. His voice, calm, smooth, continued to whisper in her ear.

'You've had a shock, that's all. I'm sorry. I thought you were ready.' His hand loosened slightly. 'I'm going to take my hand away now, sweetheart. Please be quiet for Daddy. We have to keep this as our secret. If you make a noise, Daddy will get into trouble. You understand?'

Jane nodded, tears hot on her cold face.

He took Jane's hand. 'Don't worry about her,' he said, nodding towards the woman. 'I'm going to make her better.'

Jane didn't want to see again but couldn't help herself; she turned her head towards the woman as they walked past. She was sitting up, against a tree, not quite upright; her middle sagged a bit, and she was looking down at something in her lap. Jane couldn't see her eyes anymore. The woman was quiet. Still. 'Is she going to wake up?'

'No, darling. Not here, in this world.'

Jane didn't know what he meant by that and was about to ask, but then she spotted it. 'Isn't that one of those butterflies?'

'Yes,' her daddy said. He sounded happy that Jane noticed and bent to pick it up. 'This, my princess, is a painted lady butterfly. When I make her better—' he pointed to the quiet woman '—I'll pin this to her.'

'What for?'

He beamed at Jane. 'So everyone will know.'

Jane waited for him to tell her what it was that everyone would know, but he didn't. Instead, he placed the butterfly beside the woman. 'When are you going to make her better, Daddy?'

'When you're safely tucked up in bed, I'll come back and finish her.'

Jane took her daddy's hand and they walked back out, through the trees. They walked for a long time; Jane didn't remember it taking that long to get there. Afraid they were lost, she gripped her daddy's hand tighter. Finally, she saw the car through the trees.

Before Jane knew it, she was back in bed, unable to recall the journey home. She was so sleepy, her eyes fluttering and closing.

'Night, Princess.'

'Night-night Daddy,' she whispered.

'Now, remember – you can never tell anyone where you've been tonight. Ever. It'll always be our secret.'

I wake up on the kitchen floor at 2 a.m. The house is empty. There's no one to hide my latest blackout from. My bones ache with the cold; I must've been here for a while. I got back to the house before midnight and went straight to bed, therefore it's possible I've been out of it for two hours. I really hope I haven't been anywhere. Especially in the car. It's bad enough I drive during a blackout, but to be drunk and driving during one seems so much worse. Double jeopardy. Even though it's unlikely I'll go to sleep now, I take myself off to bed. A deep ache grips me as I pass Ella's bedroom, then Alfie's. I'm nothing without them.

When the alarm goes off, I have to drag myself from the bed – a mixture of exhaustion, hangover and despair desperately trying to pin me down. What's the point in getting up? If I stay wrapped in the warmth of my duvet, I can pretend none of this is happening. Then, I remember what Abi said last night, and I'm suddenly energised. Either Nisha knows what I've been doing . . . or . . . *she* is the one leaving the mutilated animals on my doorstep. The reasons she'd do this aren't clear. We've always got on, Samir knows her well – on the surface there's nothing about her that would make me suspect she was capable of this. And I must remember, it was *my* car on the vets' CCTV footage. So maybe the hard fact is, she's covering for me.

But that doesn't feel right either. I can't imagine Nisha knowing something as unsettling as me stealing dead animals from the vets' and not uttering a word about it to me. Or anyone else. As has become obvious, she enjoys being in the thick of it – she's been actively engaged in the Olivia abduction case, keen to find out all about it, theorising who had motive and opportunity to take her. If she knew something about me coming to the practice in the early hours, rummaging around and taking animal by-products from the fridge, I'm confident she'd say something. If not directly to me, then to Samir.

Or, is that the reason Samir hasn't been himself lately? Maybe she told him and he doesn't know how to broach the subject with me. Whatever the reasons – I need to get myself into the practice early and do some digging.

The light is barely breaking as I pull into my space in the vets' empty car park. I've got about an hour before the others get here. My first task is to check the CCTV I was unable to access yesterday.

As I rush inside, I'm shocked to see Samir sitting behind the desk.

'Oh,' I say. I'm immediately deflated. Why is he here so early? 'Didn't expect to see you.'

'You need to tell me what's going on, Jen.' His face is serious, drawn.

'I was getting in early to get a head start,' I say, trying hard to stop my voice shaking.

'You look terrible.'

'Cheers.' I frown at him as he leans back in the chair and studies my face.

'Police take you away, you're acting strange – deleting CCTV files. You know they copied them all, don't you, so there's no point you doing this now.'

Panic fills me. 'What?'

'A couple of officers came to the practice after they took you and asked to see the CCTV footage.'

'And you let them? Without a warrant? Jesus.'

'Well, Jen – it's not as though I thought we had anything to hide, is it? A woman has been abducted and they thought the angle of the camera would help – why wouldn't I agree? It'd be a dick move to delay it by making them obtain a warrant first. Time is of the essence – it's been a bloody week since she was taken. I was trying to help.'

'Yes, of course, sorry. It's just . . .' I can't begin to explain all this. I'm so tired, I haven't the energy. 'Never mind. It's fine.'

'Are you going to let me in on whatever is going on, then?'

'You mean apart from my life falling apart?'

'Is it really that bad?'

'Yep. Honestly, Samir – this is about as bad as it can get. Do you believe I'm involved in Olivia's—'

'Of bloody course I don't. But you're hiding *something*.'

I decide I should tell him the whole story – minus the part about my father. 'Shall we make a drink and I'll give you a quick run-down?'

'Sure,' he says, getting up. 'Sounds like a plan.'

Before I've even taken two steps, the reception door flings open and DS Davis and DC Bishop walk in, shoulder to shoulder. My pulse thuds. Samir shoots me a wary look as they stride towards me.

'Jennifer Johnson, you are under arrest on suspicion of the abduction of Olivia Edwards. You do not have to say anything, but it may harm your defence if you do not mention when questioned something which you later rely on in court. Anything you do say may be given in evidence.'

I catch Samir's shocked expression as I'm being led out of the building. I turn to him. 'Sorry, I'm so sorry. Get Abi to cancel my clients. I'll speak to you soon.'

'This is bloody ridiculous,' he shouts after me. 'She hasn't done anything . . . You're wasting . . .' His words get swallowed up as the doors bang closed behind us. As soon as Samir mentioned the police copied the files from our computer, I knew this was inevitable. There's another police vehicle and a tow truck in the car park – a uniformed officer is overseeing the removal of my car.

'What . . . why are you taking my car?' My words stick in my throat.

'We have a warrant to seize it, as well as certain items from your property,' Davis says as she bundles me into the back of their car. Fear sweeps in as I realise what a mess I'm in. The likelihood of me being able to explain myself or my actions in a believable way are slim. Whatever I say is going to make me sound crazy.

Is this it? Am I ever going to see my children again?

If I was confident that I didn't have anything to do with Olivia's disappearance, that would be one positive – I might at least come *across* as innocent. But I can't even be sure I wasn't responsible. Thank God Mark *did* take the kids to his parents' and that I've been arrested at the practice. The thought of Ella and Alfie watching as I'm being taken away makes my stomach clench. I never want them to experience what I did.

I really hope I'm not charged. If I went to prison, their lives would follow a similar path to mine and I couldn't live with that guilt.

It's not going to come to that.

As much as I repeat that in my mind, another horrifying thought invades, crushing it.

They're going to find Olivia dead.

After all, I'm the daughter of a serial killer. Doesn't murder run in the blood?

Chapter 56

MARK

A heaviness crushes my ribcage, my chest is tightening as though a boa constrictor has wrapped itself around me. I must be having a heart attack. I claw at my shirt collar, its restriction of my throat suffocating. Hunching over my desk, sending paperwork scattering, I force myself to slow my breathing. I'm not dying. Not from any heart-related issue, anyway. Guilt, maybe.

What have I done? I bang my forehead repeatedly on the melamine surface of the desk, the hollow thudding echoing in the room. She's been arrested. Detained. She'll be in a cell. She'll be furious.

My mobile trills beside my head, and at first, I pray it's Jen – calling to tell me it's all been one huge misunderstanding and she's been released without charge. But if it were her, what would I even say to her? 'Oh, hi, love – how are you? Sorry for shopping you into the police, darling. I had no idea they'd actually arrest you. Forgive me, won't you?' I'm partly relieved to see the caller ID is Brett.

'You're a hard one to get a hold of, mate! Where've you been hiding?' he says, with his usual brashness.

'It's been . . . a trying time,' I say, my own voice flat.

'Oh? More problems with the missus?'

There's something about this immediate inference that riles me, but I know it's my fault. I'd been so drunk the other night, I obviously told him more than I should've.

'No! Why would it be that?' I fail to keep the indignation from my voice.

'Ah, sorry – hit a nerve. Was only assuming it must be that given what you said before. And her . . . well . . . her demeanour, you know, when I was there last week. Something obviously wasn't right between you; it wasn't just a blip like you suggested.'

My face burns with shame. I hadn't meant to share Jen's blackouts, let alone any of the other stuff. The fact that Brett picked up on there being deeper problems means I couldn't have been paying close enough attention to my own marriage. Although, in all honesty, I did know the bigger picture, didn't I? I'd felt it – the shift – I'd realised Jen's blackouts had been increasing, that she was hiding something from me. But I ignored it. Swept it under the carpet rather than deal with it.

Coward.

'Yeah, well. I guess you'll find out soon enough, may as well hear it from me.'

'Shit – you've separated? I'm sorry, mate. Really.'

'It's not as simple as that, unfortunately.' I give Brett a synopsis of the situation spoken as affectlessly as if I were giving a PowerPoint presentation. After I finish, I have to check he's still on the line.

'Yeah, I'm here. Hell! I don't know what to say.'

Rendering Brett incapable of comeback is no mean feat. 'Did I do the right thing?'

'You acted, that's the main thing. You didn't sit back and let things happen *to* you. That's progress. You were thinking of your kids, man. That's noble. She'd want you to do that, really. I mean, she'll hate you for it now, sure. But, in time . . .'

She will hate me; he's right about that.

'She should've told you, mate. Simple as. Because a marriage built on a foundation of lies won't thrive.' Brett seems pleased with his words of wisdom and we chat for a bit longer. I come off the phone feeling better about my decisions. Brett's right. I did what I did for our children's sakes and that's precisely what Jenny would want me to do. It's what she'd do, too, if the roles were reversed.

I ignore Jen's voice in my head, shouting: 'Yes, but why didn't you give me the chance to explain first?' Then I try and bury the answer.

Chapter 57

JENNY

I pull my sleeves over my hands to keep warm. It's not winter, but the air in the room feels to be in the minuses. Maybe it's the frosty reception created by Harper reading the detectives my prepared statement that has caused the temperature to dip. The interview room is different to the one I found myself in yesterday – somehow, this one appears more 'serious'. Like they want me to know this is where real criminals are questioned. The starkness; its oppressively dark colour; the stale, airless quality all add to the sombre atmosphere. They want me to experience as much discomfort as possible.

They're getting their wish.

I shift on the hard chair, my bottom numb. It's been at least an hour since I was dragged in here, Harper in tow. There was no way I was speaking a word without her here now I've been arrested. She sits, her posture relaxed, glaring at the detectives. If it wasn't so intense, I might laugh. Her attitude is one of confidence verging on arrogance and I like it. After I initially answered their questions with brevity, with Davis doing her best to extract even more from me at each point, Harper advised a no-comment interview. Then she called a halt to the interview so we could 'discuss' the charges in light of the evidence disclosed. We went into another room and prepared my statement.

Since then, Davis and Bishop have taken turns playing good cop, bad cop, and I've calmly stated 'no comment' every time. Now, after Davis has asked again, albeit in a different way, how I came to be in possession of Olivia's bracelet, Harper suddenly places a hand up, sliding me a smile before leaning forwards and locking her attention onto DS Davis.

'Hold on,' she says. 'It's rather convenient, is it not, that it was my client's husband, who himself had links to the victim, who brought the bracelet – the only real evidence as far as I'm aware – to you?' Harper widens her eyes. 'You only have his word for how he came across it.' DS Talia Davis's face blanches. I see it, and Harper does too. She latches on to it immediately, pressing on. 'The mere finding of my client's fingerprints on the bracelet have, I believe, been covered in her prepared statement where she clearly states that during a routine veterinary appointment, the victim's dog became anxious and tried to flee, resulting in both the victim and my client grappling with the animal. During which time my client grasped the victim's forearm. She remembers this because she then passed comment on her bracelet, saying how pretty it was, and they had a brief conversation about it. This interaction accounts for my client's *smudged* fingerprints being lifted from the item.'

Harper flashes them a triumphant smile. Then, gathering her notepad and briefcase, she stands. 'If that's all you have, detectives, I kindly ask you release my client on bail pending your further investigations.'

Davis slams back in her chair, shooting Bishop a sideways glance. Bishop leans forwards. 'Interview suspended at eleven-thirty-six,' he says, dully into the machine before hitting the stop button. Chairs scrape as Davis and Bishop prepare to leave the room.

'Stay there,' Davis says. She doesn't make eye contact as she and Bishop stride to the door. 'We'll be back in a sec.'

Harper turns to me, a wide grin showing off her neon-white teeth. 'When you get home, make sure your husband stays away.'

'Why?'

'I think we've just made him a person of interest.'

Half an hour later, I'm in a taxi on my way home.

Chapter 58

JENNY

The sheer size of this house is daunting – being here alone with nothing but the echoes of my family is breaking me. I lie on Ella's bed, contemplating my next move. I'd like to think Mark is as innocent as he's made out. In my heart I don't believe he would be capable of harming Olivia any more than I believe I could. But when you're pushed to the limit, when the very things you hold dearest, love the most, are threatened in any way – all bets are off. Anyone is capable of hurting another human being if the right set of factors are in play. Even kind, amiable, soft-hearted Mark. If there was a risk to the children, for example, he'd act. He'd fight. He'd kill for them. I have no doubt. The fact he's taken them from me, from our family home, because he doesn't trust me with them is the worst thing, yet the best thing too.

A father who would kill for their child – that's a good father isn't it?

Only, I know that's not strictly true. My father might

not have committed murder in order to protect me, save me, or anything like that – his reasons were purely selfish. He did what he did to feed the urges; to make himself feel good. There was nothing altruistic about his actions. But in his own way, he killed to make sure he controlled himself – thereby protecting my mother and me from his evil side. In his mind, he was a good father.

As a child I thought so too. His letters said as much. I didn't read them at first. The early ones were likely destroyed by Claire before I ever set eyes on them. But then he started sending them directly to me. They remained unopened, bundled together in a pink ribbon for years. Until curiosity got the better of me. Once I began reading them, I read them over and over. I pretended I was having a conversation with him in person, replying to his words out loud. I still do that. It's a way of reconnecting with the father I once loved. I spent so much time with him as a child and would get excited each time he came home and uttered the words, 'How do you fancy coming on a little adventure with me?' It was only much later that I recalled the fear those words would cause. It was only later, in my dreams, that I revisited those dark places and relived the horrors my father referred to as adventures.

He holds Jane's hand as they trip through the field – Jane sweeps her other hand out across the wheatgrass and lets it tickle her palm. They stop once they've reached the area her father says is 'the place' – it's dark, like night. She looks skyward and sees nothing but shadows of trees. They're beneath the huge blanket of them, sheltered and invisible. Jane's heart rate races along; she knows her daddy is going to show her one of his secrets.

There's a shack ahead that looks as if it's about to fall down. He explains why this was the best place to come – how it's peaceful, and no one disturbs him here. It's near a quarry but the meadow was beautiful – filled with butterflies – painted ladies, he says. It's a special place. But more than that, he says he feels comfortable in his own skin here. Jane asks him what that means, as it's the only skin he has so how can he feel uncomfortable. He bats her question away with the wave of his hand, then lifts her up into his arms, tells her to close her eyes. She feels movement, hears crunching of leaves as he walks. Then, she's falling.

When she wakes up, she's no longer in the dark wood. There are things inside the shack – Jane's seen them before; they're familiar.

Then there's her.

She's new.

The chime of the doorbell wrenches me from a dream. Sitting bolt upright, I scramble around inside my mind for something grounding to grasp hold of. I'm on Ella's bed. I must've dropped off. I can't believe I've slept at a time like this. I spend half my nights battling to drift into unconsciousness and can't manage it; now, with my life turned upside down, I fall into a slumber. The bell rings out again, accompanied by fists banging on the wooden door. I run fingertips through my hair and dash down the stairs to open it, praying it's Mark with the kids, not the police again.

It's neither.

Nisha stands on the threshold, her face unreadable. 'Can we talk?' she says, her words staccato.

I don't say anything, but swing the door wide for her to enter.

'Coffee?' I ask, flicking the switch on the machine. 'I assume it's not a flying visit.'

'Please. Thanks.' Nisha sits, her gaze roaming the kitchen. 'Nice place.'

'Thank you. I thought you'd been here before?'

'Nope.' She eyes me suspiciously. 'First time I've ever set foot here.'

The way she holds my gaze when she states this gives me the impression there's an underlying reason for her statement. She can't be aware I had a fleeting suspicion she could be the person leaving the mutilated animals on my doorstep. Yet, it feels as though she must know *something* otherwise why make a point of saying it in the way she did. I decide to go in for the kill. Not like I have anything to lose now.

'Nish, the other day, when we were chatting in the waste room, you mislabelled the yellow tub—'.

'I lost concentration for a sec, that's all. No harm done.'

'No. But, has it happened before?'

'What, sticking the wrong label on something?'

'Have you . . . *purposely* mislabelled stuff?'

'God, no! Why would you ask that?' She sits back, her mouth slack with disbelief. Then, her eyes narrow. 'Is it Abi? She told you what happened, didn't she?' Nisha leaps up from the chair and begins pacing the tiled floor. 'I knew she went behind my back.'

The sudden shift in atmosphere is alarming. A trapped animal can become agitated, vicious if it feels threatened. It can be on the defensive – attack first to ensure it comes off better. And that's just how Nisha is acting. I need to put cold water on the flames. 'Oh, well, no – it wasn't like that, Nisha,' I say. 'No one was going behind your back or trying to get you into trouble.'

'But she told you about the tabby cat that it didn't make it to the crem?'

I tilt my head to one side. Nisha's face is flushed red, but she's gone from angry to hurt and looks as though she might cry. 'She mentioned there was an issue . . .'

'It wasn't my fault, I swear. I've no clue how it could've gone missing.'

'So, the deceased tabby is lost?'

She looks uncomfortable. 'Something went wrong. I looked everywhere.'

'You could've mislabelled the tub, like you were about to when I came in.' I try and say it gently. She's coiled so tight, she might slip back into anger at any moment.

'I didn't. I'm sure. It just . . . disappeared. I thought perhaps you might've taken it?'

Here it is. The point at which I should also come clean. I ask her to sit down, to relax, and then I tell her about the gifts being left on my doorstep. She seems genuinely shocked and is adamant she has nothing to do with it and moreover didn't even consider I had been at the vet practice after hours. My theory she was covering for me because she'd seen the CCTV was wrong. I'm not altogether convinced, though – something isn't sitting right. Is she playing games with me? I've been side-tracked too – I haven't even asked her why she turned up at my door.

'Well, we don't appear to be any further forward. By the way, what was it you came for, Nisha? I've completely dominated the conversation.'

'I was worried. The detectives took you from the practice yesterday, then Samir was beside himself this morning because they arrested you. I just wanted to check you were okay.'

'How did you know I'd be here, then? I mean, if you knew I'd been arrested.'

'Oh, I went to the station first—'

'You did what? Why?'

'Because I wanted them to know I thought they'd got the wrong person.'

'What made you so sure?'

'Oh, come on, Jen. Why would you hurt anyone? You've only ever done good; you're always the first person to help others. You don't fit the profile.'

I almost laugh, but I don't want to annoy Nisha and actually, if she's telling the truth and has nothing to do with my mutilated gifts, then I need to gather all the help and support I can get.

'Okay. But when you say "profile" what do you mean and is this just some random bunch of thoughts you've had to support your suspect list that you shared with us last week?'

She gives a shrug. 'Well, sort of, I guess. I've done a fair bit of researching since this happened, though, and I have some interesting theories about the type of person who took Olivia. And maybe it's linked to the mutilated animals – the same person could be responsible for both.'

Nisha continues to relay some things that could easily relate to me, who my father is, and the way she's looking at me with her intense dark eyes disturbs me. I still can't shake the feeling she knows something else. During her internet searches has she unwittingly uncovered my past? And now she's keeping it as a trump card.

I'm suddenly uneasy. I've invited her into my house but what if she *is* the one tormenting me? I can't say I know a lot about her or her family. I'm now keen to get her out. I shouldn't trust anyone.

Once she's left, I slump down on the sofa. Although I've been released on bail, I'm obviously Davis's key suspect. Maybe I should be trying to shine the spotlight on other people – Harper has already done a good job of directing suspicion on to Mark, but saving myself by highlighting my misgivings about Nisha could offer us both some breathing space. I don't want Mark to be hauled in for questioning; I don't want him to be involved – for the sake of our children I need to do a spot of misdirection. Plus, if Nisha has uncovered the truth about who I am, others may well have done too. Relatives of my father's victims might have found me. And what if they'd like revenge?

When I discovered the truth about what my father did, I'd read everything there was so I could try to make sense of it. And, despite putting it to the back of my mind, I know the rumours, the belief at that time, was that my father had taken me along to his crime scenes. I've suppressed the memories. Now they only seep through in nightmares. But they were right – I did witness more than was ever divulged. More than I've ever allowed myself to think about.

I'm not sure why it's important, I just sense it is. I can't stay here any longer, inactive. Being proactive is the only way I can dig myself out of this hole. Mind made up, I call another taxi. The police haven't just seized my car, they've taken my laptop and home computer, so the closest option is the library. Roisin's too far away. It'll cost me time I don't have. I need to research my father's crimes again; there's something on the edge of my memory, nudging me, but right now I can't grab a hold of it.

At the library I trawl through the immense catalogue of online articles and journal entries about Paul Slater. Even seeing his name in print causes an ache deep inside me. I find each of the five murders, scanning the details in the hope something jumps out at me. After half an hour or so, I think I've found what I'm looking for.

Whoever is responsible for Olivia's abduction, whether that really is me, someone close to me, or a relative hell-bent on revenge, I think they are following the same MO as my father.

Olivia's abduction is a copycat crime.

Chapter 59

I prop the phone up and play my recollection of our meeting back, furiously scribbling notes as my voice, fast and a little distorted, emits from it. When I finish, I sit back and imagine myself sitting opposite Paul. Relaxing now, I visualise everything about the visit. This is an important part because when I first come out from seeing him at the prison, I expel as much as I can remember about what he's spoken of – but the adrenaline is still too high, so I often forget things. I always need a quiet time of reflection to put myself back there – remember the finer details. He was on good form today – keen to talk about Jane. As long as some of it was 'off the record', he said. Just between us.

I promised I wouldn't write about the parts he didn't want me to. I didn't experience any guilt as I blatantly lied to him. None of what he's said will ever make it into print – well, not in the way he's anticipating. I wonder what he'll do once he finds out he's been duped. How he'll feel. I hope he feels stupid. Humiliated. Cheated. Inconsequential. Ordinary. All the things I feel.

'The newspapers reported where the victims had been found but police never uncovered the original killing ground; the actual place where I took their lives,' he'd said, a smug look on his face. 'As they closed in on me, they found out I'd purchased an area of land. I watched as they scoured it, laughing because they weren't even close. Not even the dogs picked up the scent.'

'You must've enjoyed that – having one up on them.'

'It was satisfying, yes.'

'You wanted them to find the dead women once you'd finished with them, wanted others to appreciate what you'd done to them, but you didn't want them to find your special place?'

'That's it, you see. It was *my* special place. Mine and Jane's. Didn't want anyone else traipsing around in there.'

'Jane went there – to the actual place you killed them?'

He hesitated, stared at me intently before replying. 'I took her a few times. She didn't know exactly where it was; I couldn't risk her knowing. They'd try and extract it from her – I knew that, so had to protect her.'

'Do you think she remembers?'

'I imagine it's somewhere in her unconscious mind, yes.'

'Do you think she ever goes back to the special place?'

'I don't know. Doubtful. It's likely collapsed by now – it's been over twenty years.'

'Collapsed?'

It was at that point the atmosphere had altered. Like Paul was fighting with himself over whether he should tell me more. Wondering if he really could trust me. I was careful not to rush him. He'd back right off if I seemed desperate to know. I'd placed my hands under my thighs to stop them fidgeting. I'd smiled, encouragingly. After a few seconds, he'd carried on.

He'd told me. I'd hit the jackpot. I could've left right then; I'd everything I needed from him. I'd never have to visit him, see his smug fucking face ever again. But something seemed to click in his brain, and he gave me a look that sent an icy chill up my spine.

'You seem very interested in Jane,' he'd said, his eyes boring into mine. 'I thought you were coming here for me.'

'I guess I'm a little jealous, that's all.'

'Oh? Jealous of what?'

'Of how much you love her. How much Claire loves her. Apparently, she's never stopped trying to find Jane.'

'Claire smothered that child. She wasn't meant to be a mother – didn't have the instinct, anyone could see that. It's no surprise to me Jane left her as soon as she could. I was the one who made sure their relationship was satisfactory, so once I was out of the picture, there was no one to step in. I bet Claire made her life a living hell.'

'Maybe you're wrong – it looked to me like Claire loved your daughter very much. She was everything to Claire after you left. All she had. Can you blame your wife for latching on to the only good thing remaining in her life?'

'I guess not. But too much love can be suffocating, can't it?'

'I wouldn't know.'

I get up now and walk to the kitchen, pulling open the fridge. I gulp cold wine straight from the bottle, all the while knowing full well that getting drunk won't numb the pain.

It's galling knowing how much she's loved, how special she was and still is. It took me every ounce of self-control to remain calm when Paul was talking about her, not to shout in his stupid face. Why did she deserve it all? She didn't even care. She never visited him. She isn't dealing with any of the fallout of her decision to turn her back on everything, run away from the past. All that love and she ignored it, choosing to leave it all behind. She didn't give a damn about the victims' families, the trauma they faced daily. She didn't have to witness it all because she'd started afresh – pretending none of it happened.

But now I know what it was that she ran from. What she's been hiding all her life. And I bet aside from her and Paul, I'm the only other person who does.

Jennifer Johnson has been inside her father's killing ground. And I know just what to do with this information.

Chapter 60

JENNY

My mind whirrs as I gaze out of the rear window of the taxi on the way back home. Images and memories collide and explode like fireworks in my head. I'm not sure where to go next, who to turn to. As I've shared so much with Roisin, it makes sense to speak with her about my latest findings. Plus, I really should tell her about the arrest. Switching my attention from the scenery to my mobile, I tap on Roisin's name and listen to the ringing tone drone on.

'Come on, come on,' I mutter. My hands grip the phone as I silently plead for her to pick up. I really don't want to have to leave a message.

'Jen, good timing,' Roisin says, out of breath. 'I've just . . . got back . . . was going to call you.'

I wait for her to regain her composure before speaking. The driver is on a call of his own, a woman's voice blaring out of the hands-free, so hopefully he won't be listening in. 'I beat you to it – I've had the mother of all days so far. I was wondering if we could meet for a chat.'

'Yes, definitely. I've been doing some further investigation

– I've gone full-on private investigator – and there's something I think you should see in person anyway. I've got to pop out again now, but can you be here for seven? If Mark is okay with looking after the kids.'

I humph loudly down the phone. 'He's got the kids at his parents' place. I'll explain all when I see you.'

'Oh, that sounds a little ominous. Okay, hon, I'll see you soon.' There's a pause before she adds, 'Take care, Jen, won't you.' Then she's gone. I glance at the time display. I've got just over two hours. Time to get home, reread my letters – the ones Mark and the police didn't find – and make a plan.

The driver drops me at the top of my drive and I tap the reader with my card to pay him.

'Can I book you again, for around six-thirty?'

'You'll have to call the office to book, love. Do it nice and early; we get a flurry around teatime.'

'Okay, thanks,' I say, climbing out. I don't go inside the house; instead, I rush to the shed, go inside, unhook the shovel, then go out and around the back of it. There's a gap big enough for me to walk behind and it's here I dig. It's not long before the shovel hits against something solid. Not bothered now about getting dirty, I drop to my knees and scoop earth with my hands. A rotten smell hits me and I rear back, covering my nose.

'Oh, God!' For a moment, confusion invades my mind along with the stench, then I realise what it is.

I don't understand.

A bin liner, half opened, lies close to the top of the hole. The hole *I* dug when we first moved in. No one but me knows about it, I'm certain. So, I must've buried this bin liner. But when?

Holding my breath, I carefully take hold of the liner and pull it out, placing it beside the mound of earth while I retrieve what I came for. I lift the metal box from its grave and set it down. The last time I recall digging the box up to read the letters it contains was last year. The bin liner has been placed on top, and now, as I dare peek inside, I realise the remains of the dead rabbit are relatively fresh. Put here, I'd guess, within the last two weeks.

If I've done this, it must've been during a blackout as I have no recollection of it.

Could this be what I was doing the night Olivia was taken? When I awoke, cold and dirty, my pyjamas stained with wet earth, mud embedded under my nails – had I been digging to bury the mutilated animal? It doesn't make sense I would go to the lengths of burying it if I had been the one who'd taken the animal and left it on my own doorstep. But even more doubtful is the likelihood I'd bury it here, in my special place – where I keep the things I want to remain private. Unless I knew, even in my trance state, that I would eventually uncover it. Was I leaving a clue to my conscious self?

If I'm not the one doing this, why was I at the practice the night before finding one of these gifts? I saw myself getting out of the car on the vet CCTV – it has to be me.

My heart jolts.

I close my eyes tightly as I play over the footage in my head. I watched my car pull in, but the driver's side door was out of shot. The car jostled as a person got out. I'd immediately made the assumption it must've been me. But I *didn't* see myself.

What if someone else drove my car there?

Chapter 61

JENNY

All this time I've been fraught with worry that it was me. It was the obvious conclusion given it was my car I spotted. But Mark has access to it. He could've easily taken it that night while I was in the throes of a blackout. So, I'm back to suspecting my husband has something to do with all of this. I'm not the only one, though – even Harper overtly put him in the frame when talking to Davis and Bishop.

I keep coming back to the same question, though. *Why* would he be doing this? There's nothing other than my original ridiculous thought of them being in this together, which I can bring to mind that would make for a plausible reason. I need to get this clear in my head. No one else could've taken my car keys. Unless they have their own set. Is it possible to get a car key cut as easily as you can a house key? If someone had access to my car, they could've used it to abduct Olivia and transport her to where they're hiding her. Her DNA will be found in my car and I can't prove I wasn't the one who took her. My only way out of this is to find the real culprit myself.

A memory flashes through my mind – a flashback to seeing the scene of one of the murders.

It's not a shack I was in.

The realisation comes to me, like a wave crashing over my head. The first time I'd been there I'd blacked out, didn't remember all the details. Then, the other time, Dad blindfolded me, lifted me into his arms and carried me in.

Then down.

My God. We went *under* the ground.

The fact I hide things in a shed, and also bury secrets under the ground, means I'm like him. Or, at least, I've unconsciously picked things up from him. The closer I get to the truth of what's happening, the more afraid I'm becoming. I think I'm being set up. The real perpetrator of this crime, the copycat, wants me to believe it could be me – and certainly wants the police to believe it. I need to figure this out before Davis and Bishop build their case against me. I'm assuming that while I might be on bail, it can be revoked if they come to believe I'm a risk to the public. I might not have a lot of time to prove my innocence and give them reason to suspect someone else.

If the person leaving the dead animals is on to me – who I am – and they know more about me, my father, and his crimes than I realise, then it's likely the culprit took Olivia too. That everything is linked. Like Nisha said earlier. And a true copycat would want to replicate as much of the original crimes as possible. I've tried so hard over the years to forget what I saw. I've done a good job and for the life of me, I can't remember enough detail despite my flashback. I wouldn't be able to hazard a guess where to start looking for Olivia.

The letters.

Finding the final letter he sent me, I carefully reread it. He had owned the land where the women's bodies were discovered. He'd bought it back when he and Mum first married because he knew he'd need to continue his 'hobby' undetected. That's why he felt safe there. But he hadn't taken any chances. He'd dug underground – made his own lair a good distance away from the location he left his victims to be found.

So, where would the copycat take Olivia?

Then it dawns on me. The area of land the vet practice is situated on belongs to me and Samir. It's about fifty acres, mainly woodland. There was a heavy police presence in the surrounding fields but I'm betting they hadn't banked on there being any kind of structure *below* ground level where she could be well hidden. The initial searches would likely have been focusing on sightings of Olivia – or her body – and maybe clothing. I shudder. If this is a true copycat crime, they would certainly be looking at replicating the location type. I wonder if I'm too late – whether Olivia's already dead.

No. That's not how my father worked, though. He played with them first, toying with them. The news articles I've just read mentioned the women had been missing up to nine days before they were found. Once he'd 'made them perfect' he wanted people to see his handiwork, so he'd moved the body from the murder scene to a different location nearby. He wanted the glory, so he'd leave the women somewhere easy to find. As Olivia hasn't been discovered yet, I'm hoping that's a good sign.

The perpetrator hasn't finished yet.

But time is running out.

Chapter 62

JENNY

Blood pounds through my body, the sound thumping in my ears. I'm taking a huge risk, but it's all I can think to do. As I rush into Ella's room, a moment of panic grips me, stopping me in my tracks. What if I don't see my children again? If I can't clear my name, my fate might be the same as my father's. I force the thought away as I grab Ella's rucksack from under her bed. I tip it upside down, the contents spewing onto her bed, and run back downstairs with it.

I jam in a torch, hat and pair of gloves, then go back to the shed, unhook a trowel from the wall rack and put that inside too. It's not exactly fit for purpose, but it's better than nothing and less conspicuous than a shovel. I hesitate, my teeth chattering, but not from the cold. My only plan is to go to the vet practice and begin walking through the field to the woodland, to the densest part. It's a big area, I've no clue where to start, really. I could spend hours searching and find nothing. I need help. Not

317

only to be another pair of eyes, but someone to provide a certain level of safety. It's irresponsible of me to go it alone. If something happens to me, I'd be leaving my children behind. I make one of the quickest decisions I've ever made. There's only one person I trust who I know will also be ready and willing to help at this short notice.

'Hey,' I say down the phone. 'You know you said you take every opportunity to be out of your flat?'

'Yeees,' Abi says, her tone cautious.

'Well, how do you fancy coming on a little . . . adventure with me?' I say. A cold fist clamps around my heart as the words leave my mouth. My father used to utter the exact same phrase. I shake off the uneasy feeling as I continue to tell Abi to wrap up warm, wear walking boots and bring a torch and that I'll meet her at the vets' in twenty minutes.

'Sure. I'll see you there.' The line goes dead. Bubbles of adrenaline pop in my veins. Finally, I'm acting. I can't sit back and allow things to happen to me; I must take control.

I pull my bike from the garage and walk it to the end of the drive. Then, backpack on, I begin cycling up the hill. I reach the vet car park within ten minutes and prop my bike against the far wall, then jump up onto it to await Abi. The thought I'm playing with fire crosses my mind. If something were to happen, no one would know where I am. Which means I'm also putting Abi at risk. My desire to act right at this moment is born from selfishness, a need for self-preservation. I consider calling Abi back, telling her it's a waste of time and suggest going for a drink instead. But the other side of me, dismisses my concern.

I remember that I'm meant to be going to Roisin's. I check the time on my mobile. I'm never going to make our arrangement. I'm about to ring her, when I see Abi walk around the corner. She's dressed in a duffel coat, with a quirky bobble hat. She has walking boots on. Good, she took my instruction and came prepared. I jump off the wall, fling the backpack over my shoulder and rush towards her.

'Thank you for coming out on my whim. Where's your car?'

'Got a taxi, thought it might look odd parking in here at night.'

'I hadn't thought of that. Look, I know things have been a bit . . . mad . . . around here. I'm so, so sorry, Abi. You must be wondering what on earth you've got yourself into.'

'Honestly? This is the most excitement I've had in my life. Bring it on.' She links arms with me and drags me towards the field.

'Oh, hang on. I'm not sure where—'

'This is the way you came before,' Abi says, her eyes narrowing. 'You know – when you drove here in the dead of night?'

I look at her blankly for a moment, then realise she's seen the CCTV too. That's obviously why she thought it'd look odd her parking here. 'Right,' I say, deciding there's no point saying more, or sharing my suspicion that it wasn't me who drove the car that night. We walk on, a steely sense of purpose in our strides.

Chapter 63

MARK

The kids are subdued; they know something is wrong. I can't lie to them. It's not fair. Together with my parents we sit in the lounge while I tell them we're staying here for a while, until the police don't need Mummy's help anymore. If it comes to the worst-case scenario and Jen is convicted of Olivia's abduction – and I try not to let myself go there, but inevitably my mind does – her murder, I'll have to re-evaluate what to tell them.

After they've bathed and got into bed, I get a call from Roisin. No doubt she's heard about Jen's arrest.

'Mark,' she says, 'I can't get hold of Jen and she was meant to come to mine for seven. Is she okay?'

'I'm sorry, Roisin. I should've called before. Jen's been arrested.'

'What? Again?'

'The detectives went to the vets' this morning and—'

'No, no. I spoke to her late this afternoon, Mark. She called to arrange to see me. *What* is going on?'

I stutter and stall, confusion whipping any words from my mouth. If they released her, why didn't Talia Davis inform me? I take in a slow, juddering breath.

'Look, I'm not even sure what's happening, Roisin.' I sit heavily on the chair, struggling to make sense of this. 'Literally everything has gone haywire. I've left with the kids, for the minute at least, until . . .'

'I know. She told me when I mentioned you looking after the kids while she came to mine.' I hear Roisin let out a slow sigh. 'Why, Mark?'

'I can't trust her. I mean, for Christ's sake, I've found out so much she's kept from me for our entire bloody marriage. Did *you* know, Roisin? Am I the only one in the dark about who my wife really is?'

'She's who she's always been, Mark. And no, actually, she didn't tell me directly. That's fine by me. Her childhood is in the past – it doesn't define her. Her father's crimes aren't hers.'

'I'm not so sure about that.'

'Do the police know about your history, Mark?' My jaw slackens, unsure if this is a simple passing question, or whether there's meaning behind it. She can't know about what happened when I was at uni – the stupid mistake I made; Brett's supposed prank that went so wrong. But, she does have a point. I've never spoken about it, only Brett knows and I certainly didn't share it with Jen, much less the police. As if she's reading my mind, she continues, 'Aren't there things you've done you try and forget about? Jen didn't do anything wrong. She was treated badly; she was used. But she escaped that life and built a better one. She's a good mother. She was a good wife until you cheated.'

322

'I didn't mean to cheat.'

'Ah, yes . . . it just happened, I know.' Roisin's condescending tone fills my ears. 'You said it was a one-night stand, but you had a connection with Olivia, didn't you? It doesn't take a genius to work that out. And Jen told me she went to bed leaving you downstairs the night of Olivia's abduction. You'd been drinking. She didn't tell the police that. She was loyal. Remember that.'

I know I deserve this verbal assault and I sit back and take what she's dishing out, an overwhelming sense of guilt surging through me.

'I admit, I can't recall with any degree of certainty what I, or Jen, did that night. But you're right. She didn't let me down like I have her.'

'You can make it up to her. We need to find her because I have a nasty feeling she's taking matters into her own hands.'

Chapter 64

JENNY

We've climbed over stiles, wound through kissing gates, and trekked across fields and so far, I've seen nothing to suggest a place the copycat could be utilising to hide Olivia.

'It's almost ten,' I say. 'Maybe it's time to call it quits. It's too dark.'

'I don't think we should give up yet. You said you thought time was running out, that Olivia's life was in real danger.' I've given Abi a quick precis of my father's crimes as we've walked and, although shocked, she took it extremely well. Something tells me she thinks it's cool that I have a serial killer for a father.

'But maybe I should be leaving this to the police,' I say.

'They aren't exactly doing a good job, though, are they? I mean, so far they've arrested an innocent woman and failed to find another.'

I appreciate Abi's loyalty, her undeterred faith in me and her belief that I'm not involved in Olivia's abduction.

But I can't help wondering if she'd be as certain if she were in possession of all the facts. Being I need all the support I can get, I decide now isn't the time to arm her with them all. 'True. They haven't exactly filled people with confidence. God knows what poor Olivia's family are going through. Must be torture.'

'I still haven't managed to get it out my head.'

'What?'

'Nisha saying she thinks Olivia's dad is acting weird. That he's got something to do with it. Poor bloke – who wouldn't act weird with their daughter missing, presumed dead?'

'Well, quite. But let's not say *presumed dead*, shall we?' A shiver tracks up my back, and I rub the back of my neck.

'You know it's unlikely she'll be found alive though, right?'

I swallow hard, but the lump in my throat prevents me from answering.

We walk on in silence for a moment, carefully stepping over the uneven ground. We approach the back part of our land that adjoins the old quarry. This is the perimeter of what we own, so I don't think going beyond this point will be worthwhile. If the copycat is following my father's MO, he won't encroach on land that doesn't belong to me. If they're intent on framing me, it has to be on my property that Olivia's body is found. But the fact there's a disused quarry nearby does make my palms sweat. I remember there being a quarry where my father took me. Near to where he kept his victims – a detail that was stated in various news articles too. And there was a meadow. Not only do I recall walking through it, but I also remember Dad telling me that the painted lady butterflies live in open meadows. I cast my torch around. It doesn't shine far into the distance, but it's enough to illuminate a field ahead.

Perhaps I'm close.

'I think you should get back home, Abi. I've dragged you too far into my mess. I'll head off home too, pick this up again tomorrow when we've got light on our side.'

'I'm not leaving you here alone, Jenny. It's far too dangerous.'

'Honestly, I'll call it quits tonight too. I'm sorry for dragging you out in the cold for nothing.'

'It's not for nothing though, is it!' She stops dead in her tracks and turns to face me, shining her torch up so I can see her. 'It's life or death, Jenny.'

The intensity of her words jabs, like knives, at my gut and the added creepiness of her pale face illuminated harshly by the torch is unnerving. A moment ago, she was convinced we were looking for a body – a salvage mission not a recovery one – but I don't point that out. I want to think on the positive side. I need to. I don't want to even contemplate not finding Olivia alive.

'Are we going deeper into the woods?' Abi nudges me out of my thoughts. 'Or shall we go this way?' She indicates towards an area that seems as though a path has been forged by previous footsteps, then moves in that direction. I look that way, then to the dense woodland she shone her torch towards first. I weigh up the options.

'I think we should retrace our steps,' I say. 'We should go back the way we came. I'm worried we'll get lost out here, Abi. Then there'll be three missing women. I don't think the police will be impressed.'

Abi looks at me, disappointment etched on her face. She gives a shrug. 'Sure. You're probably right. Shame we didn't find anything though. Had a good feeling we would.' She gazes into the trees, her torchlight catching a hedgehog rustling through the leaves at the same time as an owl screeches. We both jump, the beam of light leaping before settling back on the ground.

I squint, thinking I see something, but Abi swings the torch away and points it back down the way we came. 'Bloody hell. Okay, let's go, then.' We laugh at our jitteriness. If we're skittish over a few nocturnal creatures, imagine if we found a body. An image forces itself into my mind. Pallid skin, dead eyes staring at me. Purplish hands lying limp on the ground. I've already seen dead bodies; I should know what to expect. Would I be shocked if I saw Olivia's body?

I very much hope I would.

Chapter 65

With Paul's help, I've pieced it all together. I'm confident that with what I now know, I'll be able to create the perfect crime. There's much more to do, though. This is just the background research. Part one of the plan. Initially, I considered this to be the most difficult part – having to see Paul Slater and act like I cared about his story, about him, was challenging. But as I'm coming to realise, the hard work begins now. Because next, I have to use what I know to get to Jane – aka Jennifer. Timing is going to be tricky. It'll all have to align to make the evidence against her compelling.

I can't rush this part. Patience is everything.

'Rome wasn't built in a day', as my mother likes to say.

Chapter 66

JENNY

It's gone eleven by the time we get back to the vet car park. Abi calls for a taxi. I say I'll wait with her until it arrives. I want to make sure she's in it, and on her way before I go back.

'Thanks, Abi. I can't stress enough how much it means to me that you were willing to come here and help me. Especially given I'm the prime suspect!'

'Oh, God, Jenny. You don't think I'd believe that nonsense, do you?'

'Well,' I say, sucking in breath. 'You saw the CCTV footage . . .'

'Yeah, but I also know there's odd stuff going on with a few other people, too. It's not just you acting a bit . . . *off*, is it?' She raises her eyebrows. I'm guessing she's referring to Nisha again.

'I think this whole thing has made everyone act a little weird. If we're going by that, each and every one of us looks guilty. Nisha's just, well, *invested* in the case, that's all. It's because she's literally so close to it.' I'm not sure if I'm trying to convince Abi or myself.

'Maybe.'

I've clearly not convinced Abi of Nisha's innocence. But if Abi knows my car was here in the early hours of the morning, why doesn't she suspect me as much as she does Nisha? I'm about to ask, but a car pulls up at the entrance to the car park.

'That's my ride,' Abi says.

'Thanks again, Abi. Try and get some sleep.'

'Doubt that'll happen – I'm far too pumped. Might do some research instead – see if I can dig up anything useful.'

'Okay. Thanks. Keep me posted. I won't be sleeping much either.'

Abi gives me a brief hug, then walks across to the waiting car.

Once her taxi is out of sight and I can't hear it anymore, I take my torch out of the rucksack and head back into the woods. When Abi's torchlight was waving wildly around the last area we were standing in, I thought I saw something. The need to check it out overrides my need to go home. Having already put Abi through enough tonight, I was reluctant to extend the night search. However much she said she was up for it, and did seem disappointed not to find anything, I'm sure coming across a body would've floored her. The fact that I brought a twenty-year-old on my mission finally rings alarm bells. My mental state has obviously reached saturation point if I willingly put her life at risk. I have to do this next bit alone.

I follow the line of the quarry, along the perimeter until I reach the point we had stopped to turn back. Abi had suggested following where footprints had flattened a path, rather than deeper into the woods – and I'm now at the spot where she'd swung her torch towards the trees. My legs ache from the cycling and all the walking. The tremor in my muscles is violent as I make my way over the rough ground, my feet faltering on raised tree roots, vines and slimy leaves. Exhaustion has caught up with me.

I stumble, my upper body lurching forwards as my foot makes contact with something hard. I yelp out in shock as I crash into a tree. What did I trip on? Gathering myself, I brush bark off my coat and shine the light over the raised part of ground. My breath stops before I can expel it, trapped in my lungs. Ducking down, I extend a shaky hand out to touch the funnel-type protrusion jutting from the ground.

This is the place – I feel it in my gut.

Getting the trowel from my rucksack, I dig around, removing the leaves and loose earth to uncover a large ring. It's attached to a wooden trapdoor in the ground. Adrenaline fires through my veins. Is it an old air raid shelter? There have been numerous findings in the area over the years, but I wasn't aware of one here in the woodland. Unless it's something to do with the quarry as it's so close. I don't recall seeing it on the map. How would someone know this was here? Yet, even as I think it's unlikely, at the same time I know in my heart that it has to be where Olivia is being kept captive.

But, is she alive down there?

My instinct tells me to leave, go straight to the police to inform them of my finding. Because if I go any further, open the hatch and climb inside, not only am I putting my life in danger, but I could also be ending any hope Olivia has of being saved too.

I want to bang my fists on the wood, yell down the funnel, which I can only assume is acting as an air vent ensuring Olivia gets enough oxygen to live for however long he has planned. If he's down there with her right at this moment, though, me making a noise, alerting him to my presence, would spell disaster. I must think this through. If I were to storm the killing ground, I'd be leaving my DNA all over the place. I don't need any further 'evidence' levelled against me.

Retracing my steps, I wait until I'm almost back at the car park before placing a call to DS Davis, asking her to meet me here. I hear a mix of excitement and trepidation in her voice when I relay what I think I've found and share that I think someone is trying to frame me by hiding Olivia on my land. She says she's on her way, with the 'appropriate' backup.

Whatever's lying under the ground waiting, I need her to be with me when we uncover it.

Chapter 67

JENNY

Appropriate backup entails a number of police vehicles, a fire engine and an ambulance. I watch in silence as the vet car park fills up and Talia Davis exits her car and strides towards me. She's dressed for the event – a thick, padded jacket, boots and torch in hand. There's no sign of Bishop.

'Right,' she says as she reaches me. 'I've kept this low-key for now.'

I widen my eyes. If this is low-key, I'd hate to see over-the-top. 'Sure,' I say. 'Thanks for coming, Detective Sergeant Davis.' I shift my weight from one foot to the other and keep doing it. The detective gives me a cautious glance and, realising I'm coming across as edgy, like I'm guilty of something, I consciously force my feet to still. 'It's cold, isn't it?' I say, giving a nervous cough. She doesn't respond, checking her radio's working and clicking her torch on and off instead.

'Depending on what, if anything, we find, I don't want

too much attention. It's why there's no flashing lights, no helicopters. I certainly don't need the press getting hold of this yet,' she says, her eyes blazing. 'I assume you've only told us of your finding?'

For a split second, I panic. Should I mention that I brought Abi here? But we didn't find anything then – Abi knows nothing about this, so I think I'm in the clear. 'No, just you, Detective Sergeant Davis,' I say confidently.

'Good. Oh, and, for tonight, just call me Talia instead of that mouthful.'

'Okay.' I nod and look around the car park. 'How come Detective Bishop isn't tagging along?'

'For now, I don't need him. I don't want the scene trampled over by loads of clumsy feet before I know what we're dealing with, so it's the bare minimum to start with.'

It makes sense, but I get the impression she's holding something back. I wonder if Bishop has been sent elsewhere and is awaiting Talia's instruction to move in on another suspect. God, I hope so. I really need to be off the hook on this one.

'Right, sure. It's pretty uneven ground in places; dark too.'

Talia looks skyward. 'At least there's a full moon,' she says, raising her eyebrows. 'Apt,' she adds, quietly, before turning towards an approaching uniformed officer. They exchange a few words and then she tells me that PC Jordain is the only other officer coming with us at this point. I offer a nod of acknowledgement. Jordain, standing with his feet apart, both thumbs hooked in his vest, gives me the briefest of smiles. Anxiety ripples through my already queasy stomach.

With her radio attached to her jacket, Talia follows my

lead as we trudge through fields and woodland, PC Jordain staying a distance behind. Our torchlights bob and with the moon high above casting a good glow, our path is relatively easy. I've a new-found energy now I have her with me. However, my confidence wanes as we approach the location where I believe Olivia is being held. What if I'm wrong? If this is merely an old shelter and it's empty, I have nothing. And no solid leads as to what's going on or who's responsible. Only gut feelings and possibilities. Dragging Talia Davis and the emergency services out here for no reason won't go down well at all. It won't put me on any better footing with the detectives and, in fact, I'll probably make myself an even stronger prime suspect in their eyes.

The heavy darkness is oppressive as we reach the spot where I tripped on the funnel, the canopy of trees blocking the moon's illumination. I explain to Talia how I found it, and what it led me to believe given my father's MO.

Talia puts her ear to the funnel, then moves to the hatch, which I left partially covered with leaves. She sweeps the remaining leaves from it with one swift arm movement and again puts her ear to the wood and listens. I hold my breath.

'Get back, please,' she says, waving her arm at me. I do as she says, looking around to see where officer Jordain is. I can make out his silhouette moving slowly through the trees as he follows our path. I understand the reasoning behind not disturbing evidence, but I'd have thought he and the rest of the team wouldn't be far behind. Just in case.

I turn back to see Talia, who is snapping on a pair of gloves. She grabs hold of the metal ring and begins pulling. It doesn't give and I'm itching to rush to her side to help.

'Er . . . can I at least—'

Talia cranes her neck to check where her colleague is before resuming her task, a steely look of determination on her face, while I imagine my own shows a mixture of frustration and impatience. He seems to have taken her too much at her word, though, and is hanging back so far that he can't see her looking for his help.

'Okay, you'll have to give me a hand,' she says through gritted teeth, her body arched back with the strain of pulling. I don't need to be asked twice. I tread carefully over to the hatch. Talia stops pulling and stands upright, unzipping her pocket.

'Here,' she says, handing me some gloves. The tremor in my fingers makes it difficult to feed them into the tight latex material and it takes several attempts. Then, as Talia retakes her position, I crouch down and push my fingertips between the crack of the wooden hatch and earth to help lever it up. A rush of air presses itself into my face and I gasp. There's a musty, unpleasant smell. Talia's breaths are laboured after the sustained pulling, but she's quick to recover.

'Okay, you can go back there now.' She points her torch towards the line of trees where Jordain is presumably standing. Tension tightens every muscle. The anticipation of what's to come is so great I feel I might snap.

Officer Jordain calls across to ask if she requires assistance. Talia rejects his offer, muttering something about 'too little, too late'.

'You aren't going to go down alone, are you?' I frown. 'Surely he should go with you?' I tilt my chin towards Jordain. She really is taking the no trampling by 'loads of clumsy feet' thing seriously, which makes me question why I've even been allowed this close.

Talia shakes her head. 'I'm good. Just, please, Jenny. Keep back, eh? I know what I'm doing.'

'Sure. Sorry.' With legs trembling, I take a few steps back. My heel catches in a tree root and I almost lose balance. Talia's attention is elsewhere now, so I stop where I am – still close enough to rush to her side if needed – positioned between her and the other officer. I glance in his direction, but his focus is on his torch; the beam of light is flickering like lightning. He mutters to himself as he repeatedly taps it. The fractured light catches the trees, sending ominous, creepy shadows into the night. A violent shiver judders my body and I wrap my arms around myself.

'Hello, is anyone down there?' Talia shouts into the void. The only other noises I can hear are woodland animals and crunching leaves. She calls down again, but there's no sound. No movement. Talia turns to me and in my torchlight, I catch her lowered eyebrows and tight lips. She thinks I've brought her on a wild goose chase.

'She might be unconscious?' I whisper. The real thought – 'she might be dead' – isn't one I dare say out loud.

'I'm going down,' Talia says matter-of-factly, then sighs deeply. 'If you promise to do as I instruct, and nothing more, then you can come here and hold the hatch for me.'

Glad to be doing something, I walk to her and grip the hatch tightly with my still-gloved hand, internally begging to God that Olivia is not only down there, but alive. Talia turns to me, her expression neutral. 'Will the hatch stay open?'

I push it back, as far as it'll go. It might stay open, but to be sure, I get up and hunt for a branch to wedge it.

Giving a nod of approval, Talia swings her legs over the hole in the ground and shines her torch down. 'There are steps,' she says and without another word, drops down. My heart stutters as I envisage her falling. But she immediately calls up to me as she descends. 'There's something down here.'

Then, for what feels like an hour, there's no more communication.

Then I hear a crackling. It's Talia's radio. She's giving instructions to whoever is on the other end. I turn sharply to see where officer Jordain is but he's moved from where he was. Talia's head pops back up; her breathing is shallow and rapid.

Shit, shit, shit.

She's found Olivia's body.

'What is it? Is she there? Is she *alive*?'

As Talia hauls herself out of the hole, she shakes her head. 'Back right up now, Jenny. This is officially a crime scene and I can't have you near it. Thanks for leading me here – the others are coming now, one of them will escort you back to the car park.'

'You . . . have to . . . tell me.' My words stick in my throat; I can't swallow.

Talia places her hands on my shoulders, gently pushing me back. 'Let us deal with this from here.' She turns away, her flashlight rhythmically waving to indicate our position and I glimpse Jordain leading others this way.

A sudden bolt of adrenaline shoots through me and I run. I don't care if I'm about to disturb a crime scene – I have to see this for myself. I hear Talia's stern voice yell 'no', but I'm already inside.

It is some kind of bunker. I think I was right about it

being an old air raid shelter. My torchlight illuminates something pale, naked.

Olivia is propped up against the side of the metal interior, tied, gagged, her head lolling forward.

Lifeless.

'Oh, God – no.'

Talia rushes at me, grabbing my arms. 'You can't be down here!'

'I'm too late,' I say, tears clouding my vision. 'I didn't figure it out soon enough.' My words sound strange to my ears: distant, distorted. Like someone else is speaking them from under water. An image juts into my mind – mottled skin, a body propped up but sagging in the middle, hair limply hanging forwards. My legs give and I feel Talia's hands under my arms, stopping me from falling to the ground.

'For Christ's sake,' she mutters. 'I need help in here.' I hear her shout, then a buzzing in my ears takes over before everything goes black.

Chapter 68

JENNY

The next thing I know, I'm on the back seat of a police car, a blanket wrapped around me.

My eyelids are heavy, my head woozy following my faint. Or blackout. I'm not sure which, but it took me back to when I was with my dad in his underground hideaway – the overwhelming pressure in my head, the heaviness in my legs. The smell.

'I need to be sick,' I say, clawing at the car door. 'Quick.' The policeman scrambles out of the front and opens the door in time for me to vomit on the ground. Hot bile burns my throat. So many questions buzz around in my head, but I'm retching too much to ask a single one. The policeman, young, inexperienced by what I've gathered, politely averts his gaze while I continue to spit green liquid onto the gravel of the car park. He's staying close, though, like he's in charge of me. Am I under arrest? I'm in the back of a police vehicle following the discovery of Olivia Edwards' body, and I'm a person of interest at the very least. I put my fingertips to my stinging eyelids, pressing hard to prevent the tears escaping. Is this nightmare ever going to end?

Wiping my mouth with the edge of the blanket, I sit back in the car.

'Do you want some water?' he asks, turning back now to face me.

'Please,' I rasp. He closes my door and returns to the driver's seat, grabbing a bottle from the glove compartment.

'Here you go.' He hands it to me. 'Must be a shock—'

'A shock? I'd say. I really thought I might be in time . . .' I sip the water, afraid too much will start me off being sick again.

'What do you mean?' he says, his brow furrowed.

'I thought I'd worked it out in time to save her. Am I under arrest?'

He stares at me, his expression inscrutable. Frustration bubbles, but I don't have the energy to press him further. If I don't ask questions, I can put off the inevitable for longer. My head is heavy, and I let it loll against the window. As I do, I catch a flurry of movement. I sit bolt upright, all queasiness evaporating.

'Is that . . . is that her?' I stare, wide-eyed out the back window, where I see a waiting ambulance admitting a stretcher. Not a body bag. 'But, I saw her. She was dead. Talia said . . .'

'DS Davis thought the worst when she first approached the woman, but her fears were misplaced as it goes. You must've missed it. On account of your faint, like.'

'Oh, thank God!' I slump back against the leather interior and close my eyes. She's alive. We did it. We found her. Sheer relief floods my body, making me feel weak. For a split second, a surge of hope wells inside me as I think things might now get back to normal. Then I remember. Nothing will be the same after all of this, even if Olivia has been found alive. The policeman's voice breaks my thoughts as he tells me DS Davis is heading over.

Talia opens my door and ducks down.

'How are you doing?'

'Better, thanks. Now I know Olivia's okay.'

'She's unconscious, though – so not fully out of the woods,' Talia says, then rolls her eyes. 'So to speak.' I give a half-hearted smile, which fades instantly when I realise what that means. If Olivia's been unable to tell police exactly what happened, then this still isn't anywhere near over.

'I really thought she was gone. Seeing her there like that, she looked just like . . .' I stop myself from finishing the sentence and look up at Talia's face. Her usual bright olive tone seems washed out, her eyes heavy. The dwindling adrenaline after such a rush no doubt having an effect.

'You weren't alone,' she says.

My legs, and stomach, are stronger now and I get out of the car, leaving the blanket on the back seat. Talia tells me that it took almost all the crew to get Olivia out of the underground shelter and as I watch the paramedic slam the ambulance door, I can't help but wonder how the perpetrator would've done it alone. If he was planning on killing Olivia down there, getting her dead body to the upper ground would surely be too difficult for one person. Yet, my dad did it. I suppose now, in this case, they were transporting a live woman and were concerned about her wellbeing, whereas my father didn't have to worry about handling his victim safely. Whoever's done this likely didn't plan to worry about it either if the end result was supposed to be Olivia's death.

I make my way across the car park, Talia close behind, and lean against the vet practice wall. We both follow the ambulance's progression as it drives slowly out.

'Odd, really, isn't it?' Talia pipes up.

'Which bit?'

'How you were suddenly able to find her, where all of us have failed,' Talia says. She purses her lips, letting the words hang in the space between us. I should've guessed she'd be suspicious of how I found her. It does seem coincidental. But does she *really* think I'm the culprit after all? Perhaps she believes I thought Olivia was already dead, and that's why I led her to the location. Talia eyes me cautiously. My mouth is dry again and I wish I'd brought the bottle of water with me. I don't have the energy to explain it all, yet I know I must.

'I followed my father's lead,' I say.

'He's in prison, Jenny. It's not as though it's him doing this, is it.'

'No. But someone is copying his crimes. It's what brought me here.'

Talia stares at me for a moment longer; I can sense her weighing me up. She's contemplating whether *I* am the copycat. Until Olivia regains consciousness and can tell them exactly what happened, I'm not any better off than before. I'm still far from being off the suspect list. At least Olivia is alive, though. Her family will have her back. It's the best outcome and given how things are going, it's a damn lucky one.

'Might be a good idea to keep this under wraps for

now,' Talia says. 'I don't want to go public yet. I'd appreciate it if you didn't share any of tonight's developments with a soul. You understand? Leave telling the world – and more specifically, the copycat – that Olivia's been found alive. We could use this information to our advantage.'

'What makes you think this will draw him out? Maybe he was planning on leaving her there until she died and so he won't come back here at all.'

'That's a possibility.' Talia's forehead creases, and almost to herself she says, 'If they were trying to make sure you went down for this, they're not likely to risk going back to the shelter I suppose.' She places her hand on my arm, gently guiding me towards my bike. 'Anyway, I'll drop you home before I head to the hospital.'

'No, it's fine. I'll cycle. I need my bike at my house, seeing as I have no car.'

'Really? After all that's happened tonight?' Talia gives a wry smile. She's still cautious. I imagine her detective mind is walking through *all* the possibilities in her head, not just the one where I've been framed.

'It's mostly downhill from here. And besides, it'll give me time to attempt to make sense of everything.'

'If you're sure. You were kinda out of it back there in the shelter. Should you take the risk?'

'I think we both know I'll take the risk.'

She gives me a knowing look, but doesn't say anything further. I watch her walk to her team, listen as she talks into her radio – informing someone of what's happened. As I cycle past, I give a nod in her direction. I feels eyes on my back as I slowly pedal out of the car park. I also catch the word 'surveillance' and immediately jump to the conclusion I'm going to be watched.

Chapter 69

JENNY

Thursday

'Where the *fuck* have you been? Thanks for letting me know you'd decided to renege on our plans – I've only been worried to *death* all evening, envisaging you dead in an alleyway or something.' Roisin's furious voice hurls down the line. I hold the phone at a distance to lessen the assault on my eardrum. 'Why didn't you tell me what you were planning?'

'I'm sorry, Ro. Really sorry. I should've called sooner. I didn't intend to worry you, it just all got out of hand – I was caught up in the moment.' I give a run-down of the last few hours. And despite being told not to tell a soul, I tell her we found Olivia. 'You can't disclose that to anyone though. I'll be shot at dawn.'

'Thank God,' she says. There's a pause before she says, 'I'm coming to you. Stay put.'

I open my mouth to put up an argument because it's after midnight, but the line is already dead.

The house is filled with light – I've switched on every single one in the hope it'll make me feel more secure. Safe. It still feels all wrong, being here alone, but somehow, the place is less intimidating lit up like Blackpool Illuminations.

I don't think there'll be any further gifts now, though. They served their purpose. If any more turned up it would look like someone other than me was responsible. Their aim was to make it look like it was all down to me. However, just because I don't think they'll come here for that reason, doesn't mean they aren't watching right now. Waiting in the shadows. I shiver. Looking out the large glass window upstairs, I scan the immediate area, then step away. I can't see anyone, but against the backdrop of light, no doubt I'm very visible. I pad along the landing to my bedroom. A stab of regret stalls me at the door as I look in at the undisturbed bed, the space where Mark would be now void of his body. A bubble of emotion threatens to derail me. I walk in and run my hands over the duvet, then collapse onto the bed. Finding Olivia alive is the best outcome I could've hoped for, but it still might not be the end of it. Because disturbingly, the plan to frame me for Olivia's abduction might still work.

Talia was really not convinced about how I'd found her. It's clear she thinks I was able to lead her to the underground shelter because I was the one who took Olivia there in the first place. When she said not to tell anyone, because she thought it would help draw the perpetrator out if they still believed Olivia to be alive, I got the impression that was to put me off the trail, so to speak. The surveillance I heard her ordering on the radio was meant to make me believe police would be keeping an eye on the woodland, the shelter, to lie in wait in case the culprit returns to the scene.

But I'm sure the surveillance was really for me.

Hopefully now Olivia has been found alive, albeit unconscious, it won't be long before they can get the full story from her. Until that time, though, I'm betting Talia wants to keep an eye on me to make sure I don't do a runner. Or worse, could she be thinking I may even attempt to get to Olivia in the hospital to finish her off before she regains consciousness and can give a statement? My temples throb and I put my fingertips either side of my forehead and rub in a circular motion as if the action might erase that last thought.

The doorbell echoes around the house and I jump up from the bed, ignoring the rush of blood, and run down-stairs to open the door to Roisin. I fling my arms around her and hug her so tightly that she gasps for air.

'Sorry,' I say, releasing her. 'I've never been more pleased to see you.'

Tears, pent-up emotion, relief – everything – just pours out of me. She guides me to the lounge and I plonk down on the sofa. Roisin's concerned eyes are on me as I continue to cry.

'Oh, my darling,' she mutters as she leaves the room. She returns with a drink and I cradle the mug in my hands as I let it all out, my deep sobs racking my body. She waits patiently.

'Sorry for shouting at you,' she says when I finally stop crying. 'You scared the hell out of me. And Mark.'

I snap my head up to look at her. 'Mark?' A burning

sensation grows in the pit of my stomach. 'How dare he be concerned – Christ, he was the one who got me into this whole mess!'

'I called him when you didn't show up, Jen. He explained everything.'

'Explained how he'd handed his wife to the police on a fucking platter?'

'Yes, that. Don't worry, I gave him a hard time.' She smiles. 'He knows he screwed up.'

'Bit late. He's taken my kids, Roisin.' It almost sets the tears off again, but I need to pull myself together now.

'I know, darling. I'm sorry. But this will all be cleared up soon and you can get your life back on track.' She speaks with a conviction I don't feel is justified. But I'm grateful for her positivity.

'I appreciate you coming all the way over here so late. Or, well . . .' I check the time. '*Early*. What was it that you wanted to talk to me about?'

'Ah, yes. Interesting development,' she says, reaching for her handbag. 'I know you didn't ask me to, but I carried on my *investigation*,' she says, making air quotes with her fingers, 'watching your mother from afar.'

'Oh, Ro . . . I shouldn't have asked you to do any of this—'

'No, no – it was practically on my route, had loads of rep meetings up north, so I was well up for it. Even used Harry's best camera so I could get some decent pictures from a distance. My mobile camera wasn't cutting it. Felt like one of those sleuths from *Rosemary and Thyme*.' She laughs. 'Not that I was enjoying it, of course – I was there for a serious reason.'

'It's okay, Roisin. You're allowed to get into the moment.

I'd have chosen someone younger, though, like Nancy Drew.' I smile.

'Well, anyway. I went to the park I saw Claire at before and she met up with the same woman.' She stretches her hand out, a photo in it. 'It's the clearest shot of the pictures I managed to get. It might be nothing, of course. I'm not saying this meeting is significant, but I followed her from the park – Claire walked in the opposite direction. The mystery woman got into a waiting vehicle, passenger side, and the car sped off. I didn't have time to snap the number plate, I'm afraid, but . . .'

Roisin's voice muffles as I take the photo from her. I'm aware that she's still talking but I don't hear her words as I scrutinise the image.

'Jen, are you listening?'

'Er . . . yeah. Yes, sorry.'

I shake my head, a fuzziness filling it.

'As I say, it might not mean anything. It could simply be a chat in the park. But I wondered if it might have relevance to you.'

With my lips clamped together I take a slow, deep breath in through my nostrils. I regard the photo for a few more seconds, then hand it back. 'No,' I say. 'Sadly, I can't say it does.'

'You definitely don't know who this is?'

'I don't recognise her.' I sigh and get up from the sofa, but stumble, knocking into the coffee table. My legs are weak; my entire body is. It's like my bones have all turned to rubber.

'Careful! What are you doing?' Roisin says.

'I think I need to sleep, Ro.'

'Are you okay? What is it?'

'I'm so exhausted.' I rub my eyes while yawning. 'I know you've driven all the way over here, but would you mind if I just took myself off to bed now?'

Roisin's right eyebrow arcs as she fixes her gaze on me.

'Are you certain you haven't seen this woman? She might be the one who's been sending the dead animals to you?'

I shrug. 'I really don't know,' I say, shaking my head. 'Can I take the photo, though? I'll hand it over to the police; let them deal with it.'

Ro smiles as she gives me the photo again. She wraps her arms around me, squeezing me so tightly that air hisses through my lips. 'That's the most sensible thing you've said.' She releases her grip and regards me closely.

'It happens. Occasionally,' I say, attempting a laugh that doesn't fool her. Roisin's expression is filled with concern, and I touch my hand to her cheek. 'You're amazing, Ro – you know that?'

She screws her nose up and takes a deep breath.

'Jen . . . I don't think I should leave you.'

'I'll be fine. Honestly.' I avoid her eyes.

She's silent for a moment as she contemplates this, but before she can add anything further, I thank her for all her help – for being my friend and believing in me, then bundle her out the door.

After her car disappears out of the drive, I make a brief phone call and then I grab my jacket.

Chapter 70

JENNY

Guilt sweeps through me as I leave the house and walk around the side to retrieve my bike. I hate that I lied to Roisin, especially after all the support and help she's given me. But I can't allow her to get any deeper involved. She's done enough.

I hesitate, pulling the photo from my jacket pocket to look at it again. The two women on the bench are twisted so they're facing each other. They appear to be deep in conversation.

I run a fingertip over the face of the woman with my mother, a powerful mix of anger and adrenaline surging through my veins. Their being together doesn't make any sense.

There was no point me telling Roisin the truth when she showed it to me. I could be jumping to the wrong conclusions. A meeting in the park doesn't prove they're anything to do with the dead animals or that they're responsible for Olivia's abduction. But I do need to check this out for myself. I hated it when Mark went directly to the police without bothering to ask my side first. I'm not doing that to someone else and that's just what Roisin would've made me do. And, to be honest, I want a bloody explanation face to face without police getting involved.

With a heaving sigh, I pocket the photo and get on the bike.

The inky darkness envelops me as I cycle the lanes to get to the vets' again, but I don't use the bike's headlight – the moonlight is just enough. I daren't alert the police who are likely still at the scene to my arrival. I suspect they're hoping the abductor comes back to the underground shelter. I don't want to give them what they want and put myself back in the frame for this. If I'm even out of it. I lift my bike over a gate, prop it against the hedge and make my way on foot towards the rear of the vet practice. Even if the police are covertly placed around the scene of where Olivia was found, I should go undetected.

I hesitate once I'm close to the building. There are no visible police vehicles, but maybe that's because officers are hidden at strategic points, lying in wait for the perpetrator to return. Then again, maybe I've seen too many crime dramas. When I feel as certain as I can be that I've not been followed, and I'm not being watched, I break cover and sneak in through the rear door of the vets'. I don't relock the door. It's the entry point I've asked her to use too.

Once inside, I wedge open the inner double doors and go to wait in the surgery. The emergency exit lights are always on, so I'm able to see now my eyes have adjusted to the dimness. A noise from the reception area sets my pulse racing. For God's sake, I told her to come through the back. I rush out. Hopefully, she hasn't just waltzed in the front door. I wanted some time alone with her before police get involved.

'OhmyGod, you gave me such a fright, Jenny.' She steps back, her hand on her chest.

'Likewise,' I say, breathlessly. For a moment I'm struck dumb – no words will form. I just stare at her, open-mouthed.

'Why are you here?' Her voice is high-pitched and all I can do is put my fingers to my lips to warn her to be quieter. She seems to get my message, whispering, 'Did you find something?'

I'm not sure how to react. 'I have, actually.' My mouth is dry, and the words seem to stick to the roof of my mouth.

'Me too,' she says, her eyes wide.

'We need to talk, Nisha. And quickly.'

Chapter 71

Visiting Paul came about through Claire. She was the one who got me in, although she wasn't actually aware she'd been instrumental, of course. I managed to manipulate the situation to suit me. It was about time the tables were turned. At first, I had a fear Paul would recognise me, even though we'd never met. He may well have seen photos; I don't know. But once I was confident there was no recognition in his face, unless he had the best poker face in the world, I knew I was safe to continue my plan.

It's been months now since I last saw him. I've made every excuse under the sun – but the key thing was telling him I'm working hard on his book. I said my editor needed to see an early draft and that pleased him no end. My most recent excuse is I'm researching – off on a field trip. And I am – it's the truth. I need the time to find the right place – the killing ground has to be perfect. On land Jenny owns so that it matches with Paul's MO. A copycat has to have accurate details and Paul has given me everything

I need to put things in place ahead of beginning the next stage of the plan.

I still see Claire regularly; she has her uses. Nothing has changed between us, though. Yet.

But it will.

Soon.

Chapter 72

JENNY

'You go first,' I say. 'But be quick.' I check my phone for the time. We don't have long.

'I could see lights, a convoy of them, from my bedroom, cutting through the lane and I knew it was unusual activity for around here this late. Thought it was probably police, that they must've found something. I had to investigate.'

So much for low-key. 'Okay, so is that what you found out – that the police are here somewhere?'

'No, Jen – and I'm not sure how to tell you this . . .' Nisha lowers her gaze. I know what's coming. I almost blurt it out, but I don't want to ruin her moment.

'Just say it, Nish. There's literally no time to waste here.'

'It's Abi.' Nisha takes my hands in hers. 'She's not who she says she is.'

'No,' I say. 'No, she's not.' I let out a deep sigh. 'I'm really so sorry, Nish. She planted the seed—'

'It's fine, really. I know. She's been manipulative from the start. But what I haven't found out is *why*. I was hoping I might find something here.'

'Don't worry about it now. I'm intending to discover that. But look, Nish, I know you love this stuff, but I need you to do something for me.'

'Go on.'

'She's coming here, any minute now. I've asked her to meet me for a chat. We were in the woodland earlier – long story – and I suspect the police are keeping a lookout.' I catch a confused look on her face, but plough on; now isn't the time for full explanation. 'You have to leave. I'm not putting you in danger, you hear?'

Her face slackens with disappointment. 'You shouldn't be here alone with her, Jen. She's a psychopath.'

'I can handle her. It's fine. And the police are close by. Any problems, I'll scream the place down.'

'Should I go and alert them then, let them know what we've found out?'

'I'm not sure we have enough yet to pin Olivia's abduction and intended murder on her. She's set it up so well to make it look like it's me. I'm going to record our conversation, get her to admit it all.'

'Okay, but I'm not going home.'

'You are, Nisha. Because if something happens to you, I'll never forgive myself. Go back to yours, gather every bit of evidence you have so we can go straight to DS Davis with it once I'm done here. We'll tie this up together. As soon as I have the recording, I'll come to you.'

'She'll realise what you're up to. She's not going to simply let you walk out of here.'

'If it comes to it, I may have to use some of the skills

I've been accused of having.' I have a vision of me restraining her, injecting her with sedative and locking her in the x-ray room – it's the securest place in the building.

'Go,' I say. 'I need to get a few things together.'

Nisha nods, and I usher her towards the back door. 'The police might be watching the front, so leave that way,' I say. 'But go quickly.' I don't want her bumping into Abi. I wonder if she'll get a taxi again, or whether it's even a taxi she used earlier. Roisin witnessed her getting into a car after seeing my mother at the park. Perhaps it's her boyfriend's car. He could well be helping her. It would make more sense as manoeuvring Olivia couldn't have been easy, and Abi is so petite.

Within a couple of minutes of Nisha leaving, I hear the rear door opening. I stand in the doorway of my room, every muscle tense in anticipation. I pray she's alone.

'Jenny?'

'In here,' I say. My voice is loud despite trying to be quiet. I step back inside, standing on the opposite side of the consulting bench. My phone is on the desk, partially hidden and already recording.

'What is it? Have you found something?' Her face is a mask of worry and now, given what I know, I realise she's been playing me all night. She didn't want me to find Olivia; she wanted to ensure I didn't. She knew we were in the right place, then discreetly directed us away from it.

'*Why*, Abi?'

Her brow knits. 'Er . . . you called me and asked me to meet you here.'

'No. Not why are you here now. Why have you done this to me? I don't understand.'

'Look, Jenny, it's been a long night. You're tired. You aren't making sense. Perhaps you need to get home and catch up on some sleep.'

I laugh. 'Good try. You know, I really didn't see any of this coming. None of it. Not once did I suspect you.'

'Suspect me. Oh, my God, Jenny. What are you saying?'

'You can drop the sweet, innocent Abi act now, love,' I say. Anger floods my body and I put both hands, palms flat on the table to stop them shaking. 'Who are you really?'

Whether it's because she knows it's not worth pretending otherwise, or because she had every intention of coming clean now anyway, the mask drops and she offers me a sly smile and a shrug. 'Well, I could ask you the same question,' she says, making no attempt to put up a defence.

'Yes, you could. Only I'm not the one who's been trying to frame you for an abduction.'

'Abduction?' A genuine look of bewilderment crosses her face.

For a split second I think I've got it wrong. Maybe she *is* only guilty of leaving mutilated animals on my doorstep, none of the other stuff.

'Murder, you mean,' she says. 'You took Olivia and you killed her the same way your father killed each of his five known victims.'

I don't care for the way she says 'known' victims. Like there could've been others that weren't found. Admittedly, it was something that played on my mind for years after I found out what he did, but psychologists and the like were confident there were five, no more. It wasn't his MO, they said. He liked people to see what he'd done. Find the dead women. There was no suggestion there were *unknown* victims. But, with the final murder before he was caught it *had* been suggested his MO might have been changing. That it was in the process of metamorphosis, like one of his damned butterflies.

I can't think about that now. I mustn't allow Abi to distract me from the here and now. And to what *she's* done. I assume, like Nisha said, she's guessed I'm recording this, so isn't going to give anything up easily. While Roisin and Nisha might be able to prove she was lying about her identity and that she's been seen talking in public with my mother, none of that adds up to attempted murder. I still make the best suspect, so I need to get her to admit she's behind it all.

Maybe I do have the upper hand though. Abi doesn't know Olivia's been found. Her plan must be to murder Olivia if she wants it to look like I've followed in my father's footsteps. If I'm careful, I can get her to admit her intentions and then make her panic that time is running out, that I've called the police and force her to go to the underground shelter to make sure Olivia is already dead from dehydration, or finish her off quickly before she can identify her as the abductor. That way, she directly incriminates herself by going to the scene, and I will be in possession of hard evidence backing it all up in case she says she saw *me* up there earlier and was suspicious of what I was doing, so went to check it out.

'Are you that desperate for attention that you want to carry on my father's work, Abi?'

'I don't know what you mean, Jenny. I don't even know who your father is. You never talk about him.' She smiles then casts her gaze around the room. It's too dark to see much. She won't be able to spot my phone.

'You know he wanted to be caught, don't you?' I keep on the subject of my father, hoping it will goad her enough to start telling the truth. 'He killed those women in private, but he placed their bodies publicly, so that they'd be discovered easily.'

'Is that what you plan to do too, Jenny?'

She's not falling for my baiting. I need to find her Achilles heel. I remember how she said she always felt she had to live up to expectations – how her relationship with her mother was difficult, much like my own. It could all have been bullshit, of course – a way to bond with me. She'd likely been getting information from Claire about me, my childhood, in order to get close to me. But for now, it's all I've got.

'Did you think becoming a murderer would make your mum proud of you?' I say. 'What kind of expectation were you attempting to live up to with that, Abi?'

'Hah!' Abi throws her head back and gives a sarcastic laugh. 'Now you think you're clever, bringing my mother into this.'

'No, I don't think I'm clever at all. If I were, I'd have figured out it was you ages ago. You must've gone to such great lengths to research me. You're the only person to have uncovered my true identity. The only one to have ever found me. You're the clever one, Abi.' I watch her face, so close to mine, as I say this. Her mouth twitches, then she smiles. A radiant smile, not a sarcastic one. She's happy I've told her she's clever. Perhaps I have to show admiration, make her feel superior to me. 'I'm impressed. You infiltrated my vet practice, made me bond with you. I really liked you, wanted to take you under my wing. You're so talented, Abi. I wanted the best for you, seeing as your mother didn't seem interested. That must've been hard. I know how it feels.'

'You know nothing of the sort.' Her lip curls, like a dog sending a warning signal before attacking. 'You had the perfect life—'

'Oh, get a grip,' I say, unable to stop myself. 'You know that's utter rubbish. I grew up with a manipulative, suffocating mother and a murdering father – which part of that would you consider perfect?'

'You were loved, *Jane*. Doted on.'

'How would you know? Jesus, you're a kid. You've been talking to my mother. I know that because I've seen the evidence. She's literally fed you a fairy tale. Why would you believe a word that comes out of that lying cow's mouth?'

Abi's chest heaves, her breaths deep as she wrestles with what I'm saying. I've hit a nerve – I need to keep going. 'She never *loved* me; my father never *loved* me. They owned me. You may well hate your own mum, but trust me, she's nothing like mine. As for my father, he was even more twisted than she was. Neither of them should've had children – they're both too selfish.'

'You were his *princess*,' Abi says, her eyes narrowed to slits. 'You were everything to him.'

'How would you know that?'

'I knew all about Paul Slater,' she says. 'And while everyone always had an inkling you'd witnessed his crimes, he kept the secret. For all the years behind bars, he kept shtum. To protect you. Surely you can see that's love.'

I shake my head. I can't believe what I'm hearing. 'Whatever my mother has told you about Paul Slater, I'd assume it's mostly lies. She's lied from the very beginning; the woman wouldn't know a truth if it slapped her in the face.'

'Oh, I agree,' Abi says. 'I wouldn't trust her word either. You have to feel sorry for her in some ways, though.'

'Really?' I scoff. 'What, because she was married to a serial killer?'

'That, and the fact she was your father's first victim.'

Her words catch me off-guard, and I inhale sharply. 'What are you talking about?'

'Oh, yeah, that's right,' Abi says, her eyes wide. 'I'm aware she's a good liar, but I don't think she had a clue that she was Paul's practice run; the one who started it all off. You'd consider her to be the lucky one as he didn't kill her, but maybe she was unlucky because he fell in love instead. She had to suffer for years as opposed to days.'

I gape at her, reeling, but then give myself a mental shake. There's no way Abi could know this, she's just trying to throw me off balance. 'Look, Abi. Enough of this nonsense. I'm not here to listen to your lies.' She shrugs as she shoots me a defiant gaze and for a brief moment, I allow her absurd notion to take root in my mind. Could it be true? I quickly shake it free again. No. I'm not going to listen to this *girl*'s stupid theories. And even if it were true my mother made her own decisions once my father was put behind bars and I refuse to forgive her for any of them no matter what bullshit Abi feeds me.

'I'm not lying, Jane.' She gives a wicked smile, her pupils so large her eyes look black. 'Anyway, Claire had her uses when I was trying to find you, and everything I know about you as a teenager I learned from her. But obviously for the important stuff, I knew I had to get to your father.'

'Get to him?' I swallow hard, my mind jumping ahead and not liking the obvious conclusion.

'I wanted to know exactly what he'd done. But more specifically I needed to know what you'd seen. It was easy, really. All I had to do was make him believe I was interested in him – a life in prison means a lot of men crave attention. Get their kicks from visits from pretty females. That's how it began.'

Nausea swells in my stomach. Abi has been visiting my dad in prison. Working her way into his confidence, to get information about his crimes and about me. What great lengths she's been to; I'm almost impressed. She's certainly done her homework. As difficult as this is to hear, at least she's opening up about it now – this is helping my case. She pauses, and I wonder if she's realised she's said too much already. A nudge in the right direction might start her talking again.

'I can't imagine he'd have let you in on anything that wasn't already in the public domain. Why would he give away his secrets after all this time?'

'It was easier than you think. His ego is more inflated than a bouncy castle. I just had to stroke it.'

'Right,' I say. 'How can you stroke a serial killer's ego?' I'm hoping this will be where she tells me how she planned to copy his crimes.

'By telling him you're writing a book all about him. All the time he was trying to make his victims special, he was really trying to make *himself* special. He wanted – needed – admiration. I promised to give him that in bucketloads. Once he started talking, he squealed like a pig, gave me everything I needed to frame you.'

She gives a laugh that cuts through me, winds me, like

I've been punched in the gut. My father told this . . . this *psychopath* about me. After all he had said about protecting me, how he'd not told a soul about his precious daughter, and yet, he blabbed everything to this twenty-something *girl*? I clench my fists. He's let me down again. I force myself to put that to the back of my mind as I realise Abi has done it – she's said what I wanted, and I blow out a breath in relief. Suddenly I see the irony in what she's saying about my father when she's clearly just the same. All that's important for me right now is that she's admitted it. She wanted to frame me. I'm surely vindicated. Or once Talia Davis and her team hear the voice recording, anyway.

'And there you were telling me he loved me, thought of me as his princess. Didn't take much for him to throw me to the wolves, did it?'

'Oh, he didn't realise that was what he was doing. It took weeks of visits to subtly gain the right information. I was patient and it paid off. Given the man's history – his obsession with women who he believed were sex workers or sleeping around, all I had to do was find the right victim. Someone who linked to you.'

'He didn't know where I lived; no one did. How did you find me?'

'Claire had done a lot of the groundwork from years of trying to trace you and that gave me enough information to track you down. She's getting on a bit, hasn't got the same resources I have, so it only took a bit more effort on my part. Once I found you, I took time to research your life here in Coleton Combe. I knew you deserved to be outed. Why should you be allowed to live in peace without a care in the world, when those you left behind

370

had to suffer, live with the aftermath your father created? You, and your perfect life, your perfect husband and house and little perfect kids who have everything they could ever want. Made me sick.'

'You could have that too, if you worked hard enough, Abi. You can still escape your mother's grasp and make a good life for yourself—'

'Stop! You've no idea, have you?'

'Well, you know that's not true.'

'And you think that's what you've done? Escaped Claire's clutches and made a good life? You might have left her behind physically, but she's still got a hold. Once I started digging, I realised your new life wasn't so perfect after all. There were cracks. You found out your husband was having an affair; you hid your true identity from him and everyone in the village. So wrong of you. It was exhilarating planning to bring you down. And while I was doing that by slowly making you go mad, replicating Paul's MO by abducting Olivia was the icing on the cake. I knew Paul would be impressed with my attention to detail.'

'And it was you who took the animal by-products.'

'Yep. Slack, the lot of you. It was brilliant when you happened to catch Nisha mislabelling the yellow tub – gave me the perfect scapegoat. How easily you believed one of your long-standing, loyal employees to be the one traumatising you by leaving mutilated gifts on your doorstep.'

'And you took my car.' I shake my head. To think I questioned myself. Then even believed it could be Mark.

'You have no idea what you're doing during a blackout. I didn't think it too much of a stretch that you might drive during one. Assumed you'd believe it too if you saw it with your own eyes. I made sure I parked it just in

371

sight of the vets' CCTV but not enough so you could see the driver. Once you believed yourself capable of that, I knew I could get you to question everything. Ensuring you were in possession of Olivia's bracelet was a nice touch, too, don't you think?'

'You got me good, Abi. Well done,' I sneer. 'Now what?'

The sound of a siren slices through the night air. Abi's head snaps towards its location, alarm on her face.

'Look, as good as this little rendezvous is, I'm going to have to cut it short.' Her body poises to run.

'I don't think so,' I say, lunging towards her, making a grab for her wrist. My fingertips make contact with her but she's too quick, pulling away before I can grasp it. I run around to the other side of the bench and manage to pull at the hood of her coat, dragging her back. Arms flail, nails scratch my face. I scratch hers – if I don't make it out of here alive, I'm ensuring her DNA is under my fingernails. I get pushed into the double doors, losing my balance as I fall through them onto the floor. I feel Abi's weight come down on top of me, expelling the air from my lungs. Before I can grab her again, she's up and running to the operating room. I'm slower, winded, but I follow. It's pitch-black inside. I slap my hand over the light switch, the bright strobe light temporarily blinding me. It's only for a split second, but it's enough time for Abi to attack.

A sharp pain takes my breath away, and I put my hand to my side. It's wet. I'm bleeding. As Abi's arm raises, I catch a glint of light refracting off the metal. She's armed with a scalpel. I feel weak, faint. Shit. Now I wish I'd been honest with Roisin and brought her along with me. Or let Nisha stay. Together, we could've taken Abi down.

Instead, as darkness descends, I realise she's about to win.

Chapter 73

JENNY

'You have to ruin everything, don't you?' I hear Abi say as I slump to the floor. Oh, God – I mustn't give in. I can't let her snuff out my life without at least trying to fight for it. The strobe light clicks off again, and as it does, Ella's and Alfie's smiling faces appear in my mind and give me an extra shot of adrenaline. I try to focus, making the most of the dim red light from the corridor shining through the door. I attempt to get up, but I'm too woozy and my feet slide on the floor, unable to gain purchase. They're probably slipping in blood. My blood. With my hand pressed against the wound in my side, I seek Abi in the darkness.

Movement to my left. A shadow sweeps in front of me.

Without having much idea of what I'm doing, I swing my leg to the side. Pain shoots through my body and I cry out. But I manage to catch Abi's ankle, and she stumbles. I hear the crash of her body falling against my metal trolley.

The one I placed a syringe filled with sedative on before she got here.

My brain feels as though it's waterlogged, and yet I'm getting increasingly light-headed. My ability to concentrate is fading rapidly; I want to go to sleep. I'm losing blood. I don't have a lot of time. With a huge surge of effort, I propel myself towards the fallen trolley, reaching my hand out to find the syringe. Abi realises what I'm trying and dives for it too. My fingers find it first, and just as Abi reaches down, I angle it into her arm and depress the plunger. I hear her gasp. Good, I've done it. I lie back, all strength leaving my body.

'What have you done?' Panic fills her voice. 'Seems you really are just like him.'

She says something else that I don't catch. My eyelids flutter closed.

There are dull shouts from somewhere inside the building. People yelling, but it's like I'm under a large, heavy duvet; all sounds muffled.

I'm vaguely aware of Talia Davis, her voice the loudest, bursting into the room.

There's a commotion, the sound of handcuffs being snapped on wrists. Abi saying, 'It's her. She did it. She's the one who abducted Olivia,' before falling silent. Talia's calling for assistance. Paramedics. For her, or me?

Either way, I must be safe.

Good. I can sleep now. Finally.

Chapter 74

JENNY

When I open my eyes, it's the first time for years that I actually feel rested. Like I had a good night's sleep for a change. I hadn't woken up once. And remarkably, I'm in a bed. Not on a cold floor, caked in mud. Although, I do hurt all over.

Gingerly lifting my head from the pillow, I see I'm not alone.

'Ah, good. You're finally back in the land of the living,' DS Talia Davis says. She's standing, stiff and official, side to side with DC Bishop.

'Not sure yet if that's better than the alternative,' I say. My voice is croaky. 'How long . . .'

'You've been out of it for about twelve hours. The wound to your side has been repaired under anaesthetic, so you're likely feeling a bit groggy.'

'I'm surprisingly clearheaded, actually,' I say.

'In that case, are you up to talking?' She doesn't wait for my response, just begins to explain the events that occurred at the vets' and those since I've been laid up. 'We had the DNA samples recovered from the underground shelter where Olivia was being held fast-tracked . . .' She pauses, narrowing her eyes a little. Pressure builds at my temples. 'And they are a partial match to yours, Jenny,' Talia says. I widen my eyes, horrified that after all of this, Abi has somehow got away with it.

'She must've planted it,' I say. 'She has *framed* me – you do see that, don't you?' I push up on my elbow, trying to sit, but wince with pain and collapse back down in the bed.

'Steady on, Jenny. You don't want to burst your stitches.'

'You've found the recording I made?' I ask. It's the only proof I have.

'Recording?'

My blood runs cold. Did Abi manage to dispose of my phone before Talia burst in? Without her confession, will I still be prosecuted for this? I swallow down tears of frustration.

'I put my mobile on the desk in my consulting room – it was recording our conversation. The one where she owned up to it all.'

Talia turns to Bishop. 'Anyone found the mobile?'

'Will check,' he says, swiping back the bed curtain and disappearing.

'Please, God – this can't be happening.'

'Don't worry, it would add weight to the case if we find it, but we have Abigail in custody and she's been talking. Not her real name, by the way.'

'Oh, I know *that*,' I scoff. 'She's been "under cover" this entire time.'

'You have that in common, then.' Talia tilts her head to one side, her eyes imploring.

'Well, yes,' I concede. 'All right, I admit I've also been hiding where I came from. *Who* I came from. But I think you'll find Abi's intentions were to cause harm; mine were the opposite.' I'm so glad to hear Talia knows about Abi. Even if she disposed of my mobile, it seems that evidence won't be all that is going to keep me from being wrongfully charged.

'It's not the only thing you have in common, though.' Talia pulls a plastic chair up and takes a seat beside my bed.

'Really. What else?' I wait for Talia to impart some half-baked emotional sob story – how Abi has had a difficult upbringing, that her absent father and challenging relationship with her mother contributed to her low self-esteem, blah, blah, blah.

'I think it's a good job you're lying down,' she says. I blow out a long, steadying breath to prepare myself for something bad. 'As I said, we found DNA that is a partial match to yours.'

Suddenly, I pick up on the word 'partial' and hope soars. Maybe they can't prosecute anyway unless they have an exact match. But then the true meaning of this hits me. Talia watches my face – sees a light flick on.

'No,' I say. 'That can't be right.'

'I'm afraid it is. Abi – aka Jaime – is your half-sister.'

My mind reels and I have a sudden feeling of weightlessness, as if I've just plunged down the loop of a roller coaster and up the other side. 'But she's like, twenty something,' I say.

'Yep.' Talia shrugs, sucking in breath before continuing. 'Claire Slater went on to have another baby after you left home. Seemingly, she tried to replace you. Even giving

377

her new daughter a similar-sounding name. Only, according to Jaime, her mother never recovered from loosing her precious Jane, trying everything to find you and bring you home. Jaime didn't turn out to be the replacement she was after. She wasn't good enough. And Jaime spent all her life attempting to live up to you. Or your mother's memories of you, at least.'

The conversation about Abi's mum comes back to me. It's how we'd bonded – it's what I'd used against her during the confrontation. I'd felt so much sympathy for her for having a mother who sounded so similar to mine. Not realising it was the *same* mother. 'I almost feel sorry for her now,' I say.

'A search warrant recovered items from the flat she was renting with her boyfriend, which tied up some lose ends.' Talia checks behind the curtain, then returns her attention to me. 'I shouldn't really go into details at this stage – it'll all come out in court, but suffice to say, we know you had nothing to do with Olivia's abduction. The evidence against Jaime is compelling . . .' Talia lowers her voice to a whisper. 'We found a copper-blonde wig, the one we think she used to dress up to look like you and ensure it was caught on the camera pointing towards Olivia's garden.'

'Why punish me, I wonder? Surely she could understand I went through the same as her while living with Claire?'

'She wanted to set the entire thing up to prove to Claire that you aren't the perfect daughter she's always made you out to be. All she wanted was to be as loved and well thought of as her half-sister – not forever living in your shadow as she felt condemned to be. She was certain, having spoken to Claire *and* Paul Slater, that sending the first mutilated animal with your father's signature painted lady butterfly attached, would be enough to start off your paranoia.'

'She was absolutely right about that. I questioned my own sanity.'

'Well, I'm sorry we didn't help either. We had to follow the evidence, you understand.'

'Yes. I'm just thankful it's all over. It *is* all over, isn't it? Is Olivia okay?'

'You will obviously need to give a statement as well as evidence in court. So, not exactly all over. But yes, Olivia has regained consciousness and we're confident she'll be able to give a full account of what happened and, as far as your involvement, we are certain you're in the clear.'

'And Mark, too, I assume?'

'Yes. Mark too. I realise that must be a difficult pill to swallow – him coming to me with what he'd found . . .'

'I'll choke on that for a while I expect,' I say, averting my eyes so she doesn't catch the hurt in them. I can't think about his betrayal right now – I'm in enough pain. 'Anyway, I'm so pleased Olivia's okay. Her family must be relieved.' And I am pleased. But, admittedly, I'm even more relieved that I'm okay. It wasn't me. Any of it. 'How, though? I mean, everything was timed so well – how did she know when I had a blackout, that I'd be unable to prove where I was the night Olivia was taken?'

'She's told us everything, against the advice of her solicitor, of course. We've got several hours of recording where she goes into great detail about how she masterminded the entire thing and, with the help of Claire and Paul, was able to use your affliction against you. She said she was aware stress caused you to black out, so all she had to do was help create enough, and then keep a close eye on you to know when the time was right to strike. She's been watching you for quite some time, Jenny.'

'She said she was patient.'

'She's a very creative young woman. A shame she couldn't put it to better use. She may well have earned the love and attention she so desired had she applied herself.'

'Talia,' I say, my eyebrows raised. 'I doubt anything would've impressed my . . . *our* . . . mother.'

But, no doubt my father would be impressed with Abi's ingenuity. Although, something tells me if he'd realised why she was doing it – so she could frame his princess – she might not have made it back out from within the prison walls.

Chapter 75

JENNY

'Well, look at you, Nancy Drew,' Roisin says, partially obscured by the huge bouquet of flowers she's carrying. She half-crouches to place them on the table. The nurse who's just removed the cannula from my arm ready for my discharge shoots her a stern look. 'Oh, I know,' Roisin says. 'Don't worry, I've come to pick Jenny up. I'm taking the flowers back with me.' She rolls her eyes as the nurse leaves.

'Always like to break the rules, eh?' I say.

'You're a fine one to talk. I can't believe what you did.' She sits on the end of the bed, and I see the dark circles under her eyes. 'You shouldn't have lied to me, Jen.'

'I know. And in hindsight . . .' I sigh, then give her an apologetic smile. 'I'm really sorry. I didn't want to knowingly put you in harm's way. You *are* my only friend.'

Her face softens. 'Yeah, that's true.' Her eyes crinkle at the corners as she smiles. 'And I am proud of you. Sounds like you did a pretty amazing job. Bar getting stabbed of course.'

'If it wasn't for you, I'd never have made the link. Olivia would've been killed and without a confession, I'd have remained the prime suspect.'

'I'm glad it's all over, Jen. I can't imagine how hard it's been. Do you think you'll go visit your dad, tell him how he allowed a psychopath – another one – into your life? How with his help you almost ended up in prison too?' Whilst her tone is mainly sarcastic, I hear the anger beneath.

'Don't worry, I'm not letting him back into my life, Ro. In any way, shape or form. But I hope Claire tells him everything. I hope he feels guilty that he's the one responsible for Abi getting all the inside info she needed to get to me. And there was me, always believing he was looking out for his princess.'

'People like him and Abi only have their own needs in mind, Jen. Every single thing they do is for their own agendas. If anything, you know, I'd have assumed Abi was Claire's and your father's kid together. Because it's as though she's inherited his killing gene.'

'Killing gene? Jesus, Roisin. That sounds horrifying.'

'I might've just made that up,' Roisin says, smiling as she gets up and positions the wheelchair next to my bed. 'I think it was a film. But there's definitely something in it – genetic factors and stuff.'

'Oh, right,' I say, slightly disconcerted.

Her face pales. 'I mean, *obviously* that's not the case with you. I didn't mean to suggest . . .'

'It's fine. I know what you meant. But maybe you should consider that theory when you try and get me in that thing.' I point to the wheelchair. 'I'm not being wheeled out of here.'

She laughs and pushes the wheelchair to the side. 'You're so stubborn, Mrs Johnson.'

Hearing her say my name, the one I've had for the past eleven years, fills me with sadness. 'I'm not sure I'll be Mrs Johnson for much longer.'

'Oh, love. I'm sorry Mark did what he did. But you know his intentions weren't bad. He loves those kids.'

'Yeah. And so do I.'

'Has he been to visit you?'

'Nope. He's taking the coward's way out as per.'

'I'll talk to him, Jen. The detectives told me they'd informed him of all the developments. He knows none of this was down to you.'

'Damage is done, though, isn't it? I just want my kids back now. They belong with me. It's been proven I'm not a danger to them. As long as Ella and Alfie come home, that's all I'm bothered about right now. The rest will wait.'

'Okay. Let's get you home, then.'

Roisin links her arm through mine, and together, we slowly walk out of the hospital.

Chapter 76

One week later

Mark stands on the doorstep as Ella and Alfie burst in. My husband seems different: smaller maybe, as though the events of the last few weeks have somehow shrunk him. His dark eyes are even darker, the light in them dimmed. I turn away sharply, not able to look any deeper. I refuse to feel sorry for him; he chose his path the moment he betrayed me. For the second time.

'Take it easy with Mummy, kids,' he says as they fling themselves at me. 'Remember she's had an operation.' He tries to draw them back from me, but I stop him. It's been too long since I've had this amount of love showered on me.

'I'm fine,' I say. 'I need an Ella and Alfie hug.' They wrap their arms around me, and despite the pain, it's the best feeling in the world. 'Mummy missed you.' Tears blur my vision. We all hold on to each other for a while longer, before I pull away slightly. 'You two okay?'

Alfie nods. 'We've been at Nanna's. She gave us sugar cakes every night,' he says, his eyes wide. 'They were conconut ones.'

'*Coco*-nut, Alfie. I keep telling you,' Ella says, tutting. 'Don't worry, Mum. I made sure we brushed our teeth. It was sooo much sugar, I'm sure it's made my teeth wobble.'

'You're so funny, Ella.' I glance towards the open door, to Mark, standing awkwardly, his arms limp at his sides. 'Right, you two, do you want to say goodbye to Daddy and take your bags to your room and unpack?'

They kiss Mark and drag their things behind them towards the stairs. I wait until they've disappeared before turning to the broken man at my front door. The man I married and loved. Still love, really, despite it all.

'I'm so sorry, Jen,' he says before I can speak. 'I fucked up.'

I nod. 'Yeah, Mark. You did.' I'm finding it difficult to make eye contact; the hurt is too great. But I know I wasn't without fault. 'We both played a part,' I say, finally raising my head to meet his gaze. 'I should've told you everything a long time ago.'

'Doesn't excuse what I did, though. I panicked, Jen. I found that stuff and I freaked out. Can you forgive me?'

I've thought about this for the past week. Going over and over in my head the way things have gone between us. Deciding whether we could ever put it behind us successfully enough to move on, together. I thought I'd reached a conclusion, from my side at least. Now, with Mark standing in front of me, everything falls away. It's easy to plot out a list of pros and cons when the person isn't with you. You don't have their deep-brown eyes on you, reminding you of the things you love about them the most. I have to look beyond that, though. To be fair to all of us.

'I honestly don't think it's possible, Mark.'

He nods, knowingly. I imagine he's been battling with the same pros and cons list himself.

'I'm sorry. I did what I thought was right at the time.'

'I know I made a mistake not sharing my past,' I say. 'But ultimately, I needed you to believe in me. You might not have known my background, but you know *me*. Who I am. To have handed me in without even attempting to talk with me first . . .' My voice breaks and I take a deep breath. 'You hurt me all over again, Mark. But to have taken the kids away from me!' Anger edges my words as I spit them out through gritted teeth. 'That was unforgivable. There's no trust left.'

'I guess it was already broken after what I did.' He stares down at his feet.

'Well, it certainly didn't help. I suppose I've always found it hard to fully trust people so I always hold something back for me. Doesn't mean we couldn't have rebuilt our marriage and been happy after your affair with Olivia. The four of us could've still lived a good life if only you'd stood by me.'

The power of those words seems to knock him. He takes a step back, his eyes glistening. 'We have two amazing kids. We did something right, eh?' he says, palming the gathering tears away.

'Yes.' As much as I could cry too, I hold strong, my voice firm. 'Whatever happens we'll make sure their childhood isn't affected by our decisions. Okay?'

He sniffs loudly and straightens. 'Agreed,' he says, his moment of insecurity no longer on display. 'I'm going to stay with Brett for a few weeks – sort out the business side of things. Looks like we'll be partnering up. Then, once we've a little distance between . . . events . . . maybe we could talk? Figure out how best to move forward.'

'Sounds reasonable.' The fact that he's accepting the offer of help from Brett speaks volumes. For all of this, has Mark really changed? Or is he still the person who goes along with things, getting dragged into situations he just doesn't feel able to say no to? I think he's making a mistake. I might've been wrong about Brett in that he didn't know about who I was, wasn't involved in any of the things that occurred, but he will ride roughshod over Mark; I feel sure of it.

'I do love you, you know. I never meant to let you down.'

His words catch me off-guard. I press my lips together, breathe in heavily through my nose to stop myself crying. Mark reaches a hand towards me and I quickly take a step back to avoid it. The threat of my emotion overspilling is imminent.

'Bye, Mark,' I say, without looking at him. I close the door and with my head bowed against it, I listen to his slow footsteps crunching on the gravel as he walks away. Once the sound of his car dies down, I step away. He's gone. But I'm no longer alone in this huge house.

I hear squeals coming from upstairs followed by rapid footsteps.

'Give it back, Alfie – or else.'

Alfie has obviously taken something of Ella's and she's chasing him across the landing. Normality has resumed.

I can't help but smile.

My marriage might well be over, but I've come out of this nightmare with my freedom, and my kids. I'm grateful

I've got a future. That we all have. And, thankfully, neither my mother nor father will be part of it.

I can finally put my serial killer family connection behind me. For good.

Epilogue

The delicate, wispy wing detaches with one sharp tug.

I watch on; see the pink tip of her tongue poke through the gap where her two front teeth were a few days ago. The thumb and forefinger of her right hand pin the helpless insect to the wooden picnic table as the fingers of the other dismember the twitching butterfly.

She gently places the top right wing – its two black dots like blank, dead eyes – to one side, before tearing the lower right wing from its body. She's so focused, her gaze intent, never leaving the butterfly as she lifts her other hand, releasing the vice keeping the creature trapped. She watches as the butterfly's remaining wings flutter, first furiously, then slowing.

Giving up.

A gentle breeze catches one of the severed wings and it flies across the table. I'm itching to run to her, to stop her. But I stay still; barely breathing. I need to see what she does next. She slams her hand down hard on the butterfly before it can escape, and a white, dusty powder puffs through her fingers. She shrugs her shoulders down hard in frustration.

From my position at the kitchen window, I sense her anger. Fear, mixed with a sense of inevitability, settles in my stomach. I know this type of behaviour. I've seen it first-hand, after all.

God, please, no.

Is history repeating itself?

Could it be possible that the killing gene skipped a generation?

I'll have to keep a close eye on Ella from now on, nip any psychopathic tendencies in the bud. I can't have my daughter growing up to be anything like her grandfather.

I must protect her at all costs.

THE END

Acknowledgements

I would like to thank the fabulous team at Avon, HarperCollins for their hard work – so much goes on behind the scenes and they do an amazing job. Special thanks to Helen Huthwaite and Thorne Ryan for their input in writing *The Serial Killer's Daughter*. I'm hugely appreciative for Thorne's eye for detail and invaluable editing skills in helping shape this novel.

Thanks to my agent, Anne for her continued support and for making the less fun aspects of my job so much more enjoyable. Thanks to my wonderful family and friends for everything they do to keep me sane (ish). My thanks to Kathy O'Neill for answering my vet questions. Mistakes and artistic license are all mine. My writer friends – I'm so truly thankful to have you in my life.

Huge thanks to the book reviewers and bloggers who helped make my last book, *The Serial Killer's Wife* such a huge success by spreading the book love – I'm grateful beyond words. I've been blown away by the support and kindness and am sure they'll be behind *The Serial Killer's Daughter*, too. I hope readers enjoy it just as much!

Every marriage has its secrets . . .

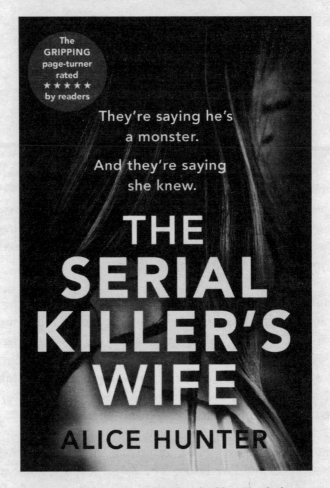

The GRIPPING page-turner rated ★ ★ ★ ★ ★ by readers

They're saying he's a monster.

And they're saying she knew.

THE SERIAL KILLER'S WIFE

ALICE HUNTER

The addictive and chilling debut crime thriller from bestselling author Alice Hunter.